VAL McDERMID

Val McDermid grew up in a Scottish mining community then read English at Oxford. She was a journalist for sixteen years, spending the last three years as Northern Bureau Chief of a national Sunday tabloid. Now a full-time writer, she lives in Cheshire.

Crack Down is the third of six novels featuring Kate Brannigan, and was shortlisted for the Crime Writers' Association Gold Dagger Award in 1994.

Val is also the author of three tense psychological thrillers featuring criminal profiler Tony Hill. The first of these, *The Mermaids Singing*, was awarded the 1995 Gold Dagger Award for Best Crime Novel of the Year, while the second, *The Wire in the Blood*, lends its name to the acclaimed ITV series featuring Robson Green as Tony Hill. She has also written two stand-alone thrillers, *Killing the Shadows* and *A Place of Execution*, and five novels featuring journalist-sleuth Lindsay Gordon.

VAL McDERMID

Crack Down

HarperCollins*Publishers*

HarperCollins*Publishers*
77–85 Fulham Palace Road
London, W6 8JB

The HarperCollins website address is:
www.**fire**and**water**.com

First published in Great Britain by
HarperCollins*Publishers* 1994

This paperback reissue edition published 2003

Copyright © Val McDermid 1994

The author asserts the moral right to
be identified as the author of this work

Typeset in Meridien by Palimpsest Book Production Limited,
Polmont, Stirlingshire

Printed and bound in Great Britain by
Bookmarque Ltd, Croydon, Surrey

For my mother,
with love and thanks

ACKNOWLEDGEMENTS

I couldn't have written this book without help from several sources. In particular: Diana Cooper, Paula Tyler and Jai Penna all contributed invaluable legal expertise and background information; Lee D'Courcy was generous with specialist knowledge in several key areas; Alison Scott provided me with medical information; Sergeant Cross at the Court Detention Centre kept me on the straight and narrow; Geoff Hardman of Gordon Ford (Horwich) filled in the gaps in my knowledge of the motor trade; and Brigid Baillie provided constructive criticism and encouragement throughout. It would have been a lot less fun without the Wisdom of Julia, the G & R team and the four-legged friends – Dusty, Malone, Molly, Macky, Mutton and Licorice.

Although the book is identifiably set in Manchester and other Northern cities, and many of the locations will be familiar to those who know the patch, all the places and people involved in criminal activities are entirely fictitious. In particular, there is no post office in Brunswick Street, nor any club quite like the Delta. Any resemblance to reality is only in the minds of those with guilty consciences.

1

If slugs could smile, they'd have no trouble finding jobs as car salesmen. Darryl Day proved that. Oozing false sincerity as shiny as a slime trail, he'd followed us round the showroom. From the start, he'd made it clear that in his book, Richard was the one who counted. I was just the bimbo wife. Now Darryl sat, separated from the pair of us by a plastic desk, grinning maniacally with that instant, superficial matiness that separates sales people from the human race. He winked at me. 'And Mrs Barclay will love that leather upholstery,' he said suggestively.

Under normal circumstances, I'd have got a lot of pleasure out of telling him his tatty sexism had just cost him the commission on a twenty grand sale, but these circumstances were so far from normal, I was beginning to feel like Ground Control to Major Tom as far as my brain was concerned. So instead, I smiled, patted Richard's arm and said sweetly, 'Nothing's too good for my Dick.' Richard twitched. I reckon he knew instinctively that one way or another, he was going to pay for this.

'Now, let me just check that we're both clear what you're buying here. You've seen it in the showroom, we've taken it on the test drive of a lifetime, and you've decided on the Gemini turbo super coupé GLXi in midnight blue, with ABS, alloy wheels . . .' As Darryl ran through the luxury spec I'd instructed Richard to go for, my partner's eyes glazed over. I almost felt sorry for him. After all, Richard's car of choice is a clapped-out, customized hot pink Volkswagen Beetle convertible. He thinks BHP is that new high-quality tape system. And isn't ABS that dance band from Wythenshawe . . . ?

Darryl paused expectantly. I kicked Richard's ankle. Only gently, though. He'd done well so far. He jerked back to reality and said, 'Er, yeah, that sounds perfect. Sorry, I was just a bit carried away, thinking about what it's going to be like driving her.' Nice one, Richard.

'You're a very lucky man, if I may say so,' Darryl smarmed, eyeing the curve of my calf under the leopard skin leggings that I'd chosen as appropriate to my exciting new role as Mrs Richard Barclay. He tore his gaze away and shuffled his paperwork. 'Top of the range, that little beauty is. But now, I'm afraid, we come to the painful bit. You've already told me you don't want to part-ex, is that right?'

Richard nodded. ''S right. My last motor got nicked, so I've got the insurance payout to put

2

down as a deposit. Which leaves me looking for six grand. Should I sort out a bank loan or what?'

Darryl looked just like the Duke of Edinburgh when he gets a stag in his sights. He measured Richard up, then flicked a casual glance over me. 'The only problem with that, Richard, is that it's going to take you a few days to get your friendly bank manager in gear. Whereas, if we can sort it out here and now, you could be driving that tasty motor tomorrow tea time.' Classic sales ploy; take it off them.

Richard did his personal version of the Fry's Five Boys gamut, from disappointment to anticipation. 'So can we do that, then, Darryl?' he asked eagerly.

Darryl already had the forms prepared. He slid them across the desk to show Richard. 'As it happens, we have an arrangement with a finance company who offer a very competitive rate of interest. If you fill in the forms now, we can sort it with a phone call. Then, tomorrow, if you bring in a banker's draft for the balance, we'll be able to complete the paperwork and the car'll be all yours to drive away.'

I looked at the form, not so easy now Darryl had reclaimed it to fill in the remaining blanks. Richmond Credit Finance. Address and phone number in Accrington. It wasn't the first time I'd seen their footprints all over this investigation. I'd meant to check the company out, but I hadn't got round to it yet. I made a mental note to get on to it as soon as I had a spare moment. I tuned back in at the bit where Darryl was asking Richard what he did for a living. This was always the best bit.

'I'm a freelance rock journalist,' Richard told him.

'Really?' Darryl asked. Interesting how his face opened up when he experienced a genuine emotion like excitement. 'Does that mean you interview all the top names and that? Like Whitney Houston and Beverley Craven?'

Richard nodded glumly. 'Sometimes.'

'God, what a great job! Hey, who's the most famous person you've ever interviewed? You ever met Madonna?'.

Richard squirmed. It's the question he hates most. There aren't that many rock stars he has much respect for, either as people or as musicians, and only a handful of them are names that most members of the public would identify as superstars. 'Depends what you mean by famous. Springsteen. Elton John. Clapton. Tina Turner. And yeah, I did meet Madonna once.'

'Wow! And is she really, you know, as, like, horny as she comes over?'

Richard forced a smile. 'Not in front of the wife, eh?' I was touched. He was really trying to make this work.

Darryl ran a hand through his neat dark hair and winked. In an adult, it would have been lewd. 'Gotcha, Richard. Now, your annual income. What would that be?'

4

I switched off again. Fiction, even the great stuff, is never as interesting when you're hearing it for the nth time. Darryl didn't hang about explaining little details like annual percentage interest rates to Richard, and within ten minutes, he was on to the finance company arranging our car loan. Thanks to the wonders of computer technology, credit companies can check out a punter and give the thumbs up or down almost instantaneously. Whatever Richmond Credit Finance pulled up on their computer, it convinced them that Richard was a sound bet for a loan. Of course, when you're relying on computers, it's important to remember that what you get out of them depends entirely on what someone else has put in.

Twenty minutes later, Richard and I were walking out of the showroom, the proud possessors, on paper at least, of the flashest set of wheels the Leo Motor Company puts on the road. 'I do all right, Mrs Barclay?' Richard asked eagerly, as we walked round the corner to where I'd parked the Peugeot 205 Mortensen and Brannigan had been leasing for the six months since my last company car had ended up looking like an installation from the Tate Gallery.

'You wish,' I snarled. 'Don't push your luck, Barclay. Let me tell you, the longer I spend pretending to be your wife, the more I understand why your first marriage didn't go the distance.'

I climbed in the car and started the engine. Richard stood on the pavement, looking hangdog,

5

his tortoiseshell glasses slipping down his nose. Exasperated, I pushed the button that lowered the passenger window. 'Oh for God's sake, get in,' I said. 'You did really well in there. Thank you.'

He smiled and jumped in. 'You're right, you know.'

'I usually am,' I said, only half teasing, as I eased the car out into the busy stream of traffic on the Bolton to Blackburn road. 'About what in particular?'

'That being a private eye is ninety-five per cent boredom coupled with five per cent fear. The first time we did that routine, I was really scared. I thought, what if I forget what I'm supposed to say, and they suss that we're setting them up,' he said earnestly.

'It wouldn't have been the end of the world,' I said absently, keeping an eye on the road signs so I didn't miss the turn off for Manchester. 'We're not dealing with the Mafia here. They wouldn't have dragged you out kicking and screaming and kneecapped you.'

'No, but you might have,' Richard said. He was serious.

I laughed. 'No way. I'd have waited till I got you home.'

Richard looked worried for a moment. Then he decided I was joking. 'Anyway,' he said, 'now when we do it, I'm not nervous any more. The only danger is that it's so repetitious I'm afraid I'll blow it out of boredom.'

'Well, I'm hoping we won't have to go through it many more times,' I said, powering down the ramp on to the dual carriageway. The little Peugeot I chose has a 1.9 litre engine, but since I got the dealership to take the identifying badges off it, it looks as innocuous as a housewife's shopping trolley. I'd be sorry to see the back of it, but once I'd finished this job, I'd be in line for a brand new sporty Leo hatchback. Freemans.

'That's a shame, in some ways. I hate to admit it, Brannigan, but I've quite enjoyed working with you.'

Wild horses wouldn't have got me to admit it, but I'd enjoyed it too. In the two years that we'd been lovers, I'd never been reluctant to use Richard as a sounding board for my investigations. He's got one of those off-the-wall minds that sometimes come up with illuminating insights into the white collar crime that makes up the bulk of the work I do with my business partner Bill Mortensen. But the opportunity to get Richard to take a more active part had never arisen before this job. I'd only gone along with Bill's suggestion to involve him precisely because I felt so certain it was a no-risk job. How could I expose to danger a man who thinks discretion is a fragrance by Calvin Klein?

This job was what we call in the trade a straight up-and-downer. The only strange thing about it was the way we'd got the job in the first place. A two-operative agency in Manchester isn't the obvious choice for an international car giant like the Leo Motor Company when they've got a problem. We'd got lucky because the new head honcho at Accredited Leo Finance was the brother-in-law of a high-class Manchester jeweller. We'd not only installed Clive Abercrombie's security system, but we'd also cracked a major gang of counterfeiters who were giving the executive chronometer brigade serious migraine. As far as Clive was concerned, Mortensen and Brannigan were *the* people to go to when you wanted a slick, discreet job.

Of course, being an arm of a multi-national, ALF couldn't bring themselves to knock on the door and pitch us the straight way. It had all started at a reception hosted by the Manchester Olympic Bid organization. Remember the Olympic Bid? They were trying to screw dosh out of local businesses to support their attempt to kick off the new millennium by holding the Games in the Rainy City. Bill and I are such a small operation, we were a bit bewildered at being invited, but I'm a sucker for free smoked salmon, and besides, I reckoned it would do no harm to flash my smile round a few potentially lucrative new contacts, so I went off to fly the flag for Mortensen and Brannigan.

I was only halfway through my first glass of Australian fizz (as good a reason as any for awarding the Olympics to Sydney) when Clive appeared at my elbow with a strange man and a sickly grin. 'Kate,' he greeted me. 'What a lovely surprise.'

I was on my guard straight away. Clive and

I have never been buddies, probably because I can't bring myself to be anything more than professionally polite to social climbers. So when the Edmund Hillary of the Cheshire set accosted me so joyously, I knew at once we were in the realms of hidden agendas. I smiled politely, shook his hand, counted my fingers and said, 'Nice to see you too, Clive.'

'Kate, can I introduce my brother-in-law, Andrew Broderick? Andrew, this is Kate Brannigan, who's a partner in Manchester's best security company. Kate, Andrew's the MD and CEO of ALF.' I must have looked blank, for Clive added hurriedly, 'You know, Kate. Accredited Leo Finance. Leo Motor Company's credit arm.'

'Thanks, Tonto,' I said.

Clive looked baffled, but Andrew Broderick laughed. 'If I'm the loan arranger, you must be Tonto. Old joke,' he explained. Clive still didn't get it. Broderick and I shook hands and weighed each other up. He wasn't a lot taller than my five feet and three inches, but Andrew Broderick looked like a man who'd learned how to fight his battles in a rugby scrum rather than a boardroom. It was just as well he could afford to have his suits hand-stitched to measure; he'd never have found that chest measurement off the peg. His nose had been broken more than once and his ears were as close to being a pair as Danny De Vito and Arnold Schwarzenegger. But his shrewd grey eyes missed nothing. I felt his ten-second assessment of me had probably covered all the salient points.

We started off innocuously enough, discussing the Games. Then, casually enough, he asked what I drove in the course of business. I found myself telling him all about Bill's new Saab convertible, the workhorse Little Rascal van we use for surveillance, and the nearly fatal accident that had robbed me of the Nova. I was mildly surprised. I don't normally talk to strangers.

'No Leos?' he asked with a quirky smile.

'No Leos,' I agreed. 'But I'm open to persuasion.'

Broderick took my elbow, smiled dismissively at Clive and gently steered me into a quiet corner behind the buffet. 'I have a problem,' he said. 'It needs a specialist, and I'm told that your organization could fit my spec. Interested?'

Call me a slut, but when it comes to business, I'm always open to offers. 'I'm interested,' I said. 'Will it keep, or do you want to thrash it out now?'

It turned out that patience wasn't Andrew Broderick's long suit. Within five minutes, we were in the lounge of the Ramada, with drinks on their way. 'How much do you know about car financing?' he asked.

'They always end up costing more than you think,' I said ruefully.

'That much, eh?' he said. 'OK. Let me explain. My company, ALF, is a wholly owned subsidiary of the Leo Motor Company. Our job is to provide

10

loans for people who want to buy Leo cars and haven't got enough cash. But Leo dealerships aren't obliged to channel all their customers through us, so we have to find ways to make ourselves sexy to the dealerships. One of the ways we do this is to offer them soft loans.'

I nodded, with him so far. 'And these low-interest loans are for what, exactly?'

'Dealerships have to pay up front when they take delivery of a car from Leo. ALF gives them a soft loan to cover the wholesale cost of the car for ninety days. After that, the interest rate rises weekly. When the car is sold, the soft loan is supposed to be paid off. That's in the contract.

'But if a dealership arranges loans for the Leos it sells via a different finance company, neither ALF nor Leo is aware that the car's been sold. The dealer can smack the money in a high-interest account for the remains of the ninety days and earn himself a tidy sum in interest before the loan has to be paid off.' The drinks arrived, as if on cue, giving me a few moments to digest what he'd said.

I tipped the bottle of grapefruit juice into my vodka, and swirled the ice cubes round in the glass to mix the drink. 'And you obviously hate this because you're cutting your own margins to supply the low-interest loans, but you're getting no benefit in return.'

Broderick nodded, taking a hefty swallow of his spritzer. 'Leo aren't crazy about it either because it skews their market share figures, particularly in high turnover months like August,' he added.

'So where do I come in?' I asked.

'I've come up with an alternative distribution system,' he said simply. Now, all I know about the car business is what I've learned from my dad, an assembly line foreman with Rover in Oxford. But even that little is enough for me to realize that what Andrew Broderick had just said was on a par with the Prime Minister announcing he was going to abolish the Civil Service.

I swallowed hard. 'We don't do bodyguard jobs,' I said.

He laughed, which was the first time I'd doubted his sanity. 'It's so simple,' he said. 'Instead of having to fill their showrooms with cars they're then under pressure to sell asap, dealers would carry only one sample of the model. The customer would specify colour, engine size, petrol or diesel, optional extras, etc. The order would then be faxed to one of several regional holding centres where the specific model would be assembled from Leo's stock.'

'Don't tell me, let me guess. Leo are fighting it tooth and nail because it involves them in initial expenditure of more than threepence ha'penny,' I said resignedly.

'And that's where you come in, Ms Brannigan. I want to prove to Leo that my system would be of ultimate financial benefit to both of us. Now, if I can prove that at least one of our bigger chains of dealerships is committing this particular fraud, then I can maybe start to get it through Leo's corporate skulls that a helluva lot of cash that should be in our business is being siphoned off. And then maybe, just maybe, they'll accept that a revamped distribution service is worth every penny.'

Which is how Richard and I came to be playing happy newly-weds round the car showrooms of England. It seemed like a good idea at the time. Three weeks into the job, it still seemed like a good idea. Which only goes to show how wrong even I can be.

2

The following afternoon, I was in my office, putting the finishing touches to a routine report on a fraudulent personal accident claim I'd been investigating on behalf of a local insurance company. As I reached the end, I glanced at my watch. Twenty-five to three. Surprise, surprise, Richard was late. I saved the file to disc, then switched off my computer. I took the disc through to the outer office, where Shelley Carmichael was filling in a stationery supplies order form. If good office management got you on to the Honours List, Shelley would be up there with a life peerage. It's a toss-up who I treat with more respect – Shelley or the local pub's Rottweiler.

She glanced up as I came through. 'Late again, is he?' she asked. I nodded. 'Want me to give him an alarm call?'

'I don't think he's in,' I said. 'He mumbled something this morning about going to a bistro in Oldham where they do live rockabilly at lunch time. It sounded so improbable it has to be true. Did you check if today's draft has come through?'

Shelley nodded. Silly question, really. 'It's at the King Street branch,' she said.

'I'll pop out and get it now,' I said. 'If Boy Wonder shows up, tell him to wait for me. None of that "I'll just pop out to the Corner House for ten minutes to have a look at their new exhibition" routine.'

I gave the lift a miss and ran downstairs. It helps me maintain the illusion of fitness. As I walked briskly up Oxford Street, I felt at peace with the world. It was a bright, sunny day, though the temperature was as low as you'd expect the week before the spring bank holiday. It's a myth about it always raining in Manchester – we only make it up to irritate all those patronizing bastards in the South with their hose-pipe bans. I could hear the comic Thomas the Tank Engine hooting of the trams in the distance. The traffic was less clogged than usual, and some of my fellow pedestrians actually had smiles on their faces. More importantly, the ALF job had gone without a hitch, and with a bit of luck, this would be the last banker's draft I'd have to collect. It had been a pretty straightforward routine, once Bill and I had decided to bring Richard in to increase the credibility of the car buying operation. It must be the first time in his life he's ever been accused of enhancing the credibility of anything. Our major target had been a garage chain with fifteen branches throughout the North. Richard and I had hit eight of them, from Stafford to York, plus four independents that Andrew also suspected of being on the fiddle.

There was nothing complicated about it. Richard and I simply rolled up to the car dealers, pretending to be a married couple, and bought a car on the spot from the range in the showroom. Broderick had called in a few favours with his buddies in the credit rating agencies that lenders used to check on their victims' creditworthiness. So, when the car sales people got the finance companies to check the names and addresses Richard gave them, they discovered he had an excellent credit rating, a sheaf of credit cards and no outstanding debt except his mortgage. The granting of the loan was then a formality. The only hard bit was getting Richard to remember what his hooky names and addresses were.

The next day, we'd go to the bank and pick up the banker's draft that Broderick had arranged for us. Then it was on to the showroom, where Richard signed the rest of the paperwork so we could take the car home. Some time in the following couple of days, a little man from ALF arrived and took it away, presumably to be resold as an ex-demonstration model. Interestingly, Andrew Broderick had been right on the button. Not one of the dealers we'd bought cars from had offered us finance through ALF. The chain had pushed all our purchases through Richmond Credit Finance, while the independents had used a variety of lenders. Now, with a dozen cast-iron cases on the stocks, all Broderick had to do was sit back and wait till the dealers finally got round to admitting they'd flogged some metal. Then it would be gumshields time in the car showrooms.

While I was queueing at the bank, the schizophrenic weather had had a personality change. A wind had sprung up from nowhere, throwing needle-sharp rain into my face as I headed back towards the office. Luckily, I was wearing low-heeled ankle boots with my twill jodhpur-cut leggings, so I could jog back without risking serious injury either to any of my major joints or to my dignity. That was my first mistake of the day. There's nothing Richard likes better than a dishevelled Brannigan. Not because it's a turn-on; no, simply because it lets him indulge in a rare bit of one-upmanship.

When I got back to the office, damp, scarlet-cheeked and out of breath, my auburn hair in rats' tails, Richard was of course sitting comfortably in an armchair, sipping a glass of Shelley's herbal tea, immaculate in the Italian leather jacket I bought him on the last day of our winter break in Florence. His hazel eyes looked at me over the top of his glasses and I could see he was losing his battle not to smile.

'Don't say a word,' I warned him. 'Not unless you want your first trip in your brand new turbo coupé to end up at the infirmary.'

He grinned. 'I don't know how you put up with all this naked aggression, Shelley,' he said.

'Once you understand it's compensatory behaviour for her low self-esteem, it's easy.' Shelley did A Level psychology at evening classes. I'm just grateful she didn't pursue it to degree level.

Ignoring the pair of them, I marched through my office and into the cupboard that doubles as darkroom and ladies' loo. I towelled my hair as dry as I could get it, then applied the exaggerated amounts of mascara, eye shadow, blusher and lipstick that Mrs Barclay required. I stared critically at the stranger in the mirror. I couldn't imagine spending my whole life behind that much camouflage. But then, I've never wanted to be irresistible to car salesmen.

We hit the garage just after four. The gleaming, midnight blue Gemini turbo super coupé was standing in splendid isolation on the concrete apron at the side of the showroom. Darryl was beside himself with joy when he actually touched the bank draft. The motor trade's so far down in the doldrums these days that paying customers are regarded with more affection than the Queen Mum, especially ones who don't spend three days in a war of attrition trying to shave the price by yet another fifty quid. He was so overjoyed, he didn't even bother to lie. 'I'm delighted to see you drive off in this beautiful car,' he confessed, clutching the bank draft with both hands and staring at it. Then he remembered himself and gave us a greasy smile. 'Because, of course, it's our pleasure to give you pleasure.'

Richard opened the passenger door for me, and, smarting, I climbed in. 'Oh, this is real luxury,' I forced out for Darryl's benefit, as I stroked the charcoal grey leather. The last thing I wanted was for him to think I was anything other than brain-dead. Richard settled in next to me, closing the door with a solid clunk. He turned the key in the ignition, and pressed the button that lowered his window. 'Thanks, Darryl,' he said. 'It's been a pleasure doing the business.'

'Pleasure's all mine, Mr Barclay,' Darryl smarmed, shuffling sideways as Richard let out the clutch and glided slowly forward. 'Remember me when Mrs Barclay's ready for a new luxury vehicle?'

In response, Richard put his foot down. In ten seconds, Darryl Day was just a bad memory. 'Wow,' he exclaimed as he moved up and down through the gears in the busy Bolton traffic. 'This is some motor! Electric wing mirrors, electric sun roof, electric seat adjustment . . .'

'Shame about the clockwork driver,' I said.

By the time we got home, Richard was in love. Although the Gemini coupé was the twelfth Leo car we'd 'bought', this was the first example of the newly launched sporty superstar. We'd had to confine ourselves to what was actually available on the premises, and we'd tended to go for the executive saloons that had made Leo one of the major suppliers of fleet cars in the UK. As we arrived outside the pair of bungalows where we live. Richard was still raving about the Gemini.

'It's like driving a dream,' he enthused, pressing the remote control that locked the car and set the alarm.

'You said that already,' I muttered as I walked up the path to my house. 'Twice.'

'No, but really, Kate, it's like nothing I've ever driven before,' Richard said, walking backwards up the path.

'That's hardly surprising,' I said. 'Considering you've never driven anything designed after Porsche came up with the Beetle in 1936. Automotive technology has moved along a bit since then.'

He followed me into the house. 'Brannigan, until I drove that, I'd never wanted to.'

'Do I gather you want me to talk to Andrew Broderick about doing you a deal to buy the Gemini?' I asked, opening the fridge. I handed Richard a cold Jupiler and took out a bottle of freshly squeezed pink grapefruit juice.

He opened the drawer for the bottle opener and popped the cap off his beer, looking disconsolate. 'Thanks, but no thanks. Can't afford it, Brannigan.'

I didn't even think about trying to change the mind of a man with an ex-wife and a son to support. I never poke my nose into his finances, and the last thing that would ever make the short journey across his mind is curiosity about my bank balance. We never have to argue about money because of the way we organize our lives. We own adjacent houses, linked by a conservatory built across the back of both of them. That way, we have all the advantages of living together and almost none of the disadvantages.

I opened the freezer and took out a bottle of Polish vodka. It was so cold, the sobs of spirit on the inside of the bottle were sluggish as syrup. I poured an inch into the bottom of a highball glass and topped it up with juice. It tasted like nectar. I put down my glass and gave Richard a hug. He rubbed his chin affectionately on the top of my head and gently massaged my neck.

'Mmm,' I murmured. 'Any plans for tonight?'

''Fraid so. There's a benefit in town for the girlfriend of that guy who got blown away last month in Moss Side. You remember? The innocent bystander who got caught up in the drugs shoot-out outside the café? Well, she's four months pregnant, so the local bands have got together to put on a bit of a performance. Can't not show, sorry.'

'But you don't have to go for a while, do you?' I asked, running my fingers over his shoulder blades in a pattern that experience has demonstrated usually distracts him from minor things like work.

'Not for ages,' he responded, nuzzling my neck as planned. Nothing like exploiting a man's weaknesses, I thought.

I wasn't the only one into the exploitation game, though. As I grabbed my drink and we did a sideways shuffle towards the bedroom, Richard murmured, 'Any chance of me taking the Gemini with me tonight?'

I jerked awake with the staring-eyed shock that comes when you've not been asleep for long. The light was still on, and my arm hurt as I peeled it off the glossy computer gaming magazine I'd fallen asleep over. I reached for the trilling telephone and barked, 'Brannigan,' into it, simultaneously checking the time on the alarm clock. 00:43.

'Did I wake you?' Richard asked.

'What do you think?'

'Sorry. That kind of answers the question,' he said cryptically.

My brain wasn't up to it. 'What question, Richard?' I demanded. 'What question's so urgent it can't wait till morning?'

'I just wondered if you were at the wind-up, that's all. But you're obviously not, so I'd better come home and call the cops.'

I was no further forward. I massaged my forehead with my spare hand, but before I could get any more sense out of him, the pips sounded and the line went dead. I contemplated going back to sleep, but I knew that was just the fantasy of a deranged mind. You don't become a private eye because you lack curiosity about the doings of your fellow man. Especially when they're as unpredictable as the man next door. Whatever Richard was up to, I was involved now too. Heaving a sigh, I got out of bed and struggled into my dressing gown. I went through to my living-room, unlocked the patio doors and walked through the conservatory to Richard's house.

As usual, his living room looked like a teenager's idea of paradise. A Nintendo console lay on top of a pile of old newspapers by the sofa. Stacks of CDs teetered on every available surface that wasn't occupied by empty beer bottles and used coffee mugs. Rock videos were piled by the TV set. A couple of rock bands' promotional T-shirts and sweat shirts were thrown over an armchair, and a lump of draw sat neatly on a pack of Silk Cut, next to a packet of Rizlas on the coffee table. If vandals ransacked the place, Richard probably wouldn't notice for a fortnight. When we first got together, I used to tidy up. Now, I've trained myself not to notice.

Two steps down the hall, I knew what to expect in the kitchen. Every few weeks, Richard decides his kitchen is a health hazard, and he does his version of spring cleaning. This involves putting crockery, cutlery and chopsticks in the dishwasher. Everything else on the worktops goes into a black plastic bin liner. He buys a bottle of bleach, a pair of rubber gloves and a pack of scouring pads and scrubs down every surface, including the inside of the microwave. For two days, the place is spotless and smells like a public swimming pool. Then he comes home stoned with a Chinese takeaway and everything goes back to normal.

I opened the dishwasher and took out the jug from the coffee maker. I got the coffee from the fridge. Richard's fridge contains only four main food groups: his international beer collection, chocolate bars for the dope-induced raging munchies, ground coffee and a half-gallon container of milk. While I was waiting for the coffee to brew, I tried not to think about the logical reason why Richard was coming home to call the police.

I realized the nightmare was true when I heard the familiar clatter of a black hack's diesel engine in the close outside. I peeped through the blind. Sure enough, there was Richard paying off the cabbie. I had a horrible feeling that the reason he was in a cab rather than the Gemini had nothing to do with the amount of alcohol he had consumed. 'Oh shit,' I muttered as I took a second mug from the dishwasher and filled it with strong Java. I walked down the hall and proffered the coffee as Richard walked through the front door.

'You're not going to believe this,' he started, taking the mug from me. He gulped a huge mouthful. Luckily, he has an asbestos throat. 'Cheers.'

'Don't tell me, let me guess,' I said, following him through to the living room, where he grabbed the phone. 'You came out of the club, the car was gone.'

He shook his head in admiration. 'Ever thought of becoming a detective, Brannigan? You don't ring 999 for a car theft, do you?'

'Not unless they also ran you over.'

'When I realized the car was on the missing list, I wished they had,' he said. 'I thought, if Brannigan doesn't kill me, the money men will. Got a number for the Dibble?'

I recited the familiar number of Greater Manchester Police's main switchboard. Contrary to popular mythology about private eyes, Bill and I do have a good working relationship with the law. Well, most of the time. Let's face it, they're so overworked these days that they're pathetically grateful to be handed a stack of evidence establishing a case that'll let them give some miserable criminal a good nicking.

Richard got through almost immediately. While he gave the brief details over the phone, I wondered whether I should call Andrew Broderick and give him the bad news. I decided against it. It's bad enough to lose twenty grand's worth of merchandise without having a night's sleep wrecked as well. I must point that out to Richard some time.

3

Two nights later, it happened again. I was about to deal Kevin Costner a fatal blow in a game of Battle Chess when an electronic chirruping disturbed our joust. Costner dissolved in a blue haze as I struggled up from the dream, groping wildly for the phone. My arm felt as heavy as if I really was wearing the weighty medieval armour of a knight in a tournament. That'll teach me to play computer games at bedtime. 'Brannigan,' I grunted into the phone.

'Kate? Sorry to wake you.' The voice was familiar, but out of context it took me a few seconds to recognize it. The voice and I came up with the answer simultaneously. 'Ruth Hunter here.'

I propped myself up on one elbow and switched on the bedside lamp. 'Ruth. Give me a second, will you?' I dropped the phone and scrabbled for my bag. I pulled out a pad and pencil, and scribbled down the time on the clock. 02:13. For a criminal solicitor to wake me at this time of night it had to be serious. Whichever one of Mortensen and Brannigan's clients had decided my beauty sleep was less important than their needs was going to pay dear for the privilege. They weren't going to get so much as ten free seconds. I picked up the phone and said, 'OK. You have my undivided attention. What is it that won't keep?'

'Kate, there is no way of making this pleasant. I'm sorry. I've just had Longsight police station's custody sergeant on to me. They've arrested Richard.' Ruth's voice was apologetic, but she was right. There was no way of making that news pleasant.

'What's he done? Had a few too many and got caught up in somebody else's war?' I asked, knowing even as I did that I was being wildly optimistic. If that was all it was, Richard would have been more interested in getting his head down for a kip in the cells than in getting the cops to call Ruth out.

'I'm afraid not, Kate. It's drugs.'

'Is that all?' I almost burst out laughing. 'This is the 1990s, Ruth. How much can they give him for a lump of draw? He never carries more on him than the makings for a couple of joints.'

'Kate, it's not cannabis.' Ruth had that tone of voice that the actors on hospital dramas use when they're about to tell someone their nearest and dearest probably isn't going to make it. 'If it was cannabis, believe me, I wouldn't have bothered calling you.'

I heard the words, but I couldn't make sense of them. The only drug Richard ever uses is draw. In the two years we've been together, I've never known him drop so much as half a tab of E, in spite of the number of raves and gigs he routinely attends. 'It's got to be a plant, then,' I said confidently. 'Someone's had it in for him and they've slipped something into his pocket.'

'I don't think so, Kate. We're talking about two kilos of crack.'

Crack. Fiercely addictive, potentially lethal, crack cocaine is the drug everybody in narcotics prevention has the heebie-jeebies about. For a moment, I couldn't take it in. I know two kilos of crack isn't exactly bulky, but you'd have to notice you had it about your person. 'He was walking around with two *kilos* of crack on him? That can't be right, Ruth,' I managed.

'Not walking around. Driving. I don't have any details yet, but he was brought in by a couple of lads from traffic. I'm afraid it gets worse, Kate. Apparently the car he was in was stolen.'

I was out of bed, pulling knickers and tights out of the top drawer. 'Well, who was he with, then? He can't have known he was in a hot motor!'

My stomach knotted as Ruth replied, 'He was on his own. No passengers.'

'This is like a bad dream,' I said. 'You know what he's like. Can you see Richard as a major-league car thief and drug dealer? Where are you now, Ruth?' I asked.

'I'm on my way out the door. The sooner I get in to see him, the sooner we can get this business straightened out. You're right. Richard's no villain,' she said reassuringly.

'Too true. Look, Ruth, thanks for letting me know. I appreciate it.' I fastened my bra and moved over to the wardrobe door.

'I'll keep you posted,' she said. 'Speak to you soon.'

Sooner than you think, I told myself as I shrugged into a cream polo-neck knitted cotton top. I grabbed my favourite knock-'em-dead suit, a lightweight wool number in a grey and moss green weave. Of course, dressing on the run, my legs tangled in the trousers as I made for the hall and I ended up sprawled on the floor, face smacked up against the skirting board, forced to recognize that it was too long since I'd cleaned the house. Cursing in a fluent monotone, I made it as far as the porch and pulled a pair of flat loafers out of the shoe cupboard. On my way out of the door, I remembered the route I was planning to go down, and hurried back into the living room, where I picked up the slim black leather briefcase I use to impress prospective clients with my businesslike qualities.

As I started the car, I noticed Richard's Beetle wasn't in its usual parking space. What in God's name was going on? If he'd gone out in his own car, what was he doing driving round in the middle of the night in a stolen car with a parcel of heavy drugs? More to the point, did the owners of the

29

drugs know who'd driven off with their merchandise? Because if they did, I didn't give much for Richard's chances of seeing his next birthday.

I pulled up in the visitors' car park at Longsight nick a couple of minutes later. There wasn't much competition for parking places that time of night. I knew I'd have at least fifteen minutes to kill, since Ruth had to drive all the way over from her house in Hale. Usually, I don't have much trouble keeping my mind occupied on stake-outs. Maybe that's because I don't have to do it too often, given the line of work Mortensen and Brannigan specialize in. A lot of private eyes have to make the bulk of their income doing mind-and-bum-numbing bread-and-butter surveillance work, but because we work mainly with computer crime and white-collar fraud, we spend a lot more of our backside-breaking hours in other people's offices than we do outside their houses. But tonight, the seventeen minutes I spent staring at the dirty red brick and tall blank windows of the rambling, mock-Gothic police station felt like hours. I suppose I was worried. I must be getting soft in my old age.

I spotted Ruth's car as soon as she turned into the car park. Her husband's in the rag trade, and he drives a white Bentley Mulsanne Turbo. When she gets dragged out of bed in the middle of the night, Ruth likes to drive the Bentley. It doesn't half get up the noses of the cops. Her regular clients love it to bits. As the dazzling headlights in my rear-view mirror dimmed to black, I was out of my car and waving to Ruth.

The driver's window slid down with an almost imperceptible hum. She didn't stick her head out; she waited for me to draw level. I grinned. Ruth didn't. 'You'll have a long wait, Kate,' she said, a warning in her voice.

I ignored the warning. 'Ruth, you and I both know you're the best criminal lawyer in the city. But we also both know that being an officer of the court means there is a whole raft of things you can't even think about doing. The kind of shit Richard seems to have got himself in, he needs someone out there ducking and diving, doing whatever it takes to dig up the information that'll get him off the hook with the cops and with the dealers. I'm the one who's going to have to do that, and the most efficient way for that process to get started is for me to sit in on your briefing.'

Give her her due, Ruth heard me out. She even paused for the count of five to create the impression she was giving some thought to my suggestion. Then she slowly shook her head. 'No way, Kate. I suspect you know the provisions of PACE as well as I do.'

I smiled ruefully. The Police and Criminal Evidence Act hadn't exactly been my bedtime reading when it became law, but I was reasonably familiar with its provisions. I knew perfectly well that the only person a suspect was entitled to have sitting in on their interview with the police was his or her solicitor. 'There is one way round it,' I said.

There's something about the mind of a criminal solicitor. They can't resist discovering any new wrinkle in the law. Dangle that as a carrot and they'll bite your arm off faster than a starving donkey. 'Go on,' Ruth said cautiously. I swear her eyes sparkled.

'Trainee solicitors who are just starting criminal work usually learn the ropes by bird-dogging a senior brief like yourself,' I said. 'And that includes sitting in on interviews in police stations.'

Ruth smiled sweetly. 'Not in the middle of the night. And you're not a trainee solicitor, Kate.'

'True, Ruth, but I did do two years of a law degree. And as you yourself pointed out not five minutes since, I do know my way around PACE. I'm not going to blow it out of ignorance of the procedures.' I couldn't remember the last time I'd had to be this persuasive. Before I knew where I was, I'd be down on my knees begging. This was going to be the most expensive night out Richard Barclay had ever had.

Ruth shook her head decisively. 'Kate, if we're going to quote each other, let me remind you of your opening speech. As an officer of the court, there are a whole lot of things I can't even think about doing. I'm afraid this is one of them.' As she spoke, the window rose again.

I stepped back to allow Ruth to open the door and get out of her living room on wheels. She let the door close with a soft, expensive click. She took a deep breath, considering. While I waited for her to say something, I couldn't help admiring her style. Ruth looked nothing like a woman whose sleep had been wrecked by the call that had dragged her out of bed. There was nothing slapdash about her understated make-up and her long blonde hair was pulled back in a neat scalp plait, the distinguished silver streaks at the temples glinting in the street lights. She was in her middle thirties, but the only giveaway was a faint cluster of laughter lines at the corners of her eyes. She wore a black frock coat over a cream silk shirt with a rolled neck, black leggings and black ankle boots with a high heel. The extra height disguised the fact that she had to be at least a size eighteen. We'd been friends ever since she'd been the guest speaker at my university Women In Law group, and I'd never seen her look anything other than immaculate. If I didn't like her so much, I'd hate her.

Now, she put a surprisingly slim hand on my arm. 'Kate, you know I sympathize. If that was Peter in there, I'd be moving heaven and earth to get him out. I have no doubt whatsoever that Richard's first demand will be that I get you on the case. And I'll back that one hundred per cent. But give me space to do what I'm best at. As soon as I'm through here, I'll come straight round and brief you, I promise.'

I shook my head. 'I hear what you're saying, but that's not enough, I'm sorry. If I'm going to do what *I'm* best at, there are questions I need to ask that won't necessarily have anything to do with what you need to know. Ruth, it's in your client's best interests.'

Ruth put an arm round my shoulder and hugged me. 'Nice try, Kate. You really should have stuck to the law, you know. You'd have made a great advocate. But the answer's still no. I'll see you later.'

She let me go and walked across the police car park towards the entrance, the heels of her boots clicking on the tarmac. 'You'd better believe it,' I said softly.

Time to exploit the irregular verb theory of life. In this case, the appropriate one seemed to be: I am creative, you exaggerate, he/she is a pathological liar. I gave Ruth ten minutes to get through the formalities. Then I walked across to the door and pressed the intercom buzzer. 'Hello?' the intercom crackled.

Giving my best impression of a panic-stricken, very junior gopher, I said, 'I'm with Hunter Butterworth. I was supposed to meet Ms Hunter here; I'm her trainee, you see, only, my car wouldn't start, and I got here late, and I saw her car outside already. Can you let me through? Only, I'm supposed to be learning how to conduct interviews by observing her, and when she rang me she said Mr Barclay's case sounded like one I could learn a lot from,' I gabbled without pause.

34

'Miss Hunter never said anything about expecting a trainee,' the distorted voice said.

'She's probably given up on me. I was supposed to meet her twenty minutes ago. Please, can you let me through? I'll be in enough trouble just for being so late. If she thinks I haven't showed up at all, my life won't be worth living. I've already had the "clients rely on us for their liberty, Ms Robinson' lecture once this week!'

I'd struck the right chord. The door buzzed and I pushed it open. I stepped inside and pushed open the barred gate. The custody sergeant grinned at me from behind his desk. 'I'm glad I'm not in your shoes,' he said. 'She can be a real tartar, your boss. I had a teacher like her once. Miss Gibson. Mind you, she got me through O Level French, which was no mean feat.'

He asked my name, and I claimed to be Kate Robinson. He made a note on the custody record, then led me down a well-lit corridor. I took care not to trip over the cracked vinyl floor tiles whose edges were starting to curl. It was hard to tell what colour they'd started out; I couldn't believe someone had actually *chosen* battleship grey mottled with khaki and bile green. Halfway along the corridor, he paused outside a door marked 'Interview 2' and knocked, opening the door before he got a reply. 'Your trainee's here, Miss Hunter,' he announced, stepping back to usher me in.

Like a true professional, Ruth didn't bat an eyelid. 'Thank you,' she said grimly. Typically,

35

it was Richard who nearly gave the show away. His whole face lit up in that familiar smile that still sends my hormones into chaos.

He got as far as, 'What are you –' before Ruth interrupted.

'I hope you don't mind, Mr Barclay, but my colleague is a trainee who is supposed to be learning the tricks of the trade,' she said loudly. 'I'd like her to sit in on our consultation, unless you have any objections?'

'N-no,' Richard stammered, looking bewildered.

I stepped into the room and the sergeant closed the door firmly behind me.

Simultaneously, Richard said, 'I don't understand,' and Ruth growled softly, 'I should walk out of here right now and leave you to it.'

'I know. I'm sorry. I couldn't not. It's too important. But look on the bright side; if I can blag my way into the secure interview room of a police station, aren't you glad you've got me on the team?' I added an apologetic smile.

Before Ruth could find an answer for that particular bit of cheek, Richard said plaintively, 'But I don't understand what you're doing here, Brannigan.'

'I'm here because you need help, Richard. I know you spend most of your time on another planet, but here on earth, it's considered to be a pretty serious offence to drive around in a stolen car with enough crack to get half Manchester out of their heads,' I told him.

'Look, I know it sounds like I'm in deep shit. But it's not like that.' He ran a hand through his hair and frowned. 'I keep trying to tell everybody. It wasn't a stolen car. It was *our* car. The one we bought in Bolton on Tuesday.'

4

Before I could pick the bones out of that, Ruth
interrupted. 'Let's just hold everything right there.
Kate, you are here on sufferance. I, on the other
hand, am here because Richard asked me to be.
I've got a job to do and I intend to do it, in spite
of your interference. So let me ask my questions,
and then if there's anything we haven't covered,
you can have your turn.'

It wasn't a suggestion, it was an instruction. I
knew what I'd done was bang out of order. I'd
taken a big risk on the strength of my friendship
with Ruth, and I didn't want to risk damaging
those bonds any further. Besides, I like watching
people who are really good at what they do. 'That's
absolutely fine with me,' I said.

'You mean she really isn't meant to be here?'
Richard asked, his grin irrepressible even in the
face of Ruth's frown.

'If you weren't facing such serious charges, I'd
have bounced her out of the door. It didn't seem

like a good time to generate even more suspicion on the part of the police. Now, Richard, let's get to it. I don't have all night.' Ruth picked up her pencil and started to write. 'Let's start at the beginning. What happened tonight?'

Richard looked uncertain. 'Well, the beginning isn't tonight. I mean, depending on what you mean, the beginning's either Tuesday night or three weeks ago.'

It was my turn to grin. I didn't envy Ruth her task. I love him dearly, but the only time Richard can tell a story in a straight line from beginning to end is when he's sat in front of a word processor with the prospect of a nice little earner at the end of the day.

Ruth squeezed the bridge of her nose. 'Maybe you could give me the short version, and I'll stop you when I don't understand something.'

'It's this job Kate's got on. I've been helping her out with it We have to buy these cars, you see, and then we give them back to the car company.' Richard paused hopefully.

Ruth's grey eyes swivelled round and fixed on me. 'Perhaps you'd like to elaborate . . . ?'

I nodded. 'My clients are the finance arm of the Leo Motor Company. They suspect some dealerships of committing fraud. It's our job to provide them with evidence, so Richard and I have been posing as a married couple, buying cars with money supplied by Leo, who then take the cars back from us,' I said.

'Thanks. So, you've been buying these cars. What happened on Tuesday night?' she asked.

'We'd picked up this really ace motor, the Gemini turbo super coupé,' Richard said enthusiastically. 'Anyway, I had to go into town, and I decided to treat myself and drive the coupé, since we'd only got it for a day or two. Then when I came out of the club, the car was gone. So I came home and reported it stolen to the police.'

Ruth looked up from her pad. 'Did they send anyone round?'

'Yeah, a copper came round about an hour later and I gave him all the details,' Richard said.

'And I informed my client first thing on Wednesday morning, if that's any help,' I added.

This time Ruth didn't scowl at me. She just made another note and said, 'So what happened next?'

Richard took off his glasses and stared up at the ceiling. A line appeared between his brows as he focused his memory. 'I went into town about nine tonight. I had to meet a couple of women in the Paradise Factory. They're the singers in a jazz fusion band, and they've just signed their first record deal. I'm doing a piece on them for one of the glossies. It was too noisy in the Factory to hear ourselves talk, so we left and went round to Manto's.' Trust Richard to spend his evening in the trendiest café bar in the North West. Looking at his outfit, I was surprised the style police had let him in. 'We stayed till closing time,' he went on. 'The girls were going on to the Hacienda, but I didn't

40

fancy it, so I went off to get my car. I'd parked it off Portland Street, and I was walking past the gardens on Sackville Street when I saw the car.' He put his glasses back on and looked expectantly at Ruth.

'Which car, Richard?' Ruth asked patiently.

'The coupé,' he said, in the injured tones of someone who thinks they've already made themselves abundantly clear. Poor misguided soul.

'You saw the car that you had reported stolen in the early hours of Wednesday morning?'

'That's right,' he said. 'Only, I wasn't sure right away if it was the same one. It was the right model and the right colour. but I couldn't see if it was the right registration number. It had trade plates on, you see.'

'Trade plates,' Ruth repeated as she scribbled. I was intrigued. Any self-respecting car thief would have smacked fake plates on a stolen car right away. I couldn't for the life of me see why they'd use the red and white plates garages use to shift untaxed cars from one place to another. It was just asking to be noticed.

'Yeah, trade plates,' Richard said impatiently. 'Anyway, I went over to this car, and I lifted up the trade plate on the front, and it was the same reg as the one that got nicked on Tuesday night,' Richard said triumphantly. He put his glasses on and grinned nervously at both of us. 'It's going to be OK, isn't it?' he added.

Ruth nodded. 'We'll get it sorted out, Richard.

Now, are you absolutely certain that this was the same car?'

'I still had the keys on my key-ring,' he said. 'It had one of those little cardboard tags on it with the number of the car, so I wasn't just relying on my memory. It was the identical number. Besides, the key I had opened the car, and there was still one of my tapes in the cassette. Isn't that proof enough?'

'Somehow, I don't think the point at issue is going to be the car,' I muttered quietly. Ruth gave me a look that would have curdled a piña colada.

'Did you call the police and tell them you'd found the car?' Ruth asked.

'Well, I figured that if I wandered off to look for a phone, the guy that had nicked it could easily have had it away again while I was busy talking to the Dibble. So I thought I'd just repo it myself and call the cops when I got home,' Richard explained. It wasn't so unreasonable. Even I had to concede that.

'What did you do next?' Ruth said.

'Well, I did what any reasonable person would have done,' Richard said. My heart sank. 'I took the trade plates off and cobbed them in the gutter.'

'You cobbed them in the gutter?' Ruth and I chorused, neck and neck in the incredulity stakes.

'Of course I did. They didn't belong to me. I'm not a thief,' Richard said with a mixture of self-righteousness and naïvety that made my fingers itch with the desire to get round his throat.

'It didn't occur to you that they might be helpful

evidence for the police in catching the car thieves?' Ruth said, all silky savagery.

'No, it didn't, I'm sorry. I'm not like you two. I don't have a criminal sort of mind.'

Ruth looked like she wanted to join me in the lynch mob. 'Go on,' she said, her voice icy. 'What did you do after you disposed of your corroboration?'

'I got in the car and set off. I was nearly home when I saw the flashing blue lights in my rear-view mirror. I didn't even pull over at first, because I wasn't speeding or anything. Anyway, they cut me up at the lights on Upper Brook Street, and I realized it was me they were after. So I stopped. I opened the window a couple of inches, but before I could say anything, one of the busies opened the door and dragged me out of the motor. Next thing I know, I'm spread-eagled over the bonnet with a pair of handcuffs on and his oppo's got the boot open.

'They kept on at me about the car being stolen, and I kept telling them, yeah, I knew that, 'cos I was the person it had been stolen off, but they just wouldn't listen. Then the guy looking in the boot came round with this Sainsbury's plastic bag, and he's waving it in my face saying, "And I suppose the villains that nicked your car decided to leave you a little something for your trouble?" Well, I had no idea what was in the boot, did I? So I told them that, and they just laughed, and bundled me into their car and brought me here. Next thing I know is they're on at me about a parcel of crack. And that's when I thought, uh-oh, I need a brief.'

Richard sat back and looked at the two of us. 'It's an unexpected bonus, getting Brannigan as well,' he added. 'How soon can you get me out of this dump, Ruth?' he asked, gesturing round the shabby interview room.

'That depends on several things. Being absolutely honest, Richard, I'm not optimistic that I can avoid them charging you, which means you won't be going anywhere until I can get you in front of a magistrate and apply for bail, which we can probably manage tomorrow morning. I still have some questions, though. Have you at any time opened the boot of the coupé?'

Richard frowned. 'I don't think so,' he said hesitantly. 'No, I'm pretty sure I haven't. I mean, why would I?'

'You didn't check it out when you bought it? Look to see if there was a spare wheel and a jack?' Ruth asked.

'The salesman showed us when we took it for a test drive,' I interjected. 'I certainly don't remember Richard ever going near it.'

He managed a grin. 'We didn't have it long enough for Brannigan to take it shopping, so we didn't need the boot.'

'Good,' Ruth said. 'This carrier bag that they produced from the boot. Had you ever seen it before?'

Richard shrugged. 'Well, I don't know. It was just an ordinary Sainsbury's carrier bag. Brannigan's got a drawer full of them. There was nothing about it to make it any different from any other one. But it wasn't in the boot when that rattlesnake showed us the car on Monday. And I didn't put it there. So I guess it's fair to say I'd never seen it before.'

'Did you touch it at all?'

'How could I? I said, I'd never seen it before,' Richard said plaintively.

'The officer didn't throw it to you, or hand it to you?' Ruth persisted.

'He couldn't, could he? His oppo had me cuffed already,' Richard replied.

'Yes, I'm a little surprised at that. Had you put up a struggle? Or had you perhaps been a little over-energetic in the verbal department?' Ruth asked carefully.

'Well, I wasn't exactly thrilled at being bodily dragged out of what was, technically, my own motor when I hadn't even been speeding and I'd been on the Diet Coke all night. So I suppose I was a bit gobby,' Richard admitted. If my heart could have sunk any further, it would have done. Add resisting arrest to the list, I thought gloomily.

Ruth was clearly as cheered as I was by this news. 'But you didn't actually offer any physical violence?' she asked, the hope in her voice as obvious as a City supporter in a United bus.

'No,' Richard said indignantly. 'What do you take me for?'

Diplomatically, neither of us answered. 'The keys for this coupé – did you have both sets?'

Richard shook his head. 'No, Brannigan had the others.'

'Have you still got them?' she asked me.

I nodded. 'They're in the kitchen drawer. No one but the two of us has had access to them.'

'Good,' Ruth said. 'These two women you were with – can you give me their names and addresses? I'll need statements from them to show you were talking about their record contract, rather than sitting in some dark corner negotiating a drug deal.'

'You're not going to like this,' Richard predicted. Correctly, as it turned out. 'I only know their stage names. Lilith Annsdaughter and Eve Uhuru. I don't have any addresses for them, just a phone number. It's in my notebook, but the boys in blue have taken that off me. Sorry.' He tried a smile, but the magic didn't work on either of us.

Ruth showed her first real sign of tiredness. Her eyes closed momentarily and her shoulders dropped. 'Leave that with me,' she said, her voice little stronger than a sigh. Then she took a deep breath, straightened her shoulders and pulled a packet of extra-long menthol cigarettes out of her briefcase. She offered them round, but got no takers. 'Do you suppose this counts as Thursday's eleventh or Friday's first?' she asked. 'Either way, it's against the rules.' She lit the cigarette, surprisingly, with a match torn from a restaurant matchbook. I'd have had Ruth marked down as a Dunhill lighter.

'One more thing,' Ruth said. 'You've got a son, haven't you, Richard?'

Richard frowned, puzzled. 'Yeah. Davy. Why?'

'What does he look like?'

'Why do you want to know that?' Richard asked. I was glad he had; it saved me the bother.

'According to the custody sergeant, when the officers searched the car more thoroughly, they found a Polaroid photograph that had slid down the side of the rear seat. It shows a young boy.' Ruth took a deep breath. 'In a rather unpleasant pose. I think they're going to want to ask some questions about that too.'

'How do you mean, a rather unpleasant pose?' I demanded.

'He's stripped down to his underpants and hand-cuffed to a bed,' Ruth said.

Richard looked thunderstruck. I knew just how he felt. 'And you think that's got something to do with *me*?' he gasped, outraged.

'The police might,' Ruth said.

'It couldn't be anything to do with us,' I butted in. 'Neither of us has been in the back seat since we got the car. The only person who'd been in the back seat that I know of is the salesman, on the test drive.'

'OK, OK,' Ruth said. 'Calm down. All I was thinking is that the photograph might possibly have an innocent explanation, and that it might have been your son.'

'So what does this kid look like?' Richard said belligerently.

'I'd say about ten, dark wavy hair, skinny.'

Richard let out a sigh. 'Well, you can count Davy out. He's only eight, average size for his age, and his hair's straight like mine, and the same colour. Light brown.' The colour of butterscotch, to be precise.

'Fine. I'm glad we've cleared that up,' Ruth said. 'Any questions, Kate?'

I nodded. Not that I had any hopes of a useful answer. 'Richard, when you were in Manto's, did you see anyone you recognized from the club the other night? Anyone a bit flash, a bit hooky, the type that just might have nicked the motor?'

Richard screwed up his eyes in concentration. Then he shook his head. 'You know me, Brannigan. I don't go places to look at the punters,' he said apologetically.

'Did you do a number on anybody about the car?'

'I didn't mention it to a soul. I'd just have looked a dick-head next week, back with my usual wheels,' he said, with rare insight.

'I don't suppose you know who's doing the heavy-duty stuff round town these days?'

Richard leaned forward and stared into my eyes. I could feel his fear. 'I've got no interest,' he said, his face tense. 'I bend over backwards to avoid taking any interest. Look, you know how much time I spend in the Moss and Cheetham Hill with new bands. Everybody knows I'm a journo. If I showed the slightest interest in the gangs and the drugs, I'd be a dead man, blown away on the steps of some newspaper office as a warning to other hacks not to get any daft ideas in their heads about running a campaign to clean up Manchester. You ask Alexis. She's supposed to be the crime correspondent. You ask her the last time there was a heavy incident in Moss Side or Cheetham Hill where she did anything more than toddle along to the police press conference! Believe me, if I thought for one minute that the gang that owns these drugs knows it was me that drove off with them, I'd be begging for protective custody a long, long way from Manchester. No, Brannigan, I do not know who's doing the heavy stuff, and for the sake of both our healths, I suggest that you remain in the same blissful state.'

I shrugged. 'You want to walk away from this? The only way you're going to do that is if we give them a body to trade,' I turned to Ruth. 'Am I right?'

'Regardless of that, you're probably going to have to spend another few days in police custody,' Ruth warned him.

Richard's face fell. 'Is there no way you can get me out sooner? I've got to get out of here, double urgent,' he said.

'Richard, in my opinion, the police will charge you with possession of a Class A drug with intent to supply, which is not a charge on which magistrates are inclined to allow bail. I'll do my best, but the chances are heavily stacked against us. Sorry about that, but there we go.' Ruth paused to savour a last mouthful of smoke before regretfully stubbing out her cigarette.

'Oh, shit,' Richard said. He took off his glasses and carefully polished them on his paisley silk shirt. He sighed. 'I suppose I'll have to go for it. But there's one slight problem I haven't mentioned that Brannigan seems to have forgotten about,' he said sheepishly, looking short-sightedly in my direction.

My turn to sigh. 'Give,' I said.

'Davy's due on the seven o'clock shuttle tonight. Remember? Half-term?'

As his words sank in, I got to my feet, shaking my head. 'Oh no, no way. Not me.'

'Please,' Richard said. 'You know how much it means to me.'

'There isn't that much dosh in the world,' I said, panicking.

'Please, Kate. That bitch is just looking for an excuse to shut me out,' he pleaded.

'That's no way to talk about the woman you married, the mother of your child, the former joy of your existence and fire of your loins,' I said, slipping defensively into our routine banter. It was no use. I knew as I looked down at the poor sod that I'd already given in. A dozen years of efficient contraception, and what does it get you? Someone else's kid, that's what.

5

I had to sit through the whole tale a second time
for the CID's preliminary taped interview with
Richard. Ruth had instructed him to co-operate
fully, in the hope that it might predispose them
towards letting his bail application go through.
Looking at their faces as they listened to Richard's
admittedly unlikely story, I didn't rate his chances
of seeing daylight for a while.

After the interview, Ruth and I went into a brief
huddle. 'Look, Kate, realistically, he's not going
to get bail tomorrow. The best chance we have
of getting him out is if you can come up with
evidence that supports his story and points to the
real criminals.' I held my tongue; Ruth is one of the
few people I allow to tell me how to suck eggs.

'The crucial thing, given the amount of drugs
involved, is that we keep him out of the main-
stream prison system so he's not in contact with
criminals who have connections into the drug
scene. What I'm going to suggest to the CID is

that they use the excuse of the "stolen" car and the possibly pornographic photograph to exploit paragraph five of the Bail Act,' she went on.

I must have looked as blank as I felt, for she deigned to explain. 'If the suspect's been arrested for one offence and the police have evidence of his implication in another, they can ask for what we call a lie-down. In other words, he remains in police custody for up to three days for the other matters to be investigated. That'll give us a bit of leeway, since the meter doesn't start running till the day after the initial hearing. That gives us Saturday, Sunday, Monday and Tuesday. He'll appear in court again on Wednesday, by which time you might have made enough headway for me to be able to argue that he should be let out.'

'Oh whoopee,' I said.. 'A schedule so tight I'll be singing soprano and an eight-year-old too. Go for it, Ruth.'

I left Ruth to her wheeling and dealing with the CID just after half past four and drove into the city centre. Chinatown was still lively, the late-night trade losing their shirts in the casinos and drunkenly scoffing Chinese meals after the clubs had closed. Less than a mile away, in the gay village round Chorlton Street bus station, the only sign of life was a few rent boys and hookers, hanging around the early-morning street corners in a triumph of hope over experience. I cruised slowly along Canal Street, the blank windows of Manto's reflecting nothing but my Peugeot. I didn't even spot anyone sleeping rough till I turned down Minshull Street towards UMIST.

The street was still. I pulled up in an empty parking meter bay. There were only three other cars in the street, one of them Richard's Beetle. I'd have to come back in the morning and collect it before some officious traffic warden had it ticketed and clamped. At least its presence supported Richard's story, if the police were inclined to check it out. I took my pocket Nikon out of my glove box, checked the date stamp was switched on and took a couple of shots of the Beetle as insurance.

Slowly, I walked round to Sackville Street, checking doorways and litter bins for the trade plates. I didn't hold out much hope. They were too good a prize for any passing criminal, never mind the guys who had stuck them on the coupé in the first place. As I'd expected, the streets were clear. On the off chance, I walked round into the little square of garden in Sackville Street and searched along the wall and in the bushes, being careful to avoid touching the unpleasant crop of used condoms. No joy. Stumbling with exhaustion, I walked back to my car and drove home. The prospect of having to take care of Davy weighed heavily on me, and I desperately wanted to crack on and make some progress towards clearing Richard. But the sensible part of me knew there was nothing I could do in the middle of the night. And if I didn't get some sleep soon, I wouldn't be fit to do what had to be done come daylight.

I set my alarm for half past eight, switched off the phones and turned down the volume on the answering machine. Unfortunately, I couldn't do the same thing with my brain. I tossed and turned, my head full of worries that wouldn't lie down and leave me in peace. I prayed Ruth's stratagem would work. While he was still in police custody, Richard was fairly safe. But as soon as he was charged and remanded to prison, the odds would turn against him. No matter how much the police tried to keep the lid on this business, it wouldn't take long in the leaky sieve of prison before the wrong people learned what he was in for. And if the drugs belonged to one of the Manchester gangs, some warlord somewhere would decide that Richard needed to be punished in ways the law has long since ceased to contemplate.

We'd both gone into this relationship with damage from past encounters. From the start, we'd been honest about our pain and our fears. As a result, we'd always kept it light, by tacit agreement. Somewhere round about dawn, I acknowledged that I couldn't live with myself if I let anything happen to him. It's a real bastard, love.

I was only dozing when the alarm went off. The first thing I did was check the answering machine. Its friendly red light was flashing, so I hit the replay button. 'Hello, Kate, it's Ruth.' Her voice was friendlier than I deserved. 'It's just before six, and I thought you'd be pleased to hear that I've manged to persuade the divisional superintendent that he has most chance of obtaining convictions from this situation if he keeps Richard's arrest under wraps. So he's agreed, very reluctantly, not to hold a press conference announcing a major drugs haul. He's not keen, but there we go. Was I put on earth to keep policemen happy? He's also receptive to the idea of a lie-down, but he wants to hang on till later in the day before he makes a final decision. Anyway, I hope you're managing some sleep, since working yourself to the point of exhaustion will not serve the interests of my client. Why don't you give me a call towards the end of the afternoon, by which time we both might have some information? Speak to you soon, darling. It'll be all right.' I wished I could share her breezy confidence.

As the coffee brewed, I called my local friendly mechanic and asked him to collect Richard's Beetle, promising to leave a set of keys under the kitchen window box. I also phoned in to the office and told Shelley what had happened. Of course, it was Richard who got the sympathy. Never mind that I'd been deprived of my sleep and landed with a task that might have caused even Clint Eastwood a few nervous moments. Oh no, that was my job, Shelley reminded me. 'You do what you've got to do to get that poor boy out of jail,' she said sternly. 'It makes me feel ill, just thinking of Richard locked up in a stinking cell with the dregs of humanity.'

'Yes, boss,' I muttered rebelliously. Shelley always

makes me feel like a bloody-minded teenager when she goes into Mother Hen mode. God knows what effect it has on her own two adolescents. 'Just tell Bill what I'm doing. I'll be on my mobile if you need me urgently,' I added.

I washed two thick slices of toast down with a couple of mugs of scalding coffee. The toast because I needed carbohydrate, the coffee because it was a more attractive option than surgery to get my eyes open. I pulled on jogging pants and a sweat shirt without showering and drove over to the Thai boxing gym in South Manchester where I punish my body on as regular a basis as my career in crime prevention allows. It might not be the Hilton, but it meets my needs. It's clean, it's cheap, the equipment is well maintained and it's mercifully free of muscle-bound macho men who think they've got the body and charm of Sylvester Stallone when in reality they don't even have the punch-drunk brains of Rocky.

I wasn't the only person working out on the weights that morning. The air was already heavy with the smell of sweat as half a dozen men and a couple of women struggled to keep time's winged chariot in the service bay. As I'd hoped, my old buddy Dennis O'Brien, burglar of this parish, was welded to the pec deck, moving more metal than the average Nissan Micra contains. He was barely breaking sweat. The bench next to him was free, so I picked up a set of dumbbells and lay back to do some tricep curls. 'Hiya, kid,' Dennis said on his next outgoing breath. 'What's the world been doing to you?'

'Don't ask. How about you?'

He grinned like a Disney wolf. 'Still doing the police's job for them,' he said. 'Got a real result last night.'

'Glad somebody did,' I said, enjoying the sensation of my flabby muscles tightening as I raised and lowered the weights.

'Fourteen grand I took off him,' Dennis told me. 'Now that's what I call a proper victim.'

He was clearly desperate to tell the tale, so I gave him the tiny spur of encouragement that was all he needed. 'Sounds like a good 'un. How d'you manage that?'

'I hear this firm from out of town are looking for a parcel of trainers. So I arrange to meet them, and I tell them I can lay my hands on an entire wagonload of Reeboks, don't I? A couple of nights later, we meet again and I show him a sample pair from this truck I'm supposed to have nicked, right? Only, I haven't nicked them, have I? I've just gone down the wholesaler's and bought them.' As he got into his story, Dennis paused in his work-out. He's physically incapable of telling a tale without his hands.

'So of course, they fall for it. Anyway, we arrange the meet for last night, out on the motorway services at Sandbach. My mate Andy and me, we get there a couple of hours before the meet and suss the place out. When these two bozos arrive, Andy's stood hiding behind a truck right the far side of the lorry park, and when the bozos park up beside my car, I make sure they see me giving him the signal, and he comes over to us, making out like he's just come out of the wagon, keys in his hand, the full monte.' Dennis was giggling between his sentences like a little lad outlining some playground scam.

I sat up and said, 'So what happens next?'

'I say to these two dummies, "Let's see the money, then. You hand over the money, and my mate'll hand over the keys to the wagon." And they do no more than hand over their fourteen grand like lambs. I'm counting the money, and when I've done, I give Andy the nod and he tosses them the keys. We jump into the motor and shoot straight off. I tell you, the last thing I see is the pair of them schmucks jumping up and down beside that wagon, their mouths opening and shutting like a pair of goldfish.' By the end of his tale, Dennis was doubled over with laughter. 'You should've seen them, Kate,' he wheezed. 'The Dennis O'Brien crime prevention programme scores another major success.'

The first time he said that to me, I'd been a bit baffled. I didn't see how ripping someone off to the tune of several grand could prevent crime. So Dennis had explained. The people he was cheating had a large sum of money that they were prepared to spend on stolen goods. So some thief would have to steal something for them to buy. But if Dennis relieved them of their wad, they wouldn't have any money to spend on stolen goods, therefore the robbery that would have had to take place was no longer necessary. Crime prevention, QED.

I moved over to a piece of equipment designed to build my quads and adjusted the weights. 'A lot of dosh, fourteen grand,' I said. 'Aren't you worried they're going to come after you?'

'Nah,' he said scornfully, returning to his exercise. 'They're from out of town. They don't know where I hang out, and nobody in Manchester would be daft enough to tell them where to find me. Besides, I was down Collar Di Salvo's car lot first thing this morning, trading the BMW in. They'll be looking for a guy in a red BM, not a silver Merc. Take a tip, Kate – don't buy a red BMW off Collar for the next few days. I don't want to see you in a case of mistaken identity!'

We both pumped iron in silence for a while. I moved around the machines, making sure I paid proper attention to the different muscle groups. By ten, I was sweating, Dennis was skipping and there were only the two of us left. I collapsed on to the mat, and enjoyed the complaints of my stomach muscles as I did some slow, warm-down exercises. 'I've got a problem,' I said in between Dennis's bounces.

Just saying that brought all the fear and misery right back. I stared hard at the off-white walls, trying to make a pattern out of the grimy handprints, black rubber skidmarks and chips from weights swung too enthusiastically. Dennis slowed to a halt and walked across to the shelves of thin towels that the management think are all we deserve. Like I said, it's cheap. I suppose it was their version of crime prevention; nobody in their right mind would steal those towels. Dennis picked up a couple, draped them over his big shoulders and sat down on the bench facing me. 'D'you want to talk about it?'

I sighed. 'To be honest, I'm not sure I can.' It wasn't that I didn't trust Dennis. Quite the opposite. I trusted his affection for me almost too much to tell him what had happened to Richard. There was no knowing what limits Dennis would go to in the attempt to take care of anyone threatening my happiness and wellbeing. Considering the different perspective we have on the law of the land, we find ourselves side by side facing in the same direction more often than not. For some reason that neither of us quite understands, we know we can rely on each other. And just as important, we like each other too.

Dennis patted my left ankle, the only part of me he could comfortably reach. 'You decide you want an ear, you let your Uncle Dennis know. What d'you need right now?'

'I'm not sure about that either.' I wiped the back of my hand over my mouth and upper lip and tasted the sharp salty sweat. 'Dennis. Why would you put trade plates on a stolen motor rather than false plates?'

'What kind of stolen motor? Joyrider material,

stolen to order, or just somebody stuck for a ride home?'

'A brand new Leo Gemini turbo super coupé. Less than a ton on the clock.'

He pondered for a moment. 'Temporary measure? To keep the busies off my back till I got it delivered where it was supposed to be going?'

'In this instance, we're talking a couple of days after the car was lifted. Plenty of time to have dropped it off with whoever, I'd have thought,' I said, shaking my head.

'In that case, you're probably talking right proper villainy,' he replied, rubbing the back of his neck with one of the towels.

'Run it past me,' I said.

Dennis pulled a packet of Bensons and a throw-away lighter out of the pocket of his sweat pants and lit up. 'They never have any bloody ashtrays in here,' he complained, looking round. The paradox clearly escaped him. 'Anyway, your professional car thief goes out on the job knowing exactly what motor he's going for. He doesn't do things on spec. He'd have a set of plates on him that he'd already matched up with another car of the same make and model, so that if some smart-arsed traffic cop put him through the computer he'd come up clean. So he wouldn't need trade plates. Your serious amateurs, they might use trade plates just to get it across town to their dealer. But they're not that easy to come by. OK so far?'

I got off the floor and squatted on a low bench.

'Clear as that Edinburgh crystal you offered me last month,' I said.

'Your loss, Kate,' he said. 'Now, on the other hand, if I wanted a fast car for a one-off job, I'd do exactly what the guy you're interested in has done. I'd nick a serious set of wheels, smack some trade plates on it from my local friendly hooky garage when I was actually using it, then dump it as soon as I'd finished the job.'

'When you say proper villainy, what exactly did you have in mind?' I asked.

'The kind of stuff I don't do. Major armed robbery, mainly. A hit, maybe.'

I began to wish I had the sense not to ask questions I wasn't going to like the answers to. 'What about drugs?'

He shrugged. 'Not the first thing that would spring to mind. But then, I don't hang out with scum like that, do I? At a guess, it'd only be worth doing if you were shifting a parcel of drugs a reasonable distance between two major players. Say, from London to Manchester. Otherwise there'd be so many cars running around with trade plates that even the coppers would notice. Also, trade plates are ten a penny on the motorway. Whereas brand new motors with or without trade plates stick out like a sore thumb on the council estates where most of the drugs get shifted. You want to get a pull these days, you just have to park up in Moss Side in anything that isn't old enough to need an MOT,' he added bitterly.

'What would you say if I told you there were a couple of kilos of crack in the boot of this car?'

Dennis got to his feet. 'Nice chatting to you, Kate. Be seeing you. That's what I'd say.'

I pulled a face and stood up too. 'Thanks, Dennis.'

Dennis put a warm hand on my wrist and gripped it tightly enough for me not to think about pulling away. 'I've never been more serious, Kate. Steer clear of them toerags. They'd eat *me* for breakfast. They wouldn't even notice you as they swallowed. Give this one the Spanish Archer.'

'The Spanish Archer?' This was a new one on me.

'El Bow.'

I smiled. 'I'll be careful. I promise.' I thought I'd grown out of promising what I can't deliver. Obviously I was wrong.

6

I walked into the office to find my partner Bill
looming over Shelley like a scene from *The Jungle
Book*. Bill is big, blond and shaggy, the antith-
esis of Shelley, petite, black and immaculately
groomed right down to the tips of her perfectly
plaited hair. He looked up and stopped speaking
in midsentence, finger pointing at something on
Shelley's screen.

'Kate, Kate, Kate,' he boomed, moving across
the room to envelop me in the kind of hug that
makes me feel like a little girl. Usually I fight my
way out, but this morning it was good to feel safe
for a moment, even if it was only an illusion. With
one hand, Bill patted my back, with the other
he rumpled my hair. Eventually, he released me.
'Shelley filled me in. I was just going to phone
you,' he said, walking over to the coffee machine
and busying himself making me a cappuccino.
'This business with Richard. What do you want
me to do?'

On paper, Bill might be the senior partner of Mortensen and Brannigan. In practice, when either of us is involved in a major case and needs help from the other, there's never any question of the gopher role going to me just because I'm the junior. Whoever started the ball rolling stays the boss. And in this instance, since it was my lover who was in the shit, it was my case.

I took the frothy coffee he handed me and slumped into one of the clients' chairs. 'I don't know what you can do,' I said. 'We've got to find out who stole the car, who the drugs belong to and to make out a strong enough case against them for the police to realize they've made a cock-up. Otherwise Richard stays in the nick and we sit back and wait for the slaughter of the innocents.'

Bill sat down opposite me. 'Shelley,' he said over his shoulder, 'stick the answering machine on, grab yourself an espresso and come and give us the benefit of your thoughts. We need every brain we've got working on this one.'

Shelley didn't need telling twice. She sat down, the inevitable notepad on her knee. Bill leaned back and linked his hands behind his head. 'Right,' he said. 'First question. Accident or intent?'

'Accident,' I said instantly.

'Why are you so sure?' Bill asked.

I took a sip of coffee while I worked out the reasons I'd been so certain. 'OK,' I said. 'First, there are too many imponderables for it to be intentional. If someone was deliberately trying to set up Richard, or me, they wouldn't have bothered with the trade plates. They'd just have left it sitting there with its own plates, so obvious that he couldn't have missed it. Why bother with all of that when they could have planted the drugs in either of our cars at any time?'

Shelley nodded and said, 'The thing that strikes me is that it's an awful lot of drugs to plant. Surely they could have achieved the same result with a lot less crack than two kilos. I don't know much about big-time drug dealers, but I can't believe they'd waste drugs they could make money out of just to set somebody up.'

'Besides,' I added, 'why in God's name would anyone want to frame Richard? I know *I* sometimes feel like murdering him, but I'm a special case. Not even his ex-wife would want him to spend the next twenty years inside, never mind be willing to splash out – what, two hundred grand?'

Bill nodded. 'Near enough,' he said.

'Well, even she wouldn't spend that kind of dosh just to get her own back on him, always supposing he paid her enough maintenance for her to afford it. It's not as if he's an investigative journalist. The only people who take offence at what he writes are record company executives, and if any of them got their hands on two kilos of crack it would be up their noses, not in the boot of Richard's car.' My voice wobbled and I ran out of steam suddenly. I kept coming up against the horrible realization that this wasn't just another case. My life was going to be irrevocably affected by whatever I did over the next few days.

Thankfully, Bill didn't notice. I don't think I could have handled any more sympathy right then. 'OK. Accident. Synchronicity. What are the leads?'

'Why does somebody always have to ask the one question you don't have the answer to?' I said shakily.

'Has his solicitor got anything from the police yet?' Bill asked. 'Who's looking after him, by the way?'

'He's got Ruth. If the cops have got anything themselves yet, they've not passed it on. But she asked me to call her this afternoon.' I stirred the froth into the remains of my coffee and watched it change colour.

'So what have we got to go at?'

'Not a lot,' I admitted. 'Frankly, Bill, there aren't enough leads on this to keep one person busy, never mind the two of us.'

'What were you planning on doing?' he asked.

'I don't know anybody on the Drugs Squad well enough to pick their brains. So that leaves Della.'

Bill nodded. 'She'll be as keen to help as me and Shelley.'

'She should be,' I agreed. Not only did Detective Chief Inspector Della Prentice owe me a substantial professional favour in return for criminals translated into prisoners. Over the past few months,

67

she'd also moved into that small group of women I count as friends. If I couldn't rely on her support, I'd better send my judgment back to the manufacturer for a major service. 'The only other thing I can think of is cruising the city centre tonight looking for another serious motor with trade plates on it.'

'The logic presumably being that if they've lost the car they were counting on, they'll need another one?' Bill asked. 'Even though the drugs have gone?'

'It's all I've got. I'm hoping that our man will be out and about, trying to find out who's got a parcel of crack they shouldn't have. But that's a one-person job, Bill. Look, leave me numbers where I can reach you, day or night. I promise, if I get anywhere and I need an extra pair of hands, I'll call you right away.'

'That's truly the only lead you've got? You're not holding out on me?' he asked suspiciously.

'Believe me, Bill, if I thought there was anything for you to do, I'd be on my hands and knees begging,' I said, only half joking.

'Well, let's see what Della has to say. Right, team, let's get some work done!' He strolled back over to Shelley's desk. 'This bit here, Shelley. Can we shift it further up the report, so all the frightening stuff hits them right at the beginning?'

Shelley rolled her eyes upwards and got to her feet, squeezing my arm supportively as she passed me on the way to her desk. 'Let me have a look,

Bill,' she said, settling into her chair.

As I headed for my own office, Bill looked up and smiled. I think it was meant to reassure me. It didn't. I closed my door and dropped into my chair like a stone. I put a hand out to switch on my computer, but there didn't seem a lot of point. I swivelled round and looked out of the window at the city skyline. The lemon geranium on the sill was drooping. Knowing my track record with plants, my best friend Alexis had given me the geranium, confidently predicting it was inde-structible. I tried not to see its impending death as an omen and turned away. Time was slipping past, and I didn't seem to be able to take any decisive action to relieve the sense of frustration that was burning inside me like indigestion.

'Come *on*, Brannigan,' I urged myself, picking up the phone. At least I could get the worst job over with. When the phone was answered, I said, 'Andrew Broderick, please.'

Moments later, a familiar voice said, 'Broderick.'

'Andrew, it's Kate Brannigan. I have good news and bad news,' I said. 'The good news is that we've found the car, undamaged.'

'That's tremendous,' he said, his astonishment obvious. 'How did you manage that?'

'Pure chance, unfortunately,' I said. 'The bad news, however, is that the police have impounded it.'

'The police? But why?'

I sighed. 'It's a bit complicated, Andrew,' I said.

Brannigan's entry for the understatement of the year contest. When I'd finished explaining, I had an extremely unhappy client.

'This is simply not on,' he growled. 'What right have they got to hang on to a car that belongs to my company?'

'It's evidence in a major drugs case.'

'Jesus Christ,' he exploded. 'If I don't get that car back, this operation is going to cost me about as much as the scam. How the hell am I going to lose that in the books?'

I didn't have the answer. I made some placatory noises, and got off the line as fast as I could. Staring at the wall, I remembered a loose end that was hanging around from Broderick's job, so I rang my local friendly finance broker.

Josh Gilbert and I have an arrangement: he runs credit checks on dodgy punters for me and I buy him dinner a lot. Anything else he can help us with we pay through the nose for.

It turned out that Josh was out of town, but his assistant Julia was around. I explained what I wanted from her and she said, 'No problem. I can't promise I'll get to it today, but I'll definitely fax it to you by Tuesday lunch time. Is that OK?'

It would have to be. The one free favour Josh had ever done me was introducing me to Detective Chief Inspector Della Prentice. My next call was to her direct line. She answered on the second ring. 'DCI Prentice,' she said crisply.

'Della, it's Kate,' I said. Even to me, my voice sounded weary.

'Kate! Thanks for getting back to me,' she said.

'Sorry? I didn't know you'd been trying to get hold of me,' I replied, shuffling the papers on my desk in case I'd missed a message.

'I spoke to your machine an hour or so ago. When I heard what had happened to Richard,' Della said. 'I just wanted you to know that I don't believe a word of it.'

I felt a lump in my throat, so I swallowed hard and concentrated very hard on the jar of pencils by my phone. 'Me neither,' I said. 'Del, I know it's not your manor, but I need all the help I can get on this one.'

'Goes without saying, Kate. Look, it's not going to be easy for me to get access to the case information or any forensic evidence, but I'll do what I can,' she promised.

'I appreciate that. But don't put your own head in the noose in the process,' I added. No matter how much they spend on advertising to tell us different, anyone who has any contact with real live police officers know that The Job is still a white, patriarchal, rigidly hierarchical organization. That makes life especially hard for women who refuse to be shunted into the ghetto of community liaison and get stuck in at the sharp end of crime fighting.

'Don't worry about me. I'll find out who's on the team and see who I know. Meanwhile, is there anything specific I can help you with?'

'I need a general backgrounder on crack. How much there is of it around, where it's turning up, who they think is pushing the stuff, how it's being distributed. Anything there is, including gossip. Off the record, of course. Any chance?' I asked.

'Give me a few hours. Can you meet me around seven?'

I pulled a face. 'Only if you can get to the airport,' I said. 'I have a plane to meet.'

'No problem.'

'Oh yes it is. Richard's son's going to be on it. And the one thing he mustn't find out is that his dad's in the nick on drugs charges.'

'Ah,' Della said. It was a short, clipped exclamation.

'I take it that response means you don't want to share the child-minding?'

'Correct. Count me out. Look, I'll dig up all I can and meet you at Domestic Arrivals in Terminal I, at the coffee counter, just as you come in. Around quarter to seven, OK?'

I didn't want to wait that long, but Della wasn't the sort to hang around either. If quarter to seven was when she wanted to meet, then quarter to seven was the soonest she could see me with the information I needed. 'I'll see you then. Oh, one other thing. I don't think it's got anything to do with the drugs, but there was a Polaroid picture of a young kid in handcuffs, you know, bondage-style, in the car. Probably just dropped by one of the villains. But maybe you could ask around and

72

see if there's anybody that Vice have in the frame
for paedophilia who's also got form for drugs.'

'Can do.'

'And Della?'

'Mmm?'

'Thanks.'

'You know what they say. A friend in need . . .'

'Is a pain in the ass,' I finished. 'See you.' I put
the phone down. At last I felt things were starting
to move.

The conversation with Della had reminded me of
the part of the problem I'd deliberately been ignoring. Davy. Not that he was in himself a problem.
It's just that I wasn't very good at keeping eight-
year-old boys happy when I was eight myself, and
I haven't improved with age. According to Richard,
Davy was the only good thing to come out of his
three-year marriage, and his ex-wife Angie seemed
more determined with each passing year to reduce
his contact with the only child he was likely to
have if he stayed with me. So it was imperative
that Davy didn't go back from his half-term holiday
with lurid tales of Daddy in the nick.

Which sounded simple if you said it very fast.
Unless we could spring Richard in the next day
or two, however, it was going to be extremely
complicated. Richard and I had agreed an initial
lie, which should hold the fort for a day or two.
After that, it was going to get complicated. While
Davy might just believe his dad had had to dash
abroad on an urgent, chance-in-a-lifetime job, it

wasn't going to be easy to explain why Richard couldn't get home again. There may be parts of the world where the transport isn't too reliable on account of wars and famine, but unfortunately most of them don't run to major rock venues. Either way, whether it took hours or days, I was going to need some assistant minders, if only to baby-sit while I rambled the city centre streets looking for fast cars with trade plates. And there aren't very many people I'd trust to do that.

I picked up the phone again and tapped in Alexis Lee's office number. '*Chronicle* crime desk,' a young man's voice informed me.

'Alexis, please.'

'Sh'not'ere,' came the snippy reply.

'I need to speak to her in a hurry. You wouldn't happen to know where I can get hold of her?' I asked, clinging to my manners by my fingernails. My Granny Brannigan always said politeness cost nothing. But then, she never had to face the humiliation of dealing with lads who still think a yuppie is something to aspire to.

''Zit'bout'story?' he demanded. 'You c'n tell me if it is.'

'Not as such,' I said through clenched teeth. I could hear my Oxford accent becoming more Gown than Town by the second. 'Not yet, anyway. Look, I know you're a very busy person, and I don't want to waste any of your precious time, but it's awfully important that I speak to Alexis. Do you know where she is?'

There's a whole generation of young lads who are either so badly educated or so thick skinned they don't even notice when they're being patronized. The guy on the phone could have featured in a sociology lecture as an exemplar of the type. 'Sh's a' lunch,' he gabbled.

'And do we know where?'

'Gone f'r a curry.'

That was all I needed to know. There might be three dozen curry restaurants strung out along the mile-long stretch of Wilmslow Road in Rusholme, but everybody has their favourite. Alexis's current choice was only too familiar. 'Thanks, sonny,' I said. 'I'll remember you in my letter to Santa.'

I was out of my seat before I'd put the phone back. I crossed my office in five strides and walked into the main office. 'Shelley, I'm off to the Golden Ganges. And before you ask how I can eat at a time like this, don't. Just don't.'

7

If the gods had struck me blind the moment I entered the Golden Ganges, I'd still have had no problem finding Alexis. That unmistakable Liverpudlian voice, a monument to Scotch and nicotine, almost drowned out the twanging sitar that was feebly trickling out of the restaurant's speakers, even though she was seated a long way from the door. The volume told me she wasn't working, just routinely showing off to her companion. When she's doing the business with one of her contacts, the sound level drops so low that even MI5 would have a job picking it up. I walked towards the table.

Alexis spotted me two steps into the room, though there was no pause in the flow of her narrative to indicate it. As I approached, she held up one finger to stop me in my tracks a few feet away, interrupting her story to say, 'Just a sec, Kate, crucial point in the anecdote.' She turned back to her companion and said, 'Thomas Wynn Ellis, a good Welsh name, you'd think you'd cracked it, yeah? I mean, she's not *crazy* about the Welsh, but at least you've got a fair chance that he's going to speak English, yeah? So she fills in all the forms to be taken on as a patient, then makes an appointment to see him about her back problem. She walks into the surgery, and what does she find? Straight from Karachi, Dr Thomas Wynn Ellis, product of the Christian orphanage, colour of a bottle of HP sauce! She was sick as a parrot!'

Alexis's companion giggled. I couldn't find a laugh, not just because I'd heard her ridicule the casual racism of her colleagues before. I sat down at the table. Luckily they'd progressed to the coffee. I don't think I could have sat at the same table as a curry, never mind eaten one. I didn't recognize the young woman sharing the table, but Alexis didn't leave me in the dark too long. 'Kate, this is Polly Patrick, she's about to take up a post at the university, doing research into psychological profiling of serial offenders. Polly, this is my best mate, Kate Brannigan, PI.'

Polly looked interested. I winced. I knew what was coming. 'You're a private investigator?' Polly asked.

'No,' Alexis butted in, unable to resist her joke of the month. 'She's Politically Incorrect!' She hooted in mirth. In anyone else, it would wind me up to some tune, but Alexis's humour is so innocently juvenile she somehow manages to be endearing, not infuriating.

This time, I managed to dredge up a smile. 'Actually, I am a private investigator. And I'd be fascinated to have a chat with you some time about what you do.'

'Ditto,' said Polly. Unusually for a psychologist, she had some people skills, for she took the barely indicated hint. 'But it'll have to be another time. I've got to dash. Perhaps the three of us could do lunch some time soon?'

We all made the appropriate farewell and let's-get-together-soon noises, and a few minutes later, Polly was just a memory. Alexis had ordered more coffee somewhere during the goodbyes, and I sat staring at the froth on mine as she lit a cigarette and settled into her seat. 'So, Sherlock,' she said. 'What's the problem?'

I reckoned I was about to ask her something that would test our friendship to the limits. But then, the last time she'd asked me a major favour, it had nearly got me killed, so I figured I didn't need to beat myself up about it too much. I took a deep breath and said, 'I need to talk to you about something important. It's personal, it's big and it's got to be off the record. Can you live with that?'

'We're friends, aren't we?'

'Yeah, and one good turn deserves the lion's share of the duvet.'

'Go on, girl, spill it,' Alexis said. She opened a shoulder bag only marginally smaller than mine and ostentatiously pressed the button that switched off her microcassette recorder. 'Your secret is safe with me.'

'Why d'you suppose that line terrifies me?' I said, in a weak attempt at our usual friendly banter.

Alexis ran a hand through her wild black hair. Coupled with her pale skin and the dark smudges under her eyes, I sometimes think she looks worryingly like one of Dracula's victims in the Francis Ford Coppola version. Luckily, her linguistic vigour usually dispels such ethereal notions pretty damn quick. 'Shit, KB, if that's the best you can do, there's clearly something serious going down here,' she said. 'C'mon, girl, spit it out.'

'Richard's been arrested,' I said. 'He was technically driving a stolen car that not so technically had two kilos of crack in the boot.'

Alexis just stared at me. She even ignored her burning cigarette. The woman who had heard it all could be shaken after all. 'You're at the wind-up,' she finally said.

I shook my head. 'I wish I was.' I gave her the full story. It didn't take long. Throughout, she kept shaking her head in disbelief, smoking so intensely it seemed to be all that was keeping her in one piece. When I'd brought her up to speed, she carried on smoking, head weaving like a Wimbledon spectator.

'It could only happen to Richard,' she finally said in tones of wonder. 'How does he do it? The poor sod!' Alexis and Richard play this game of cordially disliking each other. I'm not supposed to know it's a game; things must be bad if Alexis was letting me see she actually cared about the guy. 'I take it you want me to dig around, see what the goss is out on the streets?'

'I don't want you to take any chances,' I said, meaning it. 'You know as well as I do that most of the drug warlords in this city would blow you away at the slightest provocation. Don't tread on anybody's toes, please. I don't want you on my conscience as well as Richard. What I'm after is more practical.' I broke the news about Davy's imminent arrival.

'Sure, we'll help out. I like Davy. He's good fun. Besides, it gives me and Chris a great excuse to bunk off a weekend's labouring and have a giggle instead.' Alexis and her architect girlfriend Chris are members of a self-build scheme, which means they spend most of their spare daylight hours pushing wheelbarrows full of cement along precarious wooden planks. A dozen of them bought a piece of land, and Chris designed the houses in exchange for other people's skills in exotic areas like plumbing, wiring, bricklaying and roofing. It's my idea of hell, but they love it, though not so much that they're not glad of an excuse to give it the body swerve from time to time. I knew taking care of Davy fitted the bill perfectly; it had a high enough Goody Two Shoes element to assuage any guilt at skiving off the building site.

Hearing Alexis confirm my hopes almost brought

a genuine smile to my lips. 'So can you be at the house tonight about eight?'

Alexis frowned. 'Not tonight I can't. I'm having dinner with a contact.'

'No chance you can rearrange it?'

'Sorry. The guy's only in town for a few days.' She stubbed out her cigarette and washed the taste away with a swig of coffee. She must have felt the need to justify herself, for when I didn't respond, she carried on, 'I was at college with him, and we stayed in touch. He's one of your high-flyers, a whiz-kid with the Customs and Excise, if that's not a contradiction in terms. Anyway, he's in Manchester for a briefing session with the Vice Squad. Apparently, there's been a new range of kiddie porn mags and vids hitting the market, real hard-core stuff, and they think the source is somewhere in the North West. Can you believe it, girl? We're actually exporting this shit to Amsterdam and Denmark, that's how heavy it is. So my mate Barney's up here to tell the blue boys what they should be looking for, and I've pitched him into letting me buy him dinner. Sorry, Kate, but I've already promised the editor a splash and a feature launching a campaign for Monday's paper.'

I shrugged. 'Don't worry about it. I'll get someone else lined up for tonight, and you can weigh in when you're clear.'

'Don't do that. Chris'll see you right tonight, I'm sure she will. All she's got planned is a night in front of the soaps and a bottle of Muscadet in the bath. You got the talking brick with you?' Alexis held out her hand, and I passed her my mobile phone. I couldn't help thinking I'd be less than thrilled if Richard had offered me up for a night's baby-sitting when I'd got my heart set on a night in with *Coronation Street* and a Body Shop selection box..

'All right, darling?' Alexis began the conversation. 'Listen, Kate needs your body tonight . . . Girl, you should be so lucky. No, it's a bit of a crisis, you know? I'll fill you in later. She needs somebody she can trust to mind Davy round at Richard's . . . Eight, she said, is that OK? . . . Darlin', you'll get your reward in heaven. See you at home about six. Love you too.' Alexis pressed the 'end' button with a flourish. 'Sorted. I'll give her my keys for your house so she can let herself in.' She folded the phone closed and handed it back to me.

'I appreciate it,' I said. I meant it too. I hoped I wasn't going to run out of favours and friends before I managed to get Richard out of jail. 'One more thing – when you're chatting up your porn expert, can you ask him if there's any suggestion of a tie-in with drugs?'

'Why do you ask?' Alexis demanded, her brown eyes suddenly alert.

I groaned. 'It's not a story, trust me. It's just that there's an outside chance one of the people involved in this business of Richard's might be into paedophilia.'

'What makes you think that?' she asked, suspicious that she might be missing out on something that would plaster her by-line across the front pages of the *Chronicle*.

'It'd be cruel to tell you,' I said. 'You'd only be upset because you couldn't use it.'

Alexis shook her head, a rueful smile twitching the corners of her mouth. 'You know me too well, girl.'

I stood on the pavement outside the Golden Ganges, watching Alexis's car pull away from the kerb into a death-defying U-turn. The air was heavy with the fumes of traffic and curry spices, the sky bleak and overcast, the distant sounds of police and ambulance sirens mingling with the wail of a nearby car alarm. I turned the corner of the side-street where I'd left my car, and the ululations of the alarm increased dramatically. It took me a moment or two to realize that it was my car that was the focus of attention for the two black lads with the cordless hand-drill.

'Hey, shitheads,' I yelled in protest, breaking into a run without even thinking about it.

They looked up, uncertainty written all over their faces. It only took them seconds to weigh up the situation and decide to leg it. If it had been after dark, they probably would have brazened it out and tried to give me a good kicking for daring to challenge their right to my stereo. Shame, really. I had so much pent-up frustration in me that I'd have relished the chance to show them my Thai boxing skills weren't just for keeping fit.

By the time I reached the car, they were round the next corner. The mashed metal of the lock wasn't ever going to make sweet music with a key again. I pushed the control button that stopped the alarm shrieking. Sighing, I pulled the door open and climbed in. At least having the lock replaced would kill one of the hours I couldn't find a way to fill usefully. Before I started the engine, I called Handbrake the mechanic, checked he'd collected the Beetle without a hitch and told him I needed a new driver's door lock. That way, I wouldn't have to hang around answering his phone while he nipped out to collect the part.

I turned left on to Oxford Road and headed away from the city centre. I was clear of the curry zone in a few minutes, and straight into the heart of university residences and student bedsits. I pushed the eject button on the stereo. Goodbye Julia Fordham. Plangent and poignant was just what I didn't need right now. I raked through my cassettes and smacked the Pet Shop Boys' *Discography* into the slot. Perfect. A thrusting beat to drive me onwards and upwards, an emotional content somewhere below zero. At the Wilbraham Road lights, I cut across to Kingsway and over to Heaton Mersey where Handbrake operates out of a pair of lock-ups behind a down-at-heel block of flats. Handbrake is a mate of Dennis's who's been team mechanic to Mortensen and Brannigan for a few years now. And, for his sins, he also gets to play with Richard's Beetle. He's called Handbrake because he used to be a getaway driver for armed robbers, and he specialized in 180-degree handbrake turns when the pursuit got a bit too close for comfort. He did a six-stretch back in the early eighties, and he's gone straight ever since. Well, only a bit wobbly. Only now and again.

There was a Volkswagen Golf in one of Handbrake's two garages. As I pulled up, Handbrake emerged from under the bonnet. Anyone less likely to adopt the anonymous role of a getaway driver it would be hard to imagine. He's got flaming red curls as tight as a pensioner's perm and a face like a sad clown. He'd have no chance in an identity parade unless the cops brought in a busload of Ronald McDonalds. Handbrake wiped his hands on his overalls and gave me a smile that made him look like he was about to burst into tears.

'Gobshites get you?' he greeted me.

'Caught them in time to save the stereo,' I told him, leaving the door open behind me.

'That's saved you a few bob, then. The lad'll be back with the locks any minute,' Handbrake said, giving the door the judicious once-over. 'Nice clean job, really.'

'No problem with the Beetle?'

He shook his head. 'Nah. Piece of piss. I left it outside your house, stuck the keys back through the letter box. Mr Music out of town, is he?' I was saved from lying by the arrival of a young black kid on a mountain bike. 'All right, Dobbo?' Handbrake called out.

The lad hauled back on his handlebars to pull up in midwheelie. 'My man,' he affirmed. He shrugged out of a smart leather backpack and took a new set of locks for my Peugeot out of it. He handed it to Handbrake, quoted what seemed to be an interestingly low price and added on a tenner for delivery. Handbrake pulled a wad out of his back pocket and counted out the cash. The lad zipped it into his leather bum bag and cycled off. At the corner, he stopped and took out what looked like a mobile phone. He hadn't looked a day over fourteen.

'Don't take offence, Handbrake, but these parts aren't a little bit moody, are they?' I hate having to be such a prissy little madam, but I can't afford to be caught out with a car built from stolen spares.

Handbrake shook his head. 'Nah. Him and his mates have got a deal going with half the scrap yards in Manchester. Product of the recession. Not so much drugs around, not so much dosh to be made ferrying them round the town, so Dobbo and a couple of his mates spent some of their ill-gotten gains on a computer. One of them checks with the scrap yards every morning to see what new stock they've got in. Then when punters like me want a part, we ring in and the dispatcher works out where they can get it from and sends one of the bike boys off for it. Good game, huh?'

'You're not kidding.' I watched Handbrake pop

the remains of the lock out of my car door. 'Handbrake? You know anybody on the drugs scene that moves their merchandise in stolen motors?'

Handbrake snorted. 'Ask me another. I try not to know anything about drugs in this town. Like the man said, a little learning is a dangerous thing.' Handbrake did A Level English while he was inside. Who says prison doesn't change a man?

'OK. How would someone get hold of a set of trade plates?'

'You mean if you're not a legitimate person?'

'Why would I be asking you about legitimate people?'

He snorted again. 'Well, you can't just cobble them together in a backstreet workshop. It's only the Department of Transport that makes them, and the numbers are die-stamped into the metal, not like your regular licence plates. You'd have to beg, borrow or steal. There's enough of them around. You could nick them off a garage or a motor in transit, though that way they'd be reported stolen and you wouldn't get a lot of mileage out of them. Beg or buy a loan of a set off a delivery driver. Best way is to borrow them off a slightly dodgy garage. Why, you need some?'

Handbrake likes to wind me up by pretending he's the innocent abroad and I'm the villain. But I wasn't in the mood for it right then. 'No,' I snarled. 'But I think I might be about to deprive someone of some.'

'Better be careful where you use them, then.'

'Why?'

''Cos you'll get a tug is why. The traffic cops always pull you if you're using trade plates. Not so much on the motorway, but defo if you're cruising round. If they so much as think you're using them for anything except demos, tuition or delivery, you've had it. So you better have a good cover story.'

I was glad of the tip. I didn't think this was the right weekend for a roadside chat with the traffic division.

8

I kicked my heels for the best part of an hour in
Ruth's waiting room while she was dealing with
a client. I'd have been better employed catching up on my sleep. After I'd stood on for a
major bollocking for my outrageous behaviour
at Longsight nick, we sat glumly staring at each
other across her cluttered desk, depressed by the
lack of information we had to trade. 'I suspect the
officers actually working the case don't believe
a word Richard's saying,' Ruth said. 'All I get
is the condescending wink when I suggest that
if they really want to make a major drugs bust
they should be on the phone to every villain who's
ever grassed in his life. Anything to get a lead on
the car thieves. But of course, they don't really
believe in the car thieves,' she added cynically.
'The one lucky break we have so far is that none
of the police officers we've dealt with has made
the connection between Richard and you. At least
the superintendent is prepared to go along with the

idea of a lie-down, even though he stressed that it was for his team's benefit and not mine.'

I got to my feet. 'I suppose it's a step in the right direction. I'll let you know as soon as I get anything,' I said grimly.

Out in the street, the city carried on as usual. I cut across Deansgate and through the Victorian glass-domed elegance of the Barton Arcade into the knots of serious shoppers bustling around the designer clothes shops of St Ann's Square. Nobody had told the buskers outside the Royal Exchange that this was not a day for celebration and their cheery country rock mocked me all the way across the square and into Cross Street. I'd abandoned the car on a single yellow line round the back of the Nat West bank, and to my astonishment, I didn't have a ticket. It was the first time all day that I'd got the benefit of an even break. I had to take it as an omen.

Back home, I checked Richard's answering machine and saved the handful of messages. I returned a couple of the more urgent calls, explaining he'd had to go out of town at a moment's notice and I wasn't sure when he'd be back. I also checked his diary, and cancelled a couple of interviews he'd arranged for the early part of the coming week. Luckily, he didn't have much planned, thanks to Davy's visit. God only knew how he was going to write this week's magazine column. Frankly, it was the least of my worries.

*   *   *

Manchester's rush hour seems to have developed middle-aged spread. When I first moved to the city, it lasted a clearly definable ninety minutes, morning and evening. Now, in the evening it seems to start at four and continue till half past seven. And on Fridays, it's especially grim. Even on the wide dual carriageway of Princess Parkway, it was a major challenge to get into third. It felt like a relief to be in the airport. That's how bad it was.

I was ten minutes early for our meeting, but Della was already sitting in the domestic terminal with a coffee. When the automatic doors hissed open to let me in, she glanced up from her *Evening Chronicle*. Even from that distance I could see the anxiety in her deep-set green eyes. She jumped to her feet and pulled me into a hug as soon as I got close enough. 'Poor you,' she said with feeling, steering me gently into a seat. The sympathy was too much. Seeing the tears in my eyes, Della patted me awkwardly on the shoulder and said, 'Give me a sec, I'll get you a coffee.'

By the time she returned, I was as hard-boiled as Philip Marlowe again. 'Like the hair,' I remarked. Her shining chestnut hair, normally controlled to within an inch of its life in a thick plait, was loose around her shoulders, held back from her face with a wide, sueded silk headband.

'Thanks.' She pulled a face. 'Think it'll impress a forty-year-old merchant banker?'

'Business or pleasure?'

'He thinks pleasure, I suspect business.' Detective Chief Inspector Della Prentice is the operational head of the Regional Crime Squad's fraud task force. She's a Cambridge graduate, with all the social graces that implies, which means that when she's got some bent businessman in her sights he's more likely to think this charming woman who's so fascinated by his work is a corporate headhunter rather than a copper. The problem is, as Della once explained with a sigh, the best con men are often the most charming.

'We never sleep, eh?' I teased.

'Not with people we suspect might have their hands in a rather interesting can of worms,' Della said. 'Even if he is buying me dinner at the Thirty-Nine Steps.' I felt a momentary pang of jealousy. Since Richard only ever wants to eat Chinese food, I don't often get the chance to eat at the best fish restaurant in Manchester. As if reading my thoughts, Della said, 'But enough of my problems. Any news on Richard?'

'Not a sausage. I feel so frustrated. I just haven't got any handles to get a hold of. I don't suppose you've got anything for me?' I asked morosely.

'We . . . ell, yes, and no,' Della said cautiously, lighting a cigarette with her battered old Zippo.

The ticket-free windscreen *had* been an omen. 'Yeah?' I demanded.

'The fingerprint SOCO who went over Richard's car did some work for me a while back when I was looking into forged insurance policies, and we got quite pally. So I bought her a butty at lunch time.'

'What did she find?' I asked.

'It's what she didn't find that's significant. She was being a bit cautious. Understandably, because she's not had time yet to analyse all the prints thoroughly. But it looks like Richard's fingerprints were on all the surfaces you'd expect – door handle, gear stick, steering wheel, the cassette in the stereo. But there were none of his prints on the boot, or the carrier bag or the plastic bags that the rocks were in. In fact, there were no prints at all on any of those. Just the kind of smudges you get from latex gloves. And Richard had no gloves on his person, nor were there any in the car.' Della gave a tentative smile, and I found myself reflecting it.

'D'you know, that's the first good news I've heard all day?'

Della looked apologetic. 'I know it's not much, but it's a start. If I hear any more on the grapevine, I'll let you know. Now, as to the other thing. You owe me, Kate – I thought when I left the West Yorkshire fraud squad that I'd never have to drink with another patronizing, sexist Yorkshireman. Today I discovered they actually get worse when they're in exile on the wrong side of the Pennines. According to DCI Geoff Turnbull of the Drugs Squad, it's understandable that a nice woman like me should be interested in drugs. After all, even if I didn't manage to fulfil my womanly role by reproducing myself before my divorce, I must have contemporaries whose kids are in their late teens and therefore at that dangerous age,' Della growled through clenched teeth.

'Oh dear,' I sympathized. 'And when exactly are they letting him out of intensive care? I know a choir that's short on sopranos.'

Della managed a twisted smile. 'Once he'd finished condescending, he did actually come up with some interesting information. Apparently, when crack first started to appear in this country, it was in relatively small amounts and in quite specific areas. The obvious inference was that there were only a handful of people involved in the importing and distribution of it, and while its presence was worrying, its level of penetration wasn't seriously disturbing. However, during the last few months, small quantities of crack have been turning up all over the country along with some unusual designer drugs. The really worrying thing is that these finds have been coming out of routine operations.' Della paused expectantly.

I didn't know what she was expecting. I said, 'Why is that so worrying?'

'It's turned up where they didn't expect to find it. The operations have been targeted at something else, say Ecstasy or heroin, and they've ended up producing a small but significant amount of crack as well. And it's not localized. It's dotted all over the shop.' Della looked serious. I could see why. If small finds were appearing unexpectedly, the chances were that they were only the tip of a very large iceberg.

'Any particular geographical distribution?' I asked.

'Virtually all over the country. But it's mostly confined to bandit country.'

'Meaning?' I asked.

'The sort of areas that are semi-no-go. Inner city decayed housing, satellite council estates both in the cities and in bigger towns. The kind of traditional working-class areas where people used to leave school and go into the local industry, only there's no industry any more so they graduate straight to the dole queue, the drink and drugs habits and the petty crime that goes with them.' Della stubbed her cigarette out angrily.

'I bet your Yorkshire DCI didn't put it quite like that.'

'How did you guess?' Della said cynically. 'Anyway, the bottom line is that it looks like we've got a crack epidemic on our hands. And they suspect that whoever is dealing this crack has a very efficient distribution network.'

That ruled out the Post Office. 'And they think Richard is part of that?'

'I didn't ask. But they clearly think he's important enough to be worth sweating.' Della sighed. 'It doesn't look good, Kate, I'm bound to say.'

I nodded. She didn't have to tell me. 'Any suggestions as to where I might start looking?'

Della looked at me. Her green eyes were serious. 'You're not going to thank me for this, but I don't think you should be looking at all. These are very dangerous people. They will kill you if they think you're any kind of threat.'

'You think I don't know that? What option have I got, Della? If I can't get the real villains behind bars, they'll kill Richard. As soon as they find out just who drove off with their parcel of crack. You know they will. They can't afford not to, or every two-bit dealer in town'll think they can give them the run-around.' I swallowed the last of my coffee. I should have gone for camomile tea. The last thing I needed was to get even more hyped up.

'Did you get the chance to ask about the Polaroid?' Anything to avoid another unnerving gypsy warning.

'I spoke to a woman DS in Vice. She said she couldn't think of anyone off the top of her head, but she'd ask around. But the DCI running Richard's case doesn't seem particularly interested in it, probably because in itself it isn't technically obscene.' Della lit another cigarette, but before she could say more, bodies started flowing through the doors leading from Domestic Arrivals. Judging by the high proportion of men in suits clutching briefcases that seemed as heavy as anchors after a hard day's meetings, the London shuttle was down. I stood up. 'I think this is Davy's flight,' I said.

Della was at my side in a flash. She gave me a quick hug, threw a glance over her shoulder to make sure she wasn't about to be accosted by a small boy, and said, 'Stay in touch. I'll bell you if I hear anything.' And she was gone.

The first rush had subsided, leaving the stragglers who had had to wait for luggage from the hold. After what felt like a very long time, the double doors swung open on a woman in British Airways uniform, carrying a small holdall. By her side, Davy trotted, looking like he was auditioning for the moppet role in the next Spielberg film, hair flopping over his forehead in a slightly tousled fringe, big brown eyes eager. He was proudly wearing an outfit he'd chosen with his dad on his last visit, topped by the New York Mets jacket Richard had sent him from a recent trip to the States, still too baggy for his solid little frame. Then he saw me. All in a moment, he seemed puzzled, then disappointed. He looked around again, then realizing Richard really wasn't there, he waved uncertainly at me and half smiled. My heart sank. As far as Davy was concerned, I was clearly a poor substitute. As if I needed the confirmation.

It turned out a lot better than I expected. On the way to the car park, I told Davy the lie Richard and I had prearranged. Dad was in Bosnia; he'd had to fly off suddenly because he'd had an exclusive tip that Bob Geldof was out there organizing some sort of Bosnia Aid concert. I almost believed it myself by the time I'd finished the explanation. Davy took it very calmly. I suppose after eight years, he's grown accustomed to a dad who doesn't behave quite like other kids' fathers. At least he's not shy; that's one thing that being around Richard and his crazy buddies in rock and journalism has cured him of. 'You remember Chris and Alexis?' I asked him as we drove out of the airport towards the M56.

He nodded. 'Alexis is funny. And Chris is good at drawing and painting and building things with Lego. I like them.'

'Well, they're going to help me look after you, because I've got some work to do over the weekend.'

'Can't I come with you to work, Kate?' he wheedled. 'I want to be a private detective like you. I saw this film and it was in black and white and it had an American detective in it, Mum said he was called Humpty something, and he had a gun. Have you got a gun, Kate?'

I shook my head. Depressingly, he looked disappointed. 'I don't need one, Davy.'

'What about if you were fighting a bad man, and he had a gun? You'd need one then,' he said triumphantly.

'If I was fighting someone who had a gun, and he knew I had a gun, he'd have to shoot me to win the fight. But if he knows I haven't got a gun, he only has to hit me. That way I stay alive. And, on balance, I think I prefer being alive.'

Chris was waiting when we got home. I'd rung ahead to give her ten minutes' warning, so she was just assembling home-made cheeseburgers as we walked in. I could have kissed her. The three of us sat round the breakfast bar scoffing and telling the sort of jokes that eight-year-olds like. You know: why do bees hum? Because they've forgotten the words.

After we'd pigged out, I showed Davy the latest Commander Keen game I'd got for us both. I extracted a promise from him that he'd go to bed in half an hour when Chris told him to, and left him bouncing on his pixel pogo stick through Slug Village. Ten minutes split between the bathroom and the bedroom was enough to knock me into shape for the night. My lightweight walking boots; my ripped denim decorating jeans over multi-coloured leggings; a Bob Marley T-shirt I won at a rock charity dinner; and a baggy flannel shirt that belonged to my granddad that I keep for sentimental reasons. I tucked my auburn hair into a dayglo green baseball cap, and slapped on some make-up that made me look like an anaemic refugee from Transylvania. Grunge meets acid house. I found Chris in front of the television, watching the news. Bless her, she didn't turn a hair at the apparition. 'I really appreciate this. And believe me, Richard will need a bank loan to express his appreciation when all this is over. I take it Alexis filled you in?' I said quietly, perching on the arm of the sofa.

'She did, and it's horrifying. What's happening? Any progress?' That's probably the shortest contribution to any conversation I've ever heard Chris make.

'Not really. That's why I'm going out now. I've

got one or two leads to follow up. Are you OK to hang on here?'

Chris patted my knee. 'We're staying till this is all sorted out. I brought a bag with me, and I've moved us into Richard's room, I hope that's all right, but it seemed the most sensible thing, because then Davy can sleep in his usual bed in Richard's house so you can come and go as and when you please without worrying about waking any of us, and then we're on hand to take over the child minding as and when you need us.' I swear she's the only person I know who can talk and breathe at the same time.

I gave Chris a swift hug and stood up. 'Thanks. I'll see you in the morning then.' I walked out of the house, feeling a sense of purpose for the first time since I'd had Ruth's phone call.

9

I started off at the Delta, known to Richard and his cronies, for obvious reasons, as the 'Lousy Hand'. That's where he'd been the night the car was stolen. The Lousy Hand occupies a handful of railway arches in a narrow cul-de-sac between the GMEX exhibition centre and the Hacienda Club. Since it was only half past nine, there was no queue, so I sailed straight in.

The décor in the Lousy Hand has been scientifically designed to make you think you've dropped a tab of acid even when you're straight. God knows what it does to the kids who are really out of their heads. Everywhere I looked there were psychedelic fractals mingling at random with *trompe-l'œil* Bridget Riley-style monochrome pop art extravaganzas. There were only a few dozen punters in that early, but most of them were already on the dance floor, mindlessly happy as only those high on Ecstasy can be. The dancing was something else, too. Scarcely co-ordinated, the dancers looked like a motley assortment of marionettes jerked around by a five-year-old puppet master with all the elegance and skill of Skippy the bush kangaroo. The music had the irritating insistence of a bluebottle at a window, the heavy bass beat so loud it seemed to thump inside my chest. I'd have sold my soul to be back home with a nice restful video like *Terminator 2*.

Feeling about a hundred and five, I crossed to the bar. As well as the usual designer beers, the optics of spirits and the Tracy-and-Sharon specials like Malibu and Byzance, the Lousy Hand boasted possibly the best range of soft drinks outside Harrods Food Hall. From carrot juice to an obscure Peruvian mineral water, they had it all, and most of it was carbonated. No, officer, of course we don't have a drug problem here. None of our clients would dream of abusing illegal substances. And I am Marie of Rumania.

The bar staff looked like leftovers from the club's previous existence as a bog-standard eighties yuppie nightclub. The women and the men were dressed identically in open-necked, wing-collar white dress shirts and tight-fitting black dress trousers. The principal differences were that the men probably had marginally more gel, wax and mousse on their hair, and their earrings were more stylish. I leaned my elbows on the bar and waited. There weren't enough customers to occupy all the staff, but I still had to hang on for the obligatory thirty seconds. God forbid I should think they had nothing better to do than serve me.

The beautiful youth who halted opposite me raised his eyebrows. 'Just a Diet Coke, please,' I said. He looked disappointed to be asked for something so conventional. He swivelled on one toe, opened the door of a chill cabinet and lifted a can off the shelf, all in one graceful movement. I don't know why he bothered. I couldn't have looked less like a talent scout from MTV.

'Wanna glass?' he asked, dumping the can in front of me. I shook my head and paid him.

When he came back with my change, I said, 'You know the street outside? Is it safe to park there? Only, I'm parked right up near the dead end and there's no streetlights, and I wondered if a lot of cars get nicked from out there?'

He shrugged. 'Cars get nicked. Outside here's no worse than anywhere else in town. A thousand cars a week get stolen in Manchester, did you know that?' I shook my head. 'And two-thirds of them are never recovered. Bet you didn't know that.' Never mind the Mr Cool image, this guy had the soul of a train spotter in an anorak.

Ignoring him, I went on, 'Only, it's not really my car, it's my boyfriend's and he'd kill me if anything happened to it.'

'What kind is it?' he asked.

'Peugeot 205. Nothing fancy, just the standard one.'

'You're probably all right, then.' He leaned his

elbows on the bar and elegantly crossed his legs. I prepared myself for a lecture. 'Six months ago, you couldn't park a hot hatch anywhere between Stockport and Bury and expect to find it there when you went back to it. But with these new insurance weightings, the bottom's dropped out of the second-hand market for boy-racer cars. So the professionals gave up on the sports jobs and started nicking boring old family cars instead. Less risk as well. I mean, if you was the Old Bill, would you think the Nissan Sunny cruising past you was being driven by any self-respecting car thief?'

I giggled. Not because he was funny, but because he clearly expected it. 'Only,' I persisted, 'my boyfriend's mate had his car nicked from outside here the other night, and he was really pissed off because he'd only bought it that day. And it was a beauty. A brand new Leo Gemini turbo super coupé.'

'I heard about that,' he said, pushing himself upright again. 'That was the night they had the benefit, wasn't it?'

'I dunno.'

'Yeah, that's right. The gig was finished, because we'd shut up the bar and the lights were up. The guy came storming back in, ranting about his precious motor and demanding a phone.' So much for not mentioning the car to a soul. 'Mate of yours then, was he?' the barman asked.

I nodded. 'Mate of my boyfriend's. He reckoned

somebody saw him parking it up and coming in here. He said he thought they must have been coming to the club too, or else why would they be down the cul-de-sac?'

The barman grinned, unselfconscious for the first time. 'Well, he'd have plenty thieves to choose from that night. Half Moss Side was in here. Drug barons, car ringers, the lot. You name it, we had them.'

With a flick of his pony tail, he was gone to batter someone else's brain with his statistics. I swigged the Coke and looked around me. While I'd been standing at the bar, there had been a steady stream of punters arriving behind me. Already, the place looked a lot fuller than it had when I entered. If I was going to have a word with the bouncers before they had more important things to think about, I'd better make a move.

There were two of them in the foyer, flanking the narrow doorway that had been cut in the huge wooden door that filled the end of one of the arches occupied by the club. They both wore the bouncer's uniform: ill-fitting tux; ready-made velvet bow tie that had seen better days. As I approached, the older and bulkier one slipped through the door and into the street. Intrigued, I got my hand stamped with a pass-out and followed him. He walked about fifty yards up towards the dead end. I slipped into the shadows beyond the club and watched him. He looked around, then simply turned and walked back, carrying on past the club for another fifty yards or so before strolling back inside.

I stuck my head round the door and said, 'Where's the best place to park around here? Only, I don't want to get the car nicked. It's my boyfriend's.'

The smaller bouncer flashed a 'Right one we've got here' look at his oppo. 'Darling, you don't look like the kind of girl who'd have a boyfriend with a car worth nicking,' he said, smoothing back his hair with a smirk.

'Mind you don't wear out the rug,' I snarled back, pointing to his head. Although he was only in his early twenties, his dark hair was already thinning so it was a fair bet that would be a tender spot.

Right on the button. He scowled. 'Piss off,' he quipped wittily.

'Does the management know you're this helpful to customers who only want to avoid giving the club a worse name than it's already got?' I asked sweetly.

'Don't push it,' the bouncer with the wanderlust said coldly, glowering down at me. Now I could see him in the light, he seemed familiar, but I couldn't place him, which surprised me. I don't often forget guys that menacing. He was a couple of inches over six feet, thick dark hair cut in an almost military short back and sides. He wasn't bad looking if you ignored the thread-thin white scar that ran from the end of his left eyebrow to just underneath his ear lobe. But his eyes wrecked any illusion of attractiveness. They were cold and blank. They showed as much connection to the rest of humanity as a pair of camera lenses.

'Look, I just don't want to get my car nicked, OK?' I gabbled. 'It seems to happen a lot around here, that's all.'

The big bouncer nodded, satisfied I'd backed down. 'You want to be safe, leave it on one of the main drags where there's decent street-lighting.'

'You want to be really safe, don't bring the car into town. In fact, why don't you do us all a favour and leave yourself at home as well?' the balding Mr Charm sneered.

I winked and cocked one finger at him like a pistol. 'I might just take your advice.' I let the door bang shut behind me and walked back to my car. Even if anyone at the Lousy Hand knew anything about the coupé's disappearance, I couldn't see a way of getting them to talk to me. It had been a long shot anyway. Sighing, I climbed into the car and started cruising the city centre streets. There were plenty of clubs for the dedicated seeker of pleasure to choose from, and even more restaurants catering to the late-night trade, which gave me plenty of kerbs to crawl. I prayed the Vice Squad weren't doing one of their occasional random trawls of the red-light zones. The last thing I needed was to have to explain to a copper why I was doing an impersonation of a dirty old man.

I drove systematically down the streets and back

alleys for a good couple of hours without spotting a single red-and-white trade plate. If I'd been working for a client, I'd have given up right then. But this was different. This was personal, and the man lying in a cell worrying about the charges he was facing was the man I'd chosen to share my life with. I might not be getting anywhere out on the streets, but I could no more jack it in and go home to bed than I could set Richard free with one mighty bound.

Just before midnight, I realized I was ravenous. I'd been so hyped up on adrenaline all evening that I was suddenly right on the edge of a low blood sugar collapse. I phoned an order through, then drove back through Chinatown, double parked outside the Yang Sing and picked up some salt and pepper ribs, paper wrapped prawns and pork dumplings. I couldn't help a pang of guilt, thinking about prison food and Richard's conviction that if it didn't come out of China or Burger King it can't be edible.

I drove back to the Lousy Hand. If the car thief plied a regular patch, I might just catch him at it. It was as good a place to eat my takeaway as any. I drove slowly up the culde-sac, looking for a space. Nothing. I turned round in the dead end and drove back down. I got lucky. Someone was pulling out just as I passed. I tucked the car in against the kerb and opened the sun roof so the smell of the Chinese wouldn't linger in the car for the next six months. I started on the prawns, wanting to polish them off before they became soggy.

I looked around as I ate. Nothing much was moving. There was a short queue outside the Lousy Hand, but it seemed to be static. The only car I could see worth stealing was a new Ford Escort Cosworth, but its ridiculous spoiler, like the tail of a blue whale, was so obvious that I couldn't imagine many thieves having the bottle to go for it. Besides, it was bright red and you know what they say about red cars and male sexual problems . . .

In my wing mirror, I noticed the man mountain bouncer emerging from the Lousy Hand again. Clearly time for another walkabout. As he reconnoitred the street, I thought he still looked nigglingly familiar, but I couldn't think where from, unless we'd had a brief encounter one night when I'd been on the town with Richard. After all, bouncers shift around the clubs about as fast as cocktail waitresses, and I wasn't always one hundred per cent *compos mentis* when we crawled out of clubs in the small hours.

He headed in my direction. Instinctively, I slid down in my seat till I was below window level. I heard his footsteps on the pavement, then, when he was level with me, he stopped. I held my breath. I don't know what I expected, but it wasn't the familiar bleating of a mobile phone being dialled. I inched carefully up till I could just see him. He had his back to me and a slimline phone to his ear.

'Hiya,' he said, his voice low. 'Ford Escort

Cosworth. Foxtrot alarm system. Been in about ten minutes . . . No problem.' The phone beeped once as he ended the call. I slid back down below eye level as he turned back towards the club. Valet parking I'd heard of. But valet stealing?

I watched in the wing mirror till he was safely back indoors, then I pulled off the dayglo cap and got out of the Peugeot, still clutching my Chinese. I melted into the shadows of one of the railway arches which had a deep door recess. I could hardly believe it wasn't already occupied by one of the city's cardboard-box kids. I didn't have long to wait. I still had half my spare ribs left when a black hack coughed up the cul-de-sac. It stopped outside the Lousy Hand, and a man got out. In the lights of the club entrance, I got a quick look. Thirtyish, medium height, slim build. He walked into the club, fast, like a man with a purpose other than a dance, a drink and a legover.

He was out again in seconds, carrying a small holdall. He walked briskly towards the Cosworth. As he came closer, I clocked a heavy thatch of dark hair, high cheekbones, hollow cheeks, surprisingly full lips, a double-breasted suit that hung like it was made to measure. He stopped a few feet away from the Cosworth, flashed a quick, penetrating glance around him then crouched down. Through the gap between cars, I could just see him take something out of the holdall. It looked a bit like an old-fashioned TV remote, bulky, with buttons. I couldn't see any details, but he seemed to be hitting buttons and moving a slider switch on the side. This routine lasted the best part of a minute. Then, three sharp electronic exclamations came from the Cosworth, the hazard lights flashed twice and I heard the door locks shift to 'open'. He dropped the black box back into the holdall and took out a pair of trade plates.

The man stood up and gave that quick, frowning glance round again. Still clear, he thought. One plate went on the back of the car, hiding the existing number. He fastened the other over the front plate, then almost ran to the driver's door. He was in the car in seconds. It took less than a minute for the engine to roar into life. The car shot out of the parking space. Rather than drive to the end of the cul-de-sac and do a time-wasting three point turn, as I'd expected, he simply shot back down the street in reverse.

Caught flat-footed, I leapt for the Peugeot. By the time he'd reversed on to the main drag and headed off towards Oxford Road, I was behind him, just far enough for him not to get twitchy. Interestingly, he didn't drive the Cosworth like a boy racer. If anything, he drove like my father, a man who has never had an accident in twenty-three years of driving. Mind you, he's seen dozens in his rear-view mirror . . . The speedo didn't rise above twenty-eight, he stopped on amber and he didn't even attempt any traffic-light grand prix stuff. We crossed Oxford Road and carried on sedately down Whitworth Street, into Aytoun Street and past

Piccadilly station. Then it was time for a quick whizz through the back doubles before he pulled up outside Sacha's nightclub and blasted the horn. Luckily I was far enough behind him to stay tucked away on the corner. I cut my lights and waited.

Not for long. If the speed of her response was anything to go by, patience wasn't her boyfriend's strong suit. Depressingly, she looked like she'd walked straight off the bottle-blonde production line. Expensive bimbo, but bimbo nevertheless. Bimbos are the last women in the world wearing crippling high heels and make-up that could camouflage a Chieftain tank. This one must have had enough hair spray on her carefully tumbled locks to lacquer a Chinese cabinet, since it didn't even move in the chill wind that had sprung up in the last hour.

She jumped into the waiting Cosworth and we were off again. He was still driving like a pursuer's dream. I dumped the Pet Shop Boys and let Annie Lennox entertain me instead. Round Piccadilly, down Portland Street, down to Deansgate, out along Regent Road. I had to hang well back now, because there wasn't a lot of traffic around, and the thief was driving so law-abidingly that any reasonable driver would have overtaken him long ago. At the end of the dual carriageway, instead of heading straight on down the motorway, he hung a left, heading towards Salford Quays. I can't say I was totally surprised. He looked the sort.

The Quays used to be, unromantically, Salford Docks. Then the eighties happened, and water-fronts suddenly became trendy. London, Liverpool, Glasgow, Newcastle, Manchester. They all discovered how easy it was to part fools and their money when you threw in a view of a bit of polluted water-way. Salford Quays was Manchester's version of greed chic. It's got it all: the multi-screen cinema, the identikit international hotel for jet-set business people, more saunas per head of population than Scandinavia, it's very own scaled-down World Trade Centre for scaled-down yuppie losers and more *Penthouses* than penthouses. The only thing it lacks is any kind of human ambience.

I noticed that the Cosworth was slowing. I pulled into the parking bay of a small block of flats and killed my lights just as he drew up. He'd stopped outside a long block of narrow three-storey town houses with integral garages on the ground floor.

He got out of the Cosworth, but I could see a whisper of exhaust in the cold night air that told me the engine was still running. He waved a hand in the direction of the garage door and it rose slowly to reveal a two-year-old black Toyota Supra. He swapped the cars over, leaving the Supra on the hard standing and the Cosworth tucked safely away inside the garage.

I watched for another twenty minutes or so as lights went on and off in various rooms. When the house went dark, I decided that if Richard's car thief was entitled to sleep, so was I.

I got home just after two. The house was silent, the bed chilly. If I didn't get him out of jail soon, I was going to have to buy a hot-water bottle.

10

I dreamed I was walking down a corridor filled with breakfast cereal, going snap, crackle and pop with every step. Cautiously, I opened one eye. It was only half a dream. Davy was sitting on the edge of the bed, tucking into a bowl of one of Richard's noisier cereals, a tumbler of orange juice on the bedside table next to him. He was watching me, and as he registered the rising eyelid, he smiled uncertainly.

'Did I wake you?' he asked. 'I didn't want to miss you.'

I propped myself up on one elbow and shook my head. 'Not really,' I lied. Things were bad enough without me giving Davy a bad time. I glanced at the clock. Five past seven. I couldn't even summon up the energy to groan.

'Have you got to work today?' he asked.

'I'm afraid so,' I said.

He looked crestfallen. 'Can't I come with you?' he asked wistfully. 'I could help.'

'Sorry, hon, not today. But I don't have to go out for a couple of hours yet, so we could play some computer games first, if you want?'

He didn't have to be asked twice. When Chris and Alexis stumbled through the conservatory just after half past eight looking like Beauty and the Beast, Davy and I were absorbed in a game of Lemmings. Alexis threatened to pull the plug out of the socket unless we reverted to normal English usage. Guess which one is the Beast?

I got up and said I had to go. Before Davy's disappointment could turn into a sulk, Alexis asked if he'd brought his trunks and if he fancied spending the afternoon at a fun pool. Nobody invited me, which is probably just as well, since the temptation of playing on the slides and surfing in the wave pool might just have proved too much.

Before the grown-ups could go into a huddle about how we were going to amuse him till lunch time, Davy solved the problem. 'Kate, is it all right if I go out and play this morning?' he asked.

'Who with?' I asked, trying to act like a responsible co-parent. Judging by the look on Davy's face, he was afraid I was turning into the wicked stepmother.

'Daniel and Wayne, from the estate. I *always* play with them when I come and see my dad.'

I didn't see a problem, and as soon as the deal was struck, Davy was gone. 'I've got to run too,' I said, heading for the shower.

'What's happening with Richard?' Alexis demanded,

following me down the hall as Chris disappeared into the kitchen and started brewing some more coffee.

'They've charged him with possession with intent to supply,' I shouted over the sound of the spray and the pump from my new power shower.

'Oh shit,' Alexis said.

'I'm hopeful we can keep the lid on it,' I said. 'Will there be any reporters in the magistrates' court this morning?'

'Well, if I don't go down, there won't be anyone from the *Chron*,' Alexis said. 'And with it being a bank holiday weekend, the court agency probably won't bother with cover either. You might just get away with it. If you do drop unlucky, there are two courts sitting. If there is a reporter kicking around, ask your solicitor to get the case called in one court while the reporter's in the other one. Shouldn't be a problem. I take it that Plan A is for you to find the evidence that will clear Richard before his next court appearance?'

'Got it in one,' I said. 'And unless you've got any bright ideas about how I'm going to do that, sod off and let me have my shower in peace.'

Alexis chuckled. 'OK. I'm going in to the office in a bit to write up my copy from dinner last night. That'll be my alibi for ignoring the mags. If anybody asks me, I'll say I checked it out with the clerk and there was nothing of any interest coming up. I'll be at my desk till lunch time if you need me for anything.'

'Thanks. I might just take you up on that. How did your evening go, by the way?'

Alexis pulled a face. 'That depends on whether you're asking the cold-hearted bastard journalist or the human being. As a journo, it was a major coup. There is definitely a big-time child porn ring operating somewhere in Greater Manchester, and I'm the only journo that knows about it. We're talking million-pound industry here. But Barney showed me some of their stock in trade. And as a human being, I have to say it was one of the nastiest experiences of my life. It made me fucking glad I don't have kids of my own to worry about.'

'I don't need child porn to make me feel like that,' I said gloomily. 'Temporary custody of Davy's quite enough. Did you ask him about any tie-ins with drugs?'

'I did, and if there are any, he doesn't know about them. Most likely, one of your drug dealers is a pervert. Which doesn't really help, does it?'

I love to start the day with the good news.

Saturday morning, Manchester Magistrates' Court. The one day of the week the marble corridors of the court don't resemble the supermarket chill cabinet – there's hardly a headless chicken in sight. The only cases dealt with at the Saturday court are the overnighters – breaches of the peace, drunk and disorderly, soliciting, the occasional assault. And Richard. Because his was such a major charge

118

and he was arrested after midnight, the police hadn't been inclined to process the paperwork fast enough for him to appear at Friday's court, so he'd spilled over into Saturday. Although it probably didn't feel like it to Richard, that had its advantages. As Alexis had confirmed, the chances were good that it would escape press attention, so the people whose drugs Richard had driven off with wouldn't be picking up their *Evening Chronicle* and finding 'Rock journalist charged with massive drug haul' splashed all over the front page.

According to Ruth, Richard had been moved the night before from the nick at Longsight into the custom-built secure detention cells inside the magistrates' court building. As we'd arranged, I made my way to the duty solicitor's interview room on the fifth floor. Normally at quarter to ten on a court morning, the place is heaving with defendants, their families, their kids and their harassed lawyers. The air's usually thick with cigarette smoke and recriminations. Today, while it wasn't as silent as the executive floor lobby of a multinational, it was a lot quieter than weekdays.

I pushed open the glass door of the small office and sat on the far side of the round table, commanding a view of the entire length of the foyer outside the courtrooms. It was nearly ten when Ruth swept into sight, a nervous-looking man almost trotting to keep up with her. Ruth shoved the door open and subsided into the chair opposite me with a huge sigh. 'God, that holding area depresses the knickers off me,' she complained, lighting a cigarette. 'Kate,' she added through a mouthful of smoke, 'this is Norman Undercroft, the duty solicitor. Norman, this is Kate Brannigan, my client's partner.'

Norman ducked his head politely, looking up at me from under mousey brows. Close to, he looked a lot older than my first impression. His papery skin was covered in a network of fine lines, placing him in his late forties. He opened his mouth to speak, but Ruth beat him to it. 'Right, Kate. Listen very carefully, I only have time to run this past you once. This morning, Richard will be represented by Norman here. Norman will get up on his hind legs and tell the court that this is a complicated matter about which his client has not yet had the opportunity to consult his own solicitor fully. Therefore, Norman will be asking the court to remand Richard in custody for the weekend. The prosecution will leap to their feet indignantly and respond that Richard is a menace to society, and furthermore, the police are investigating other serious charges in relation to him. They'll ask for a lie-down so that these matters can be resolved. And the mags will smile sweetly and agree. Any questions?'

'When can I see him?' I asked.

'Between seven and nine in the evening. Any visit is at the discretion of the duty inspector, so don't be stroppy. You go round to the back entrance in Gartside Street opposite the car park.

That it? Sorry to be so abrupt, but I've got twenty for lunch and Peter has not got the knack of getting the caterers to do any work.' She got to her feet. 'Have you made any progress, by the way?'

'It's early days yet, but I think I might just be getting somewhere.'

'OK. Look, I've arranged to see Richard tomorrow morning. Why don't we meet afterwards? Say eleven, in the Ramada. You can buy me brunch.'

'Make it Salford Quays,' I called after her. 'I might need to be down there.'

'The Quays it is,' she tossed over her shoulder as she disappeared round the corner. The room seemed to double in size now only Norman and I were left. I gave him a friendly smile.

'Overwhelming,' I said.

'Mmm,' said Norman. 'Good, though. I'd choose her if I was ever charged with anything, especially if I'd done it.'

I hoped everyone else wouldn't assume Richard was guilty just because he'd hired the best criminal lawyer in town. Wearily, I followed Norman round to Court 9. There didn't seem to be a journalist in the court, unless the court reporting agency had taken to hiring elderly women who look one step away from bag ladies and have such excellent powers of recall that they don't need a notebook.

I sat on one of the flip-down seats at the back of the courtroom. There were two magistrates on the bench, a man and a woman, both middle-aged, both decidedly middle class. After two breaches of the peace and a soliciting, I decided she was a teacher and he owned his own small business. She had that unmistakable air of wanting to tell them all to behave, and he had the blunt style of the self-made man who has no conception of why everybody can't be like him.

Richard was the last case of the morning. Watching him walk into the dock, I realized just how hard it is for people to get justice. After thirty-six hours in custody wearing the same clothes, not having shaved or showered, he looked like a bad lad even to me, and I was on his side. The very structure of the court itself made the accused appear to be some sort of desperado. Richard stood in the reinforced dock, behind a barrier of heavy perspex slats, the door into the court locked to avoid any possibility of him escaping. Behind him stood an alert prison officer. The system made it clear who was the sinner here.

Although he was familiar enough with court procedures from his days as a local paper journalist, Richard looked around the court with all the bewilderment of an animal that went to sleep in the jungle and woke up in the zoo. His hair seemed to have gone lank and dead overnight, and he pushed it back from his forehead in a gesture I'd noticed hundreds of times when he was working. When he saw me, one corner of his mouth twitched in a half-smile. That was a half more than I could manage.

There was no chance for Richard even to protest his innocence. He was treated like a parcel that has to be processed. As Ruth had predicted, the magistrates made little difficulty about remanding Richard in custody. The prosecuting solicitor obligingly explained that not only were the police pursuing further inquiries but they were also keen that Richard be kept away from other prisoners to avoid any collusion with his alleged co-conspirators. They all looked as if the very idea of a bail application on a charge like this was the best joke they'd heard since Margaret Thatcher announced the National Health Service was safe in her hands. The whole thing took nine and a half minutes. As Richard's prison officer escort led him out of the dock, he turned his back to the bench, wiggled his fingers at me and blew a kiss. I could have wept.

Instead, I thanked Norman Undercroft politely for his efforts and walked briskly out into the fresh air. Since I was only round the corner from Alexis's office, I cut through Crown Square and entered the building via the underground car park. I had wheedled the door combination out of Alexis ages ago; you never know when you're going to need a bacon sandwich at four in the morning, and the motto of the canteen staff of the Manchester *Morning Sentinel* and *Evening Chronicle* is 'We never run out'.

I took the lift up to the editorial floor. Things were fairly peaceful. Most of the sports staff hadn't come in yet, and Saturdays are such quiet news days that there's only ever a skeleton team in the newsroom. Alexis sat hunched over her keyboard in a quiet corner cut off from the rest of the room by a dense thicket of various interesting green things. I recognized the devil's ivy and the sweetheart plant. I've killed cuttings from both of them. I edged round the plants. Alexis flapped a hand at me, indicating I should sit down and shut up. I did.

With a flurry of fingers over the keyboard, Alexis reached the end of her train of thought, leaned back, narrowed her eyes and re-read her last paragraph, absently reaching out for the cigarette in her ashtray. It had already burned down to the tip, and she looked at it in astonishment. Only then did I merit any attention. 'All right?' she asked.

'As predicted. Remanded till Wednesday to allow for further police inquiries relating to other serious crimes. And unless the court agency has taken to hiring the Invisible Man for Saturday shifts, we're clear there too.'

'It's only a matter of time before somebody gets a whisper.' Alexis warned. 'It's too good a story for the Old Bill to sit on. It's not every day they capture a parcel that size.'

'So let's get a move on,' I said.

'What's with the "us"? Isn't unpaid childminding enough?'

'That's only the start. I need to look at your copy of the electoral roll.'

Alexis nodded and tipped back dangerously in

her chair till she could reach the filing cabinet behind her. She pulled out the bottom drawer. 'Help yourself,' she said. I don't know exactly where she gets it from, but Alexis always has an up-to-date copy of the city voters' list. She keeps it next to another interesting document which fell off the back of a British Telecom lorry, a list of Greater Manchester names and addresses sorted by phone number. In other words, if you've got the number, you can look up the address and name of the subscriber. Very handy, especially when you're dealing with the kind of dodgy customer Alexis and I are always running up against.

I looked up the relevant street in the electoral roll and discovered the occupant was listed as Terence Fitzgerald. The phone book revealed no listing for Terence Fitzgerald, but I checked Directory Inquiries on my mobile phone and discovered there was a mobile listed for him.

'Find what you wanted?' Alexis asked.

'Maybe,' I said. I had a way to go before I could be sure that the car thief and Terence Fitzgerald were one and the same. Thanks to the poll tax fiasco, the electoral roll has ceased to be an accurate guide to who actually lives at any particular address.

'Time for a coffee?' Alexis asked.

I shook my head. 'Places to go, people to see. Thanks all the same.'

For the briefest possible time, she looked concerned. 'Take care of yourself, KB.'

'I'll be fine,' I lied. I waved goodbye and headed for the lifts. As I drove out of the car park, I stared up at the grim concrete façade of the court building and tried not to think about Richard sitting in a windowless cell, nothing to do but stare at the walls and sweat with fear. I'd once been behind the heavy iron bars of the CDC, while I'd still thought that being a lawyer was a fit and proper job for a grown-up. A criminal solicitor friend had let me shadow him for a day's duty. I'd woken up sweating for weeks afterwards.

Luckily, fighting with the city traffic didn't give me much opportunity to brood. It was just after eleven when I tucked myself into the little parking bay that gave me a perfect view of Terence Fitzgerald's town house. The black Supra was still sitting on the drive, and the bedroom curtains were still shut.

I took my Nikon out of the glove box and fitted a stubby telephoto lens to it. Then I settled back to wait and watch. God knows, it was a thin enough lead. But it was all I had. I'd give it today and see what turned up. If nothing did, it looked like a bit of breaking and entering might be on the agenda.

11

I have friends who believe we can transmit psychic energy that reaches out and touches other people, impelling them to follow certain courses of action. They'd reckon their theory gained credibility when Terence Fitzgerald's bedroom curtains opened five minutes after I took up station outside his house. Me, I think it probably had more to do with Terence's alarm clock than the waves of anxiety and urgency I was generating.

Twenty minutes later, Terence emerged, hair still damp from the shower. He wore a chocolate leather blouson over baggy brown trousers, cream shirt and splashy tie. I banged off a couple of shots as he got into the car, then I started my engine. He passed me without a second glance, and I tucked into the traffic a couple of cars behind him as we hit the main road. He headed towards town, turning off at the big new Harry Ramsden's fish and chip shop at Castlefield, an area on the edge of the city centre which the powers that be are desperately trying to transform from post-industrial desert into tourist attraction. So far they've got the chippie, a couple of museums and Granadaland, Manchester's dusty answer to Disneyland and Universal Studios. And, of course, the expensive hotels that British tourists can't actually afford.

I pulled into the garage just beyond Harry Ramsden's and pretended to check my tyre pressures while I kept watch. He came out of the takeaway section a few minutes later with an open package which he carefully laid on the passenger seat as he got back into the car. Just the thought of the fish and chips had me salivating.

He shot back into the traffic again, and we were soon belting down the Hyde Road. No grandad driving today. The only time my speedo dropped below forty-five was at the traffic lights. I nearly lost him when he went through an amber as it turned to red but I put my foot down and caught him at the next set of lights, just before the motorway. It looked like we were heading over the Woodhead Pass to Sheffield. There was no chance to take in the magnificent scenery today. I was too busy concentrating on keeping the car on the road as I powered round the bends and up the long moorland inclines in the wake of the Supra. We hit the outskirts of Sheffield around one, and Terence slowed down, clearly less familiar with the steel city than he was with Manchester.

We skirted Hillsborough, driving more carefully

now since the police were already out in force for a Sheffield Wednesday home game. I can't understand how anybody can bear to go there to watch football these days. I know *I'll* never forget those newspaper photographs of dying Liverpool fans, nearly a hundred of them, crushed to death on a sunny spring afternoon just like this one. I tried to clear the morbid memories by focusing on the Supra's rear end, twitching now-you-see-it-now-you-don't round the next corner like a rabbit's tail.

We cut through backstreets lined with blank, silent buildings, monuments to an industry that once employed a city and made Sheffield steel world-famous. The captains of industry tell us that Sheffield produces more steel than ever before, and with a quarter of the old workforce. It just doesn't feel like it, driving through what appears to be an industrial graveyard.

Beyond the mills, we climbed steeply. Like Rome, Sheffield's a city built on seven hills. Difference is, you get better pizzas in Sheffield. Soon, we were engulfed by a sprawling council estate, sixties terraces and low-rise maisonette blocks as far as the eye could see. Terence seemed to know where he was now, for he speeded up again, scattering mongrels as he went. It was becoming more difficult to maintain an unobtrusive tail, since virtually every car in sight looked like it had at least one wheel in the grave.

The Supra signalled a right turn as it approached

a large asphalted area beside a low, square building. I carried straight on, turning into the first side-street. I gave it a few minutes, then I headed back the way I'd come. A couple of hundred yards from the building, I parked the car, made sure the alarm was on, and walked the rest of the way on foot. As I got closer, I could see a battered sign which told me that Suzane was a slag, that Wayne shags great and that Fairwood Community Centre had been opened in 1969. All the casual visitor needed to know, really.

There was a blackboard outside the centre, surrounded by a knot of teenagers who looked like Sheffield's entry for the Wasted Youth of the Year contest. I'd have felt threatened if I didn't know I could kick the feet out from under any of them. As it was, I was wary, avoiding eye contact as I glanced at the blackboard. On it was written in sprawling capitals, 'Q Here 4 Sale. 3pm and 6pm. Bargins Galore.' Stapled to the corner was a bundle of flyers. I detached one as I walked on by and stuffed it into my pocket.

I rounded the corner of the community centre to the sound of a wolf whistle and a couple of suggestions as to what the youth of Sheffield would like to do to me. In the car park, as well as the Supra, there was a Cavalier and a three-ton truck. The truck was reversed hard up against the hall, its doors opened back parallel with the wall. I crouched down to tie my shoelace and sneaked a look under the van. Beyond it, the double doors of what was obviously the hall's fire exit were open. Short of crawling under the truck and into the hall, there was no way I could see what was in either of them.

I was about to walk back to the car when my phone chirruped. I felt incredibly exposed, answering a mobile phone right there, so I hurried round to the far side of the truck. At least I was out of sight from the road now. Irritated with myself for not having the sense to remember to leave the phone in the car, I barked, 'Brannigan,' into the phone.

'Kate? Where are you? Are you near home?' It was Alexis, but Alexis as I'd never heard her before. Even in those few words, I could hear panic. And panic meant only one thing.

'Davy?' I said, my fear rising instantly to equal hers.

'Kate, can you get home? Now?'

'What's happened?' I was already skirting round the back of the community centre, crossing a scrubby playing field and heading back to the car. 'He's not . . . gone missing?' My immediate terror was that, somehow, someone had discovered who had driven off with the drugs and that Davy was either a hostage or the potential victim of a vicious reprisal.

'No, nothing like that. It's just . . .'

I could hear Chris's voice saying in the background, 'For God's sake, Alex, give me the phone, you're only winding her up.' Then Chris's voice replaced Alexis's. 'Don't panic,' she said. 'Davy's come back to the house and he's in a bit of a state,

131

like he's high on something. I think he might have been given drugs or something, and I think we ought to take him to hospital. How long will it take you to get home?'

I was at the car, switching the alarm off, shoving the key in the ignition, all on automatic pilot while I digested what Chris was saying. I felt as if I'd been punched in the stomach. Taking Davy to hospital was the nightmare scenario. There was no way we could do it without everything coming on top. Angie would discover that not only was her ex-husband in jail but her son had been put at risk by said ex-husband's fancy woman and her lesbian friends. The chances of Richard ever seeing his son again without a social worker shrank to the size of a terrorist's conscience.

Chris cut into my racing thoughts. 'Hello? Kate? Are you still there?'

'Yeah, I'm here,' I said, powering down the street and heading back towards the Manchester road. 'Look, you can't take him to hospital. Oh shit, this is the worst possible thing . . . Give me a minute.' I thought furiously. On the other hand, if he was really ill, we couldn't *not* take him to hospital. The one thing Richard would never forgive was if I let anything happen to Davy. Come to that, I'd have a hard job forgiving myself. 'How bad is he?' I asked.

'One minute he's shivering, the next he's sweating. He keeps going off into crazy giggling fits and he keeps pointing at nothing really and giggling and then cuddling up to us,' Chris said. There was a note of desperation in her carefully controlled voice.

My brain had finally accessed the relevant information. 'Give me five minutes, Chris,' I said.

'I don't know,' she said. 'He's not at all well, Kate.'

'Please. Five minutes, max.' I cut off the connection before Chris could argue any more. I pulled up with a screech of rubber and the blast of a horn from the car behind. I flipped open my filofax and found the number I was looking for. I punched the number into the phone and moved back into the traffic. Sinful, I know, but getting to Davy was a greater imperative than the interests of other road users.

If anyone could help me, it was Dr Beth Taylor. Beth divides her time between an inner-city group practice and a part-time lectureship at the university in medical ethics. A few years ago, she had a fling with Bill which lasted about three months, which is probably a record for my business partner. Now, she's Mortensen and Brannigan's first port of call whenever we're investigating medical insurance claims. She also repairs broken bits of Brannigan from time to time.

The phone answered on the second ring. 'This is Beth,' the distant voice said. 'I'm not here right now, but if you want me to call you back you can leave a message after the tone. If it's urgent, you can try me on my mobile, which is . . .' I keyed the number into the phone as she recited it, then ended the call and dialled her mobile, praying to God she not only had it with her but was also in a decent reception area.

The phone rang once, twice, three times. 'Hello, Beth Taylor.' I'd never heard a more welcome sound.

'Beth? It's Kate Brannigan.'

'Hi, Kate! Long time no see. Which I suppose is a good thing, in your case. Is this a professional call? Only, I'm on my way to play hockey.'

I bit back the frustrated sigh. 'It's an emergency, Beth.'

'What have you done this time?' Underneath the warm humour in her voice, there was no mistaking the concern.

'It's not me. It's my partner's son. The friends who are looking after him think he might have been given drugs.'

'Then it's not me you want, Kate, it's the casualty department at MRI. You should know that.'

'Beth, I can't. Look, I can't explain now, not because I'm not prepared to, but because there isn't time. Please, Beth, I *need* this favour. I'm on my way back to my house now, and as soon as I get there, I'll tell you why I can't take him to hospital unless it's a matter of life and death,' I pleaded.

'If it's drugs, it could well be that,' Beth warned.

'I know, I know. But please, you're the only doctor I know well enough to trust with this.'

There was a moment's silence. 'I shouldn't do

134

this,' she said with a sigh. 'It's against all my better judgement.'

'You'll go?'

'I'll go. Where is he?'

'He's at my house. You remember it?'

'I remember,' Beth said. 'I'll be there in about ten minutes. Oh, and Kate?'

'Yeah?'

'You owe Crumpsall Ladies Hockey Club a round of drinks for every five minutes I'm late for the game.' The phone went dead before I could tell Beth it would be worth every penny.

I rang Chris straight back and told her Beth was on her way. The relief in her voice told me exactly how much fear she'd been hiding when she'd spoken to me before. 'Thank God!' she exclaimed. 'He's just been sick. We're really scared, Kate.'

'It's not your fault, Chris. This would have happened whether Richard had been there or not, believe me. Look, phone me if there's any change, OK? I'll be back as soon as I can.'

I might have broken all records driving to Sheffield. But I shattered them driving back.

I barrelled through my front door like the Incredible Hulk on speed. There wasn't a sound from anywhere, and it took me less than ten seconds to discover they weren't in the house. I ran through the conservatory and yanked open the patio doors leading to Richard's living room. Still no one. By now, I was convinced they'd had to rush him to hospital. All the way home, I'd been plagued by a vision of Davy lying in the subdued lighting of intensive care, more tubes than Central London coursing in and out of his little body.

I crossed the room in half a dozen strides and hauled the door open, cannoning into Chris, who stepped backwards into Beth, who continued the domino effect with Alexis. 'Ssh,' Beth said before I could say a word. I backed into the living room and the other three trooped behind me. Alexis shut the door.

'How is he? What's happening?' I demanded.

'Calm down,' Beth instructed. 'Three deep breaths.' I did what she told me. I even sat down. 'Davy's going to be fine. I've just given him a mild sedative and tranquillizer which have calmed him down and sent him to sleep. He'll probably be more or less zonked out till morning. He might feel a bit groggy tomorrow, but basically he'll be OK.'

'What was the matter? What happened?' I asked.

'He presented like someone who has absorbed a significant amount of an hallucinogenic drug,' Beth said. 'Nothing life-threatening, thank God.'

'But how? Where did he get it from? He only went out to play with a couple of other kids from the estate! Who'd feed drugs like that to kids?'

'I said "absorbed" advisedly,' Beth said. She ran a hand through her spiky blonde hair and frowned. 'You know those temporary tattoos that kids use? They wet the transfers and the pictures slide off on to their skin?'

I nodded impatiently. 'Yeah, yeah, Davy loves them. Some nights he gets in the bath looking like the Illustrated Man.'

'Did he have any transfers on his body this morning when he went out?'

'Not that I noticed,' I said. 'Did either of you notice last night?'

Chris and Alexis both shook their heads.

'He must have thirty or forty on his arms or chest now,' Beth said. 'And that's the source of the problem, I reckon. I've heard of a couple of cases like this, though I've not actually seen one before.'

'But I don't understand. It can't be something in the transfers, surely. He often has them covering the whole of his arms and his chest. He's crazy about them, like I said. He'll put on as many as Richard will buy for him.'

Beth sighed. 'You're right, it's not the transfers as such. It's what's been done to them. They've been doctored. They've been impregnated with a drug not unlike acid or Ecstasy, probably one that's been designed to provide a feeling of mild euphoria, general friendliness and energy. But taken in the dose Davy seems to have absorbed, it also produces hallucinations. We dumped him in the bath and washed them all off so he won't absorb any more, and luckily he seems to have had a pleasant trip rather than a terrifying one.'

Beth's words seemed to reverberate long after she'd finished speaking. None of us seemed able to come up with an adequate response. Finally, it was Alexis's journalistic instincts that hit the ground running ahead of my private investigator's. 'What do they look like, these transfers?' she asked.

'Some are geometric. Blue and gold stars, about the size of a 10p. Red and pink triangles, too. Others have pictures of clowns, cars, Batman and Superman logos and dinosaurs. The only difference between them and the straight ones is the packaging, so I've been told. Apparently the dodgy ones come in little foil packets, like those individual biscuits you get on aeroplanes. Sorry, I don't know any more than that.'

'I can't believe I've not heard about this on the grapevine,' Alexis said, outraged.

'She's a journo,' I explained to Beth.

'Why haven't there been any warnings about this?' Alexis continued. 'It's scandalous.'

'Presumably, the powers that be didn't want to start a panic,' Beth said. 'I can understand why, since it seems to be such a rarity.'

'Never mind the story, Alexis. What about Davy? Will he definitely be OK?' Chris demanded.

'He'll be absolutely fine, I promise you. In future, make sure he finds another bunch of friends to play with. Look, I've got to run. My hockey match starts in ten minutes. I'll swing by tomorrow morning, just to be on the safe side, but the best thing you can do is let him sleep it off in peace.'

Beth's departure left us in an awkward silence. Alexis broke it. 'It's nobody's fault,' she said.

'We're all going to beat ourselves up, we'll all be fighting each other to take the blame, but it's nobody's fault.'

'I know,' I said. I got to my feet. 'I just want to take a look at him.' I walked down the hall to the spare room and pushed the door open. Davy was lying on his back, arms above his head, legs in a tangle of kicked-off duvet. There was a smile on his sleeping face. I leaned over and pulled the cover up over him. He stirred slightly, grunting. I didn't know what else to do so, feeling awkward, I backed out of the room and closed the door behind me.

I went back through to the kitchen. Alexis was sitting on her own, rolling a modest joint from Richard's stash. 'Don't you think there's been enough drug-taking for one day around here?' I asked. I was teasing, but only just.

Alexis shrugged. 'The doctor says too much stress is bad for me. Chris is making a pot of coffee. You got time for a cup before you go back to wherever you were before you were so rudely interrupted?'

I raised my eyebrows. 'I wasn't planning on going back.'

'Why? Had you finished what you were doing?'

'Well, no,' I admitted.

'So get back on the road. There's nothing you can do here. Davy's zonko. Beth said he'd sleep till morning. Anybody can baby-sit a sleeping kid. But you're the only one that can get Dick out of jail.'

'Don't call him Dick,' I said automatically. 'You

139

know how it depresses me.' I looked at my watch and sighed. I had plenty of time to drive back to Sheffield and still be in time for the six o'clock sale. With luck, it would be over early enough for me to get back to Manchester in time to visit Richard. I got to my feet just as Chris came in with a tray of coffee.

'Aren't you stopping for a brew?' she asked.

I put on my FBI face. 'You expect me to drink coffee at a time like this?' I asked sternly. 'People, a girl's got to do what a girl's got to do.'

Chris giggled. Alexis guffawed. I don't know why it is that people just don't take me seriously.

12

Literary critics punt the theory that private eyes are society's outsiders. That might have been true in 1940s Los Angeles, but it's a joke in 1990s Britain. These days, if you want to last more than five minutes as a private investigator, you've got to have the instincts of a chameleon. Gumshoes that stand out in a crowd are as much use to the client as a chocolate chip pan. I've had to pass as everything from lawyer to temp, including high-class hooker and journalist, sometimes both on the same day. At least tonight I'd already cased the venue, which gave me a pretty substantial clue as to dress code.

I pulled the crumpled flyer out of my pocket and gave it the once-over. Whoever had put it together wasn't going to win any awards for grammar or graphic design. The one-day sale promised bargains of a lifetime – video recorders for £69.99, camcorders for £99.99, microwaves for £49.99, plus hundreds of other exclusive, unique, etc.

Already, and for free, we'd been presented with more exclamation marks than any reasonable person could use in a decade. With all this in mind, I dressed for the occasion. Tight faded Levis, a black Tina Turner *Simply the Best* sweat shirt (because black always makes me look like I have a major vitamin deficiency), and Richard's three-sizes-too-big Washington Red Sox jacket. I finished the ensemble with a pair of white stilettos with a two-inch heel, bought, I hasten to add, solely for professional purposes. I gathered my auburn hair into a top knot and held it in place with a gold lurex elasticated band. Never mind a million dollars, I looked about threepence halfpenny. I'd fit in like a flea in a cattery.

I was back in Shelfield for half past five. I dumped the car in a city-centre car park and found a cab to take me out to the council estate. I tipped the cabbie a fiver, which persuaded him to come back for me later. At quarter to six, I joined the queue snaking along the pavement outside the community centre. There were getting on for a hundred punters, and none of them looked like they'd be allowed to carry a donor card, never mind a gold card. I reckoned the youngest were under two, slumped slack-mouthed and sleeping in their pushchairs. The oldest were never going to see seventy again. The rest included harassed-looking women, middle-aged at twenty-five, to lads who looked fifteen till you clocked the eyes. I'd calculated well. Nobody gave me a second glance.

At ten to six, the doors opened and we streamed in. The hall was brightly lit, empty except for a raised dais in front of the Fire Exit sign. On the dais was a high counter, piled higher still with cardboard boxes claiming to be filled with microwaves, camcorders, videos and TVs. Other boxes had garish pictures of pan sets, dinner services, game consoles, canteens of cutlery, radio alarms, toasters, battery chargers and socket sets. It looked like a cut-price Aladdin's cave. Behind the stack of boxes I could see a burly man with a perm like a 1970s footballer. If his suit had been any sharper he'd have been arrested for possession of an offensive weapon. He fiddled with a mike, clipping it on to a tie so loud I expected a shriek of feedback. 'Ladies and gentlemen,' he cajoled, 'don't hang back. Come right down to the front where I can see you, and I mean that especially for you lovely ladies. I want to feast my eyes on your charms, because I have to tell you that even though I'm supposed to stand up here being scrupulously fair with you ladies and gentlemen, I'm only human. And I'd have to be more than human to resist some of the lovely ladies I can see in here tonight.' Unbelievable. Even more unbelievable, they obeyed. Like lemmings.

Sticking with the flow of the crowd, I moved forward, edging out towards the side of the hall. I looked around, searching for Terence. I spotted him after a few moments, one of several men flanking the dais. Their ages varied from late teens to early forties. I wouldn't have trusted one of them to hold the dog while I went for a pee. I reached the far wall and stopped about ten feet away from the platform. I took a good look round. The punters were eager, many of them patting the pockets that held their money, reassuring themselves it was still there. It wouldn't be for much longer, I suspected, and not because of pickpockets, either.

Now, most of the men by the platform, including Terence, were fanning out among the crowd, keeping one eye on the auctioneer as he 'entertained' the audience with a steady stream of patter consisting of *risqué* remarks, old jokes and jocular encouragement to the crowd to move forward and prepare to enjoy themselves. I tuned back in. 'I want you to promise me one thing tonight, ladies and gentlemen. I want you to promise me that you'll be good to yourselves. You're going to be offered the bargains of a lifetime here tonight, and I don't want to see you holding back because you don't think you deserve them. I am here tonight to treat you, and I want you to promise me you won't be afraid to treat yourselves. Is that a promise? Will you do that for me?'

'Yeah,' they roared back. I couldn't believe it. The guy looked like they'd minted the word 'spiv' just for him, yet the punters lapped it up like free beer.

'Now, who wants to start the ball rolling with me tonight? Who needs a cigarette lighter?' A few hands shot in the air. 'Who could use a pack of five blank cassettes?' A forest of hands joined them. 'And is there anyone out there who would like a pack of three brand-new video tapes?' I was probably the only person in the room not waving wildly. I buried my pride and stuck my hand up. The salesman grinned. 'Now if it was up to me, I'd be giving these items away, but unfortunately, the law of the land forbids me from exercising my natural generosity. So, you need to give me a token payment for these little tasters of what's to come.'

He paused for dramatic effect. The crowd hung on his words, rapt as a nineteenth-century congregation in thrall to some lunatic visionary minister. 'I'm going to be as fair as I can be. My team of lads are keeping a careful eye on you all, to see who qualifies. Now, I've got twenty of these disposable lighters here, and the first twenty to stick their hands in the air . . .' he paused again, and half a hundred arms flew wildly into the air. 'The first twenty to stick their hands in the air *after* I give the word, those lucky people can purchase a lighter for only one penny. Now, I can't say fairer than that, can I?'

The crowd obviously thought not. The salesman waved a ridiculous gavel in the air. 'Now, I'm going to bang me little hammer three times, and when I hit the counter the third time, that's the signal. Then the lucky twenty will be privileged to be allowed to buy a cigarette lighter for only one penny.' There was a pregnant pause. The hammer

145

descended once, then twice. Half the hands in the room flailed in the air at the moment the hammer should have fallen the third time. Embarrassed, they dropped their hands again. 'Don't be greedy now,' the salesman admonished. 'I promise you, everybody who wants a bargain here tonight will get one.' As he ended his sentence, the hammer banged for the third time, and a thicket of hands straggled into the air. The salesman made a pretence of looking around to see who was first, nodding histrionically as he caught the eye of his henchmen scattered round the room. Twenty punters with waving hands were selected for the cigarette-lighter bargain. It looked to me as if they'd been chosen at random. As we progressed through the cassette tapes (fifty pence), the videos (one pound) and non-stick frying pans developed as a by-product of the American space programme (two pounds), the same arbitrary selections were made. The salesman's assistants only seemed interested in checking out the contents of people's wallets.

The salesman had them in the palm of his hand now. The initial loss leaders had convinced them that tonight they really were going to get bargains. The salesman tossed back his curls and fastened the top button of his jacket, as if to signal it was time to get down to serious business. 'Ladies and gentlemen, I'm not going to insult your intelligence here tonight. I bet you all watch *That's Life*. You know that there are unscrupulous people out there who

146

want to part you and your money. Now, I'm not like that. So here's what I'll do. If you put your trust in me now, I will see to it that your trust does not go unrewarded. Ladies, this is something that will change your lives. Gentlemen, this is something that will change your luck. Every now and again, in the perfume laboratories of Paris, men in white coats come up with something that transforms the woman who wears it from the everyday to the absolutely sensational. With the right perfume, any housewife can make the man in her life feel like she's Liz Taylor, Joan Collins and Michelle Pfeiffer rolled into one. It's a scientific fact. They did it with Chanel No. 5. They did it with Giorgio. Now, they've done it with this!'

He brandished a box in the air. Candyfloss pink and silver stripes. It looked unlike anything I'd ever seen before. 'Here it is, ladies and gentlemen. My brother is in the import/export business, and he has secured a case of this unique Parisian perfume for my customers before it goes on general sale. This exclusive perfume, Eau d'Ego, will be the subject of a major advertising campaign right through the summer, ladies and gentlemen. It's going to be the hottest seller this Christmas, I promise you that. And tonight, you can be the very first people in Britain to own a bottle of Eau d'Ego.'

I struggled to keep a straight face. My French might not be up to much, but when Richard and I had spent a romantic weekend in Paris, we'd done a tour of the city sewers. I don't think you'd find many chic Parisians wearing a perfume whose name sounds suspiciously like *eau d'égout* – sewage.

The salesman was still in full flow, however. 'Now, we have a massive selection of bargains here tonight. But inevitably, we don't have enough of our most popular items to go around. My boss puts limits on me. I mean, how many of you would like to buy a camcorder for under a hundred pounds?'

Nearly half the punters waved frantically at him. He gave a satisfied smirk. 'Exactly. Now, my boss would sack me if I was to sell more than three of our bargain camcorders in one evening. So I have to ration you. Now, I have fifty bottles of Eau d'Ego here on this platform tonight. If you trust me enough to buy a bottle of this exclusive Parisian fragrance, I will give you first refusal on the lots I'm selling here tonight. I'm not saying you *can't* buy a camcorder if you don't buy the perfume, because that would be illegal, ladies and gentlemen. What I am saying is that the people who trust me enough to become my customers now will be given priority when it comes to buying the lots where we have restricted numbers. Now, I think you'll agree, I can't say fairer than that.' His tone left no space for argument. It wasn't a particularly clever pitch, and he wasn't the world's greatest spieler, but they loved it.

'I warn you, ladies, if you get a taste for Eau d'Ego, you are never going to be called a cheap date again. When this marvellous perfume goes on sale in the shops, it will have a recommended retail price of forty-nine pounds ninety-five. Now, I'm not expecting you to pay forty-nine pounds ninety-five tonight. After all, you've not seen the advertising campaign, you've not read all the magazines raving about it, you've not seen the effect it has on me. All you've got is my word. And if I tell you that the wife helped herself to a bottle and I've gone home every night since, that should tell you something!' He winked. I winced.

'I'm not even asking you to pay half-price for the privilege of wearing this fragrance. Ten pounds, that's all. For only a tenner, you can be among the first women to wear a perfume that's des tined to be the scent of the stars. Now, when my hammer falls for the third time, my assistants will have their eagle eyes peeled and the first fifty hands in the air will be given this exclusive opportunity.' This time, there was no pause. The hammer banged once, twice, three times. The audience proved Pavlov's theory of stimulus-response, the hands high above their heads as soon as the hammer hit.

All the assistants ran around distributing perfume and grabbing tenners. Terence seemed to be doing exactly the same as everyone else. At least, I couldn't see any difference. I began to wonder if I was wasting my time.

The salesman had moved on from the perfume.

Now, he was putting together bundles of items. I reckoned I could buy their equivalent down any high street in the land for less than they were asking. But common sense had died somewhere in the salesman's pitch, and he had stomped the corpse into the dust with his patter. They were *fighting* to be allowed to pay over the odds for crap that would explode, disintegrate, tarnish, break or all of the above within weeks.

The hysteria rose as he went through the charade of selling serious bargain lots to five hand-picked mug punters. I had to admire his style as he relieved them of between a hundred and fifty and three hundred pounds for bundles of goods they thought they'd bought at a huge discount. I wouldn't mind betting that at the end of the sale, they'd find that they hadn't been granted the special lots at all. All they'd get would be goods worth rather less than they'd paid, and a wide-eyed assurance that the parcel they'd 'bought' had been sold to that (non-existent) man standing right behind them . . . I was watching carefully, and I'd lost track of what was going on. The mug punters had no chance.

But the most extraordinary was yet to come. 'Have I been good to you tonight, or have I been good to you tonight?' the salesman demanded. He was greeted with a reasonably warm murmur. 'Do you think I'm someone you can trust? You, madam – would you trust me?' He went through half a dozen members of the audience, pinning them with his stare, demanding their loyalty. Every last one of them bleated a 'yeah' like so many sheep.

He smiled, revealing what he'd been doing with some of the profits. 'I told you about my brother earlier, didn't I? The one in import and export? Well, he knows how I love to treat you people, so he's always on the look-out for bargains that I can pass on to my customers. Now, a lot of these things come from outside the EEC, and according to EEC regulations, we can't display them in the same way. So what we do is we make them up into parcels. Even I don't know what's in these parcels, because we make them up at random. But I can guarantee that each of these parcels contains goods to a value well in excess of what I'm asking for them. All I ask of you is that you take the goods home with you before you unwrap them. Not because we want you to buy a pig in a poke but because the contents vary so much. If the person standing next to you sees you've got a state-of-the-art food processor for a tenner and he's only got a toasted-sandwich maker, a set of heated rollers and a clock radio, it can often cause jealousy, and the last thing we want is fights breaking out because some of our bargains are such outrageously good value for money. Now, I'm going to start with ten-pound parcels. Who's spent money with me here tonight and would like to take advantage of my insane generosity?'

I couldn't help myself. My mouth fell open. A

couple of dozen people were waving their bottles of perfume in the air. Most of them looked like Giro day was the biggest financial event in their lives. Yet they were shelling out hard-hoarded cash on a black bin liner that could have contained a bag of sugar and a half-brick. I wouldn't have believed it if someone had told me about it. Then, as the salesman moved on to fifty-pound lucky bags, I noticed a change in the pattern. It was hardly noticeable, but it was enough. For the first time that evening, I began to believe I was in the right place at the right time.

13

I drove back to Manchester, replaying what I'd just seen, wondering what it meant. If I hadn't been totally focused, I could so easily have missed the tiny alteration to the pattern. It had happened just after the fifty-pound lots had started. Terence had emerged from behind the platform with a black bin liner, just like all the others. Then he'd snaked through the crowd to a short guy in his early twenties with a red baseball cap and a black leather jacket. Even though the guy didn't have his hand stuck in the air, Terence had passed over the bag in exchange for a fat brown envelope. It looked to me like it contained a lot more than fifty pounds, unless the guy in the red hat was paying in roubles.

They said nothing to each other, and the whole exchange took the same few seconds every other transaction had taken. Terence was back serving punters within the minute. But unlike the other mugs, the guy in the red hat wasn't sticking around. As soon as he'd collected his bag of goodies, he was off, shouldering his way through the crowd towards the door, pulling off the red hat and stuffing it inside his jacket. I contemplated following him, but I had no wheels, and besides, I wanted to carry on watching Terence to see what else he'd get up to.

The answer was, nothing. For the short time that remained, he did exactly the same as the other floor men, dishing out black bin liners in exchange for crumpled notes, fending off punters who thought they'd not had the treat they'd been promised at the start of the evening.

Then, with bewildering suddenness, it was over. While the salesman was still speaking, most of his assistants switched their attention from the audience to the platform. With astonishing speed, the boxes that remained on the dais disappeared into the back of the van. By the time his closing speech was over, the platform was bare as my fridge the day before I hit the supermarket.

I worked my way back to the door, joining the punters who were slowly coming back down to planet earth to the depressing realization that they'd been comprehensively ripped off in a completely legal way with no comeback. By the time I made it outside the hall, the satisfied murmurs had turned into discontented mutterings, growing in volume as people began to examine the contents of their blind buying spree. My taxi was waiting, and I didn't hang around to watch them turn into a lynch mob. Neither did the sales crew. As my taxi pulled away from the kerb, I saw the van and the two cars move across the car park. By the time the crowd got angry enough to do anything about it, the lads'd be halfway back across the Pennines.

I pondered all the way to Manchester. It was still almost too slender even to be called circumstantial, but all my instincts told me I was following the right track. I was pretty sure I'd just witnessed the handover of a parcel of illegal substances. I just hoped that it wasn't wishful thinking that was shunting my instincts down the trail of Terence Fitzgerald.

It was nearly twenty to nine when I abandoned the Peugeot on a double yellow line a couple of streets away from the sprawling court complex round Crown Square. I was cutting it fine, since visiting ended at nine. I'd covered my back by phoning ahead *en route* from Sheffield, telling the duty inspector I'd been delayed by a puncture but that I would definitely be there within visiting hours. Looking on the bright side, I'd only have been allowed fifteen minutes anyway. I kicked off the tart's shoes and pulled on the pair of Reeboks I always keep in the car, yanked off the hair band and shook my wavy auburn hair free. I grabbed the plastic bag I'd packed in Richard's bungalow, then I jogged round to the back of the Magistrates' Court building.

I slowed down as I entered the covered walkway

that cuts into the ground floor of the building, and into the range of the video cameras. I didn't want to look like I was storming the building. I pressed the door intercom buzzer. 'Can I help you?' asked a voice with more static than a taxi radio.

'I'm here to visit a prisoner. Richard Barclay. I'm his girlfriend,' I said.

'Go through the double doors to the lift and press the button for the seventh floor,' the voice told me as the door buzzed and the lock was released.

The lift door opened on a different world from the spiffy smartness of the courts. No wood panelling or cool marble floors here. The paintwork was chipped and dirty, the floors pocked with cigarette burns, the walls adorned only with anti-crime posters to intimidate the visitors. I was signed in by a cheerful police officer who ushered me into a tiny cubicle, with two low stools bolted to the floor. The cubicle was divided in half by a metal-topped counter beneath a thick perspex screen. On each side of the counter, there was a telephone handset. I stared through the screen. The other side was identical, except that there was no handle on the inside of the door. I could get up and go any time I wanted, but the prisoner didn't even have that amount of control. I glanced at my watch. It was just after quarter to.

The door opened and Richard walked in, giving a depressing little wave. He sat down, and I found myself noticing all the things I had come to take for granted. The smooth, fluidity of his movements. The way his smile starts on the left side of his mouth before becoming symmetrically cute. I blinked hard and nailed a smile on. His mouth moved, but I couldn't hear a thing. I picked up the phone, waving at him to do the same thing. 'I was beginning to think you weren't coming,' I heard through the earpiece. It wasn't an accusation. His voice sounded strange, disembodied but immediate, not like a normal phone conversation.

'Sorry, but it was your fault I'm so late. I was out there on the mean streets working for you,' I said with a ghost of our usual sparring.

'How's Davy?' he asked.

I swallowed. 'He's fine,' I lied, hoping it didn't show. 'He's in bed asleep.' That bit was true at least.

His eyebrows rose in perfect arcs, just like Paul McCartney's. 'Before nine o'clock? On a Saturday night?'

'Alexis runs a tight ship,' I said confidently. 'She's having so much fun childminding that she's worn him out. Movies, computer games, swimming, enough thick shakes to eliminate the EC milk mountain. Or should that be lake?'

'Depends if it's gone sour yet,' he said. 'Is he missing me?'

'When he has the time to notice you're not there,' I said drily. 'I'm the one that's missing you.'

This time, the smile only made it halfway. 'I

feel like Tom Jones in "The Green, Green Grass of Home",' he said. He rubbed a hand over his face. He looked exhausted.

'You don't look like him, thank God,' I told him. 'They treating you OK?'

He shrugged. 'I guess. I've got a cell to myself, which is an improvement on last night. And the food's just about edible. It's the boredom. It's doing my head in. I'd kill for a decent book and a clean shirt.'

I waved the plastic bag. 'Clean shirt, boxers, socks and a couple of books. Alexis chose them.' He looked bemused. I wasn't surprised. 'She says it doesn't mean anything's changed between you,' I added.

He relaxed. 'Thank God for that. I can stand most things, but I don't know if I could bear to go through the rest of my life being grateful to Alexis. Thanks, Brannigan. I appreciate it.'

'You better had,' I growled. 'I don't do this for my clients, you know. You're going to be working flat out till Christmas as it is just to pay me.' I brought him up to speed, stressing how tentative it all was. That didn't stop him looking like a kid who was expecting Santa to turn up with a ten-speed mountain bike *and* a Sega Megadrive.

'OK, I hear you. Gimme the bottom line. Are you going to get me out of here in time to spend some time with Davy?' he asked. The trust I could read in his eyes pushed my stress levels into the stratosphere.

'I sincerely hope so.' I had a horrible feeling that if I didn't, my failure would mean more than one disappointed kid.

Leaving Richard wasn't something I'd relished. But the fresh air outside the court building was. I breathed deep, staring up at the sky, not caring that there was a blur of light rain in the air. I can't remember the last time I felt so low. I checked in with the baby-sitters and Chris told me Davy was still spark out. I drove round by Terence Fitzgerald's house, but the place was in darkness and there was no car outside. I contemplated a bit of burglary, but I knew it was madness. The second rule of successful burglary is: Always make sure you know enough about their lives to know when they're likely to come back. I didn't know nearly enough about Terence's nasty habits. And I didn't relish the thought of being trapped on the top floor with no visible means of escape.

I didn't feel like going home yet. I gunned the car engine into life and cruised back into town. Almost without thinking, I headed for Strangeways. In the long shadow of the Victorian prison commerce thrives. The narrow streets are packed with whole-salers' warehouses, lock-ups and shop fronts, selling casual clothes, electrical goods, jewellery, beauty supplies and furniture. They're mostly family busi-nesses, and the ages of the businesses are like the strata in a geological map. The Jews were here first, then the Cypriots, then the Asians, then a handful of boat people. We're expecting the Bosnians any day now.

A lot of the business that goes on in Strangeways is entirely legitimate. And then, a lot of it isn't. A diligent Trading Standards Officer spending a Sunday poking around the market could find enough infringements to keep a court busy for a week. They regularly do. Only nobody ever answers the summonses.

On a Saturday night, Strangeways looks as empty, dark and moody as a Hollywood film set. Except for the Jewish café, that is. Formally the Warehouse Diner, it's an unpretentious dive frequented by the traders, petty criminals and occasional visitors like me. It's the only decent eating place outside Chinatown that stays open till four in the morning, which makes it handy for all sorts of reasons. Besides, they do the best salt beef sandwiches in town, and the best fry-ups. Some dickhead nominated it for one of those 'cheap and cheerful' good food guides, which means that every now and again a bunch of tourists arrives to gawp at the regulars. I've always enjoyed the atmosphere, though if you want certain items, you have to pick your time carefully. The rabbi's a regular visitor, and the mornings he's due there's no bacon butties and only beef sausages.

I'd hit a lull; the early trade had eaten and gone and the nighthawks weren't in yet. As I'd expected, there were a few familiar faces in the diner. The one I was most pleased to see was

Dennis. He waved to me to join him and his two buddies, but what I wanted to talk about wasn't for public consumption. I shook my head and sat at a table on my own. As my tea and sandwich arrived, so did Dennis. 'What do you know, Kate?' he greeted me, pulling out the chair opposite me.

'Not a lot. Life's a bitch and then you die.' I said wearily.

'Nah,' he said. 'Life's a bitch and then you marry one.'

'That's no way to talk about the love of your life.'

He grinned. 'Me and the wife, we're modern. Into all the latest fashions. That's what keeps a marriage alive. These days we have an S&M relationship.'

I knew I was walking into it, but I walked anyway. 'S&M?'

'Sex and meals.' Dennis roared with laughter. It wasn't that funny, but it was great camouflage. Now everyone would think I was just another victim of Dennis's funny stories.

'Nice one. You know a bloke called Terence Fitzgerald? Lives on the Quays. Drives a black Toyota.'

'Terry Fitz? We were in Durham together.' He didn't mean on holiday. Durham jail is one of the meanest, bleakest places a man can do time. They don't send you there for nonpayment of fines.

'What was he in for?'

'A blag with a shooter. He was the wheels man.

161

Like Handbrake, only nasty. They never got him for it but he run over an old dear when they was having it away on their toes after a job in Skelmersdale, and he never stopped. Slag,' Dennis added contemptuously.

'He been out long?'

Dennis shrugged. 'A year or so. I don't know what he's doing these days.'

'I do,' I said. 'He's working as a floor man for an outfit doing hall sales.' I handed Dennis the crumpled flyer. 'This outfit.'

Dennis nodded sagely. 'This is his brother-in-law's team. Tank Molloy. He married Fitz's sister Leanne. Good operation he's got there. Makes a lot of money. And he does it all dead legal. He shafts them, but he shafts them within the letter of the law. The BBC had a team following him round for weeks, trying to turn him over, but they couldn't get nothing on him except for being immoral so they had to back off. Burly bloke, hair like a poodle, terrible taste in ties, that's Tank. He's usually the top man.'

I raised one eyebrow. 'The top man?'

'The one that does the patter.'

I nodded. 'Sounds like him. Any drug connection?'

Dennis looked shocked. 'What? Tank Molloy? No way. He's an old-fashioned villain, Tank. He's like me. Wouldn't touch drugs with a bargepole. I mean, where's the challenge in that?'

'What about Terry Fitz?'

Dennis took his time lighting a cigarette. 'Fitz has got no scruples. And he don't give a shit who he works with. If he's got in with the drug boys, you don't want to tangle. He's sharp, Fitz. The only thing he's stupid about is shooters. He thinks they're a tool of the trade. He wouldn't think twice about blowing you away if there was just you standing between him and a good living.'

14

It's a piece of cake, being a lawyer or a doctor
or a computer systems analyst or an accountant.
Libraries are full of books telling you how to do
it. The only textbooks for private eyes are on the
fiction shelves, and I don't remember ever reading
one that told me how to interrogate an eight-year-
old without feeling like I was auditioning for the
Gestapo. It didn't help that Alexis was standing in
the doorway like a Scouse Boadicea, arms folded,
a frown on her face, ready to step in as soon as I
stepped out of line.

Davy sat in bed, looking a bit pale, but otherwise
normal. I figured if he was well enough to wolf
scrambled eggs and cheese cabanos, he was well
enough to answer a few simple questions. Somehow, it didn't work out that straightforwardly. I
sat on the bed and eventually we established that
he was feeling OK, that I wasn't going to tell his
mum and we'd negotiate about his dad at a later
stage. Already, I felt exhausted.

'Where did you get the transfers from?'

'A boy,' he said.

'Did you know the boy?' I asked.

Davy shook his head. He risked a quick glance at me from under his fringe. I could see he was going to grow up with the same lethal cuteness as his father. However, since I've yet to discover any maternal instincts and I'm not into little boys till they're old enough to have their own credit card, the charm didn't work on me. I stayed firm and relentless. 'You don't usually take presents from strangers, do you, Davy?'

Again, the shake of the head. This time, he mumbled, 'He wasn't a proper stranger.'

'How do you mean?' I pounced.

'Daniel and Wayne knew him,' he said defiantly 'I wasn't going to, but they said it was all right.'

'Were you playing with Daniel and Wayne?'

This time he nodded. His head came up and he looked me in the eye. He was on surer ground now. Daniel and Wayne were two of the kids from the council estate. He knew I knew who he was talking about. I stood up. 'OK. In future, don't take things from people unless *you* know them. Is that a deal?'

Looking stubborn rather than chastened, he nodded. 'OK,' he dragged out.

'I'm really not cut out for this game,' I muttered to Alexis as I left.

'It shows,' she growled. Walking down the hall, I heard her say, 'You going to lie in your pit all day, soft lad? Only there's a pair of skates at Ice World with your name on, and if you're not ready in half an hour I'm going to have to go on my own.'

'Can't we go later, Alexis?' I heard Davy plead.

'You're not going to lie there half the day, are you?'

'No. But I want to go and watch my dad's team playing football this morning. We always go and watch them when I'm here.'

Silence. I bet standing on a freezing touchline watching the local pub team kick a ball badly round a muddy pitch was as much Alexis's idea of hell as it was mine. I smiled as I headed through the conservatory and back into my own territory. It was nice to know that even Alexis got stiffed now and again. I pulled on last night's jeans. I opened the wardrobe and realized I wasn't going to be able to take a rain check on my date with the iron for much longer. I'd hire someone to do it, but on past experience it only causes me more grief because they never, but never, get the creases in the right places.

Irritated, I grabbed a Black Watch tartan shirt, a leftover from my brief excursion into grunge fashion, hastily abandoned when Della told me I looked like a refugee from an Irish folk group. At least it gave me an excuse to wear the battered old cowboy boots that are more comfortable than every pair of trainers I possess. I put a white T-shirt on under the tartan and headed out the door in search of Daniel and Wayne's mum.

I crossed the common to the rows of four-storey council flats where Cherie Roberts lived. After all this time, I'm still capable of being surprised by the contrast with the neat little enclave where I live. At the risk of sounding like Methuselah at twenty-eight, I can remember council estates where the Rottweilers didn't go around in pairs for security. Oxford isn't famous for its pleasant public housing, but I had school friends who lived out on Blackbird Leys when it was the biggest council housing estate in Western Europe, and it was OK. I don't remember obscene graffiti everywhere, lifts awash with piss and shit, and enough rubbish blowing in the wind between the canyons of flats to mistake the place for the municipal dump. Thank you, Mrs Thatcher.

I walked on to the corner and looked down the narrow cul-de-sac, trying to remember which block Cherie's flat was in. I knew it was on the top floor and on the left-hand side. I'd know it when I saw it, but if I could avoid climbing six sets of stairs, I'd be happier. There was nobody around to ask either. Half past nine on a Sunday morning isn't a busy time on the streets where I live. I set off, chewing over what I knew of Daniel and Wayne's mum.

Cherie was a pale thirty-year-old who looked forty-except when she smiled and her bright blue eyes sparked. She didn't smile that often. She was a single parent. She hadn't ever been anything else in practice, even though she'd been married to Eddy Roberts for eight years. Eddy was a Para who'd fallen in love with violence long before Cherie ever got a look-in. They'd married in a moment of madness when he was waiting to be shipped to the Falklands to help win Mrs Thatcher's second term. He'd come back with his head full of Goose Green and gone just crazy enough for them to invalid him out. He stuck around for the few days it took to impregnate Cherie, but before Daniel was much more than a tadpole, her soldier of fortune was off fighting somebody else's war in Southern Africa. He dropped in a year later for long enough to give her a couple of black eyes and another baby before he vanished into Central America.

Davy is the reason I know all this. He'd been coming up to visit regularly for a few months when Cherie turned up on my doorstep one night. Davy had obviously been boasting about my brilliance as a private eye, for Cherie had a task for me. She explained, right up front, that she couldn't afford to pay me in money but she was offering a skill swap. Her cleaning and ironing for my detecting. I was tempted, till she told me about the job. She wanted me to find Eddy. Not because she wanted him back, but because she wanted a divorce.

I'd explained gently that Mortensen and Brannigan don't handle missing persons, which happens to be no less than the truth. I could tell she didn't believe me, even though I spent an hour outlining a few suggestions on how and where she might track down her errant husband. Relations between us weren't helped when the agency was all over the papers a couple of months later because of a very high-profile missing person case that I'd cracked . . . Since then, whenever we'd met in the Post Office or in the dentist's waiting room she'd been frigidly polite, and I guess I'd stood on my dignity. Not the most promising history for a successful interview.

I struck lucky on the third attempt. I recognized Cheric's door as soon as I hit the landing. Daniel's Ninja Turtle stickers were unmistakable, and obviously difficult to remove. Nothing so embarrassing to a kid as the evidence of last year's cult. Taking a deep breath, I knocked. No reply. I banged the letter box, and was rewarded with a scurrying behind the door. The handle turned and the door swung open a couple of inches on a chain and the sound of the TV blasted me, but I couldn't see anybody. Then a small voice said, 'Hiya,' and I adjusted my eye level.

'Hiya, Daniel,' I said to the pyjama-clad figure. I had a fifty per cent chance of being right.

'I'm Wayne,' he said. I hoped that wasn't a sign from the gods.

'Sorry. Hiya, Wayne. Is your mum in?'

He shrugged. 'She's in bed.'

Before he could say more, I saw a pale blue shape in the background and heard Cherie's voice say sharply, 'Wayne. Come away from there. Who is it?'

I cocked my head round the crack in the door

and said, 'Hi, Cherie. It's me, Kate Brannigan. Sorry to wake you, but I wondered if I could have a word.'

Cherie appeared at the door in a faded towelling dressing gown and shoved Wayne out of the way. 'I wasn't asleep.'

I was glad about that. She'd have had to be seriously hearing impaired to have slept through the volume her kids seemed to need from the TV. 'Yeah, right,' I said diplomatically.

'What is it?' she asked.

'I just wanted a word. Em . . . Can I come in?'

Cherie looked defensive. 'If you want,' she said, grudging every word.

'I don't want the whole neighbourhood to hear me,' I said, trying desperately not to sound like I was about to give her a bad time.

'I've nothing to be ashamed of,' she said defensively. She let the chain off and opened the door wide enough to let me in. After I'd entered, she stuck her head out and gave the landing the quick one-two to check who had spotted me.

I pressed against the wall to let her pass and lead me into the living room. 'Out,' she said curtly. Daniel reluctantly uncurled himself from the sofa and walked out of the room. Cherie switched off the TV and stared aggressively at me. 'D'you want a brew, then?' It was a challenge.

I accepted. While she was in the kitchen, I looked around. The room was scrupulously clean and as tidy as my place on a good day. Given she had two kids, it was impressive. It was a shame she didn't have enough cash to upgrade from shabby. The leatherette upholstery of the sofa was mended with parcel tape in places, and in others it had completely worn away. The walls were covered in blown vinyl in a selection of patterns, clearly a job lot of odd rolls. But the paint was still white, if not quite brilliant, and she'd pitched some video shop manager into letting her have some film posters to brighten the place up.

'Seen enough?' Cherie demanded, returning from the kitchen on bare and silent feet. There was nothing I could say about her home that wouldn't sound patronizing, so I said nothing, meekly accepting the mug of tea she held out to me. 'There's no sugar,' she said. 'I don't keep it in.'

'That's OK, I don't use it.'

The door opened a couple of inches and Daniel's head and one shoulder appeared. 'We're going round to Jason's to watch a video,' he said.

'OK. Behave yourselves, you hear me?'

Daniel grinned. 'You wish, Mum,' he giggled. 'See ya.'

Cherie turned her attention back to me. She'd found a moment to drag a brush through her shoulder-length mouse-coloured hair, but it hadn't improved the image a whole lot. She still looked more like a woman at the end of her day rather than the beginning. 'So what's this word you wanted to have with me?'

I swallowed a mouthful of strong tea and dived in at the deep end. 'I'm really worried about something that happened yesterday, and I think you probably will be too. Davy's up for the week. He was out playing yesterday morning for a couple of hours, and when he came in, he was in a hell of a state. He was really hyper, he was sick, and his temperature was all over the place. I got a friend of mine who's a doctor to come around and have a look at him. The bottom line is, he was out of his head on drugs.'

The words were barely out of my mouth before Cherie jumped in. 'And it has to be something to do with my kids, doesn't it? It couldn't be any of those nice middle-class kids from your street, could it? How do you think kids around here get the money for drugs?'

That wasn't one I was prepared to answer. Reminding her of the muggings, burglaries and dole frauds that are the everyday currency of life at the bottom of the heap wasn't going to earn me the answers I was looking for. 'I'm not blaming your lads, Cherie. From what I can gather, they're as likely to be victims as Davy was.'

That wasn't the right response either. 'Don't you accuse my lads of taking drugs,' she said dangerously, her eyes glinting like black ice. 'We might not have much compared to you, but I take care of my kids. You've no shame, have you?'

That was when I lost it. 'Will you for Christ's sake listen to me, Cherie?' I snarled. 'I've not come

172

here to have a go at you or your kids. Something scary, something dangerous, happened to Davy and I don't want it happening to any other kids. Not yours, not anybody's. You and me smacking each other over the heads with our prejudices isn't going to sort things out.'

In the silence that followed, Cherie gave me the hard stare. Gradually, the sullen look left her face. But the suspicion was still there in her eyes. 'OK. You got somebody else's kicking. I had them bastards from the Social round the other day, doing a number about how Eddy's not paying any maintenance and I must know where he is.'

I pulled a face. 'Pick a war, any war.'

'That's more or less what I told them. So, what's all this business with Davy got to do with me?' The adrenaline rush had subsided and her eyes had dulled again, emphasizing the dark blue shadows beneath them. She sat on the arm of the sofa, keeping her eyes firmly fixed on mine.

'These drugs were absorbed through the skin. From those tattoo transfers that the kids stick all over themselves. According to my doctor friend, the tattoos are impregnated with drugs. I don't know why. Maybe it's to give kids the taste for it. You know, a few freebies to get them into the habit, then it's sorry, you've got to cough up some readies.'

Cherie pulled a pack of cheap cigarettes out of her dressing-gown pocket and lit up. 'I've seen my two with a few transfers,' she admitted. 'I know they must have got them from one of the other kids because I don't buy them the stickers, and they've had them some times when they've not had spends. But I've never seen them out of their heads, or anything like it. Mind you, the way they wind each other up, you probably couldn't tell,' she added, in a grim joke.

I mirrored her thin smile. 'The problem seems to have arisen because Davy OD'd on the transfers. He loves them, you see. Given half a chance and a year's pocket money, he'd cover himself from head to foot with them. Especially if they were *Thunderbirds* ones. Now, Davy says he was playing with Wayne and Daniel yesterday. A boy he didn't know gave him the transfers, and he seems to have handed over as many as Davy wanted. He says he thought it was OK to take the transfers from the boy because Wayne and Daniel knew him,' I said.

'I suppose you want to ask my pair who this lad was,' Cherie said with the resignation of a woman who's accustomed to having her autonomy well and truly usurped by the middle-class bastards. Once upon a time I'd have been insulted to be taken for one of them, but even I can't kid myself that I'm still a working-class hero.

I shook my head. 'If you don't mind, I'd rather you asked them. I think you're more likely to get the truth out of them than me. They'd only think I was going to bollock them.'

Cherie snorted. 'They'll *know* I'm going to bollock

them. OK, I'll ask them when I see them. It'll be a few hours, mind you. Once they get stuck into a pile of videos, they lose all track of time.'

'Great. If you get anywhere, can you let me know? I'm going to be in and out a lot, but there'll probably be somebody in next door in Richard's. Or else stick a note through the door. I'd really appreciate it.' I got to my feet.

'You going to hand the slags over to the cops?' Cherie asked. Behind her bravado, I could sense apprehension.

'I don't think people that hand out drugs to kids should be out on the street, do you?'

Cherie shook her head, a despairing look on her face. 'Put them away, another one jumps in to take their place.'

'So we just let them carry on?'

'No way. I just thought you'd know the kind of people that'd put them off drug dealing for life. And put off anybody else that was thinking it would be a good career move.'

People get strange ideas in their heads about the kind of person a private eye hangs out with. The worrying thing for me was that Cherie was absolutely right. I knew just the person to call.

15

Ruth hadn't hung around waiting for me in reception. I spotted her behind the *Independent on Sunday* from the other side of the coffee lounge. There was already a basket of croissants and a selection of cold meats and cheeses on the table. Whipped cream in Alpine peaks was gently subsiding into her hot chocolate, and somehow she'd managed to get a whole jug of freshly squeezed orange juice all to herself. Luckily, she'd chosen a window table which commanded a view of the Quays. On the way to meet her, I'd swung round by Terry Fitz's flat and been relieved to see the Supra sitting on the drive and the curtains still firmly closed. From the hotel, I'd be able to see if he left home.

I sat down and said, 'If I rush off suddenly, it's not because of something you've said.'

She lowered the paper and groaned. 'Oh God, not melodrama over Sunday brunch? Frankly, I can see why you copped out of the law. Not nearly exciting enough to keep you going.'

'I'm not grandstanding,' I bristled. 'I'm trying to get Richard out of jail.'

'You and me both,' Ruth said calmly, dumping her paper, reaching for a croissant and dunking it into her chocolate. I felt faintly sick. 'Any progress?' she asked.

I brought her up to speed. It didn't even fill the gap between me ordering coffee and wholemeal toast and them arriving. Ruth listened attentively in between mouthfuls of soggy croissant. 'How fascinating. It's a novel way of distributing drugs. This sounds very promising for Richard,' she said as I ground to a halt. 'But you're going to need a lot more than that before we can persuade the Drugs Squad that Richard was merely an innocent abroad.'

'What are the next moves, from your point of view?' I asked.

'That depends to some extent on you. If you can come up with enough by Tuesday morning for the Drugs Squad to get going, then I've got a slight chance of getting bail on Wednesday.'

'How slight?' I asked.

Ruth studied the cold meat and speared a slice of smoked ham. 'I'd be lying if I said it looked good. Failing that, what I can go for is a short remand, say an overnight or a couple of days, arguing that investigations are in progress which may produce a significantly different picture within twenty-four hours. If the Drugs Squad then mount a successful operation based on information received from you, the chances are we can then get Richard out on bail. It'll take a little longer to get the charges dropped, but at least he won't be languishing in the CDC while I'm working on it.' She split a croissant and loaded it with ham, followed by a slice of cheese. I envied her appetite. I stared morosely at the toast and poured myself a coffee.

I didn't even have time to add milk. A flash of light as the sun hit the windscreen of Terry Fitz's car alerted me. He was turning out of his drive. I hit the ground running. 'Sorry!' I called back to Ruth. 'Send me the bill.'

'Don't worry about it,' she shouted. 'I'll charge it to the client.'

And I thought I padded my bills. One thing about hanging out with lawyers: they don't half make you feel virtuous.

This time, we headed up the M6. I had no trouble with the tail at first, since half of the North West of England had decided the only place to be on the sunny Sunday of a bank holiday weekend was in a traffic jam on the motorway. Things improved after Blackpool, but there were still a lot of families having the traditional bank holiday argument all the way to the Lakes. The Supra was an impatient outside-lane hogger and flasher of lights, but he had few chances to hammer it till the traffic thinned out after the Windermere turn-off. Then he was off. I prayed he was keeping a look-out for traffic cops up ahead as I watched the speedo creep up past a ton. The last thing I needed was a driving ban.

He slowed as we approached the Carlisle turning, and I hung back till the last minute before I shot off in his wake. His destination was only five minutes off the motorway, a sprawling concrete pillbox of a pub sandwiched between a post-war council estate of two-up two-down flats built to look like semis, and a seventies estate of little 'executive' boxes occupied by sales reps, factory foremen and retail managers struggling with their mortgages. I drifted past the Harvester Moon Inn, watching as he parked the Supra by the truck I recognized from the previous day. I slowed to a halt, twisted my rear-view mirror round and watched Terry Fitz climb out of his car, pick up a black bin liner from the rear seat well and head into the pub.

I parked round the corner from the pub and walked back. The blackboard stood outside the main entrance, announcing today's sales at two p.m. and five p.m. in the pub's upstairs function room. Depressed at the very thought of it, I dragged myself into the pub. It was a huge barn of a place, arbitrarily divided into bar and lounge by a wooden partition at head height. Well, head height for someone with a bit more than my five feet and three inches. The whole place was in dire need of a face-lift, but judging by the desperate tone of the notices on the walls, it wasn't making enough to persuade the brewery to spend the necessary cash. Monday night was 'the best trivia night in town', Tuesday was 'Darts Open Night, cash prizes', Wednesday was 'Ladies Night! With Special House Cocktails', Thursday offered 'Laser Karaoke, genuine opportunities for Talent!', while Friday was 'Disco Dancing! Do the Lambada with Lenny. The Harvester's very own king of the turntables'. And people say Manchester's provincial.

The clientele was marginally up-market of the down-at-heel decor. There were, naturally, more men than women, since somebody has to baste the chicken. I felt out of place, not because of my gender, but because I was the only person who wasn't part of the locals' tribal rituals. The customers sat or stood in tight groups, taking part in what was clearly a regular Sunday lunch-time session with unvarying companions. I carried on walking past the bar, gathering a few inquisitive stares on the way, and through a door at the rear marked 'Harvest Home Lounge'. It led to a small foyer, with stairs climbing upwards, and a set of double doors leading out into the car park. With half an hour to go before the sale, I'd clearly beaten the Carlisle crowds to the draw.

I walked back to the car and headed into the town centre till I found a Chinese chippy next to a corner shop. I drove back crunching worryingly cubic sweet-and-sour chicken, with a bag of apples for afters to make me feel virtuous. I joined the queue for the sale with only a few minutes to go. This time, I hung back as we filed in so I could have

a good view of the rest of the punters. The sale followed the same pattern as the previous evening's.
The only change was that Molloy, the top man,
only offered forty bottles of perfume. I put that
down to the slightly smaller crowd that they had
drawn. When we got down to the pig-in-a-poke
lots, I kept my eyes fixed on Terry Fitz.

The night before hadn't been a fluke. Soon
as Molloy announced the fifty-pound lots, Terry
appeared with a black bin liner that looked identical to the others. But he took it straight over
to a punter I'd already singled out as the man
most likely to. Just like the previous night's mark,
he was wearing a black leather jacket and a red
baseball cap. It was a different guy, there was no
question about it. But the clothes were identical.

As soon as I saw the handover, I eased myself
away from the audience and ran downstairs. I
slipped inside the door leading to the pub and
held it open a crack. As I'd expected, Red Cap was
only moments behind me. He didn't even pause
to look around him, just headed straight out into
the car park. I was behind him before he'd gone a
hundred yards.

He wasn't hard to tail. He bounced on his expensive hi-tops with a swagger, his red cap jauntily
bobbing from side to side. Across the car park,
over the road and into the council estate. We
walked for half a mile or so through the estate
until we came to three blocks of low-rise flats
arranged in an H-shape. Red Cap went for the

middle block, disappearing into a stairwell. Cautiously, I followed, keeping a clear flight below him as he climbed. I caught a glimpse of his jacket as he turned out of the stairs on the third floor, and I ran the last flight. I cleared the stairs and hit the gallery in time to see a door close behind him. Trying to look as if I belonged, I strolled along the gallery. His was the third door. The glass had been painted over and heavy curtains obscured the windows. I turned and walked back, my eyes flicking from side to side, desperately seeking a vantage point.

One of the legs of the H looked as if it was in the process of being refurbished or demolished. The windows were mostly boarded up and there was no sign of life. I hurried back down the stairs and across to the deserted block. Sure enough, the stairwell was boarded up. It had been padlocked, but the housing had been crowbarred off, some time ago, by the looks of it. I pulled the door open far enough to squeeze round it and cautiously made my way up the gloomy stairs. From what little I could see, it looked like HIV alley, condoms slithering and syringes crunching underfoot. Once I passed the first floor it became lighter and cleaner. I went all the way up to the fourth floor and emerged on the gallery at an oblique angle to Red Cap's front door. Then I settled down to wait.

Half an hour later, there had been four visits to the flat: two separate youths, one couple in their teens and a pair of lads with a girl in tow. Red Cap had opened the door to all of them, and they'd slipped inside, only to emerge less than five minutes later looking a lot happier. I've seen chemists' shops with fewer customers. After the fourth visit, I thought it was time to risk collecting some firm evidence, so I left my sentry post and jogged back to the car. I drove into the private housing estate and headed in the general direction of the flats. I didn't want to leave the car in an exposed place like a pub car park once I'd revealed that it held more than yesterday's newspapers. I parked in a quiet side-street and opened my photographic bag. I put on the khaki gilet Richard brought me back from a business trip to LA. It's got more pockets than a snooker club. I put the Nikon body with the motor drive in one, and slipped my telephoto lens and doubler into inside pockets.

Within ten minutes, I was back on the fourth floor, the long lens resting on the edge of the balcony, focused on Red Cap's front door, motor drive switched on. I didn't have long to wait. In less than an hour, I had six separate groups on film. If I didn't win the Drugs Squad's Woman of the Year award, it wouldn't be for want of trying.

16

I called it a day on the surveillance at half past four and walked back to the car. I swapped cameras, choosing a miniature Japanese one that slots into a pocket in the gilet. The pocket has a hole in it that corresponds to the lens of the camera. I loaded the camera with superfast film so it would capture an image without the need for flash, plugged in the remote shutter release cable and threaded it through the lining so the button sat snugly in the pocket I'd have my hand stuffed into. Before I set off for the five o'clock sale, I called home. There was no reply, either at my house or Richard's, so I assumed everybody was having a good time.

The five o'clock sale ran to the same formula. If I had to do this many more times, I'd be able to take over the top man's job. This time, I'd got near the front of the queue and waited till the red cap and the black leather jacket appeared. This time, it wasn't a man. Nice to see that equal opps is finally making its way into criminal circles. She was about my age, taller, bottle blonde and pale as Normandy butter. I manoeuvred my way through the crowd till I was standing at an angle to her, perfectly positioned for my camera to do the business. The handover came right on cue, the bulky envelope exchanged for a black bin liner. This time, Terry Fitz winked. I'm not sure if it was because she was a woman, or because he knew her, but it was the first time I'd seen him display any kind of recognition towards the happy recipients of his little parcels.

I thought about following the woman, but decided I'd rather stay with Terry Fitz. I knew where the drugs were going now; what I didn't know was where they were coming from. With his record, I couldn't see Terry Fitz standing on for having them stashed in his house. I waited till the woman in the red baseball cap was well clear, then I nipped out ahead of the masses and got my car in position between the pub and the motorway.

Just before eight, Terry Fitz shot past me at a disgraceful speed. On the way back, the bank holiday traffic trapped us again, but in spite of that we were still back in Salford by half past nine. As we turned into the Quays, I hung back. I was a good half-mile away when he pulled up on the street outside his house. He jumped out of the car, trotted up the path and opened the garage, re-emerging seconds later behind the wheel of the Escort Cosworth, still with its trade plates.

I waited till it zoomed past me sounding like

Concorde with a frog in its throat before I spun the Peugeot round and sped off in its wake. Back down the motorway, on to the M63, this time heading south towards Stockport. As we drove over Barton Bridge, the elevated section above the Manchester Shit Canal (so called because of the sewage works that huddle along its banks), I stayed right over in the fast lane. I came rather too close to checking out whether or not there's an afterlife one night on Barton Bridge, and it left me more than a little wary of trusting in the crash barriers.

As we descended the long curve of the bridge, I let my breath out again. I stayed with his tail-lights past Trafford Park and Sale, but I nearly missed him as he cut across three lanes of traffic to shoot off on the slip road for the M56 and the airport. We didn't stay on the motorway for long. He came off at the junction for the sprawling council estate of Wythenshawe, bypassed the shopping centre and made for the far side of the airport, over towards the cargo holding areas. The job suddenly got awkward.

The Cosworth turned right down a narrow lane that wound alongside the perimeter fence of the airport. Following it down there was a risky venture. Sighing, I doused my lights and turned right. My car was black, which meant I had less chance of being spotted. The downside was that anything coming in the opposite direction wouldn't see me either. The things we do for love.

The lane was fairly straight, so I managed easily

to keep the lights of the Cosworth in sight for a mile or so, then, abruptly, they disappeared sharply on the right. Time for a gamble. Since that was the airport side of the road, I didn't think Terry Fitz had turned off on to another minor road. I decided he'd arrived at a rendezvous. I spotted a field gateway a couple of hundred yards ahead on the left, and pulled into it, killing the engine fast. I got out of the car and pushed the door gently to. The click of the lock made me jump, but I told myself it wouldn't carry far, not so close to the airport.

I took a good look round before I crossed the road and moved cautiously towards the spot where the Cosworth had vanished. There was a narrow gap in the hedgerow, and I edged my head round. A rutted, stony track led a few yards off the road, angling round sharply to the double doors of a wooden building. Small barn, large garage, take your pick. The Cosworth was outside, parked next to a Mercedes 300SL with the personalized plate TON 1K. I could see a thin line of yellow light along the top of the door, but nothing more. The side of the lock-up was only feet away from the airport fence.

I felt seriously exposed where I was, so I slipped across the track and inched up to the corner, checking the hedge as I went. Just on the corner, there was a bit of give and I wriggled into the bushes, trying not to think of all the nocturnal creatures that lurk in the English countryside. If you ask me, extinct is quite the best state for mice and rats and most other small furry animals with sharp teeth. Not to mention all the creepy insects that would take one look at my hair and decide it was a better habitat than the filthy maze of the hedgerow.

I gave an involuntary shudder that rippled through the hedge with a noise like *Wuthering Heights* meets *The Wind in the Willows*. 'Get a grip, Brannigan,' I muttered under my breath. I took a deep breath and my nose filled with dust. Predictably, just like the worst kind of wimpy heroine, I felt a sneeze welling up inside. I pinched the bridge of my nose so tight my eyes watered, but not so much that I missed the garage door opening. Terry Fitz appeared in the doorway, called back, 'No problem, speak to you in the week,' and walked briskly to the Cosworth.

He was carrying three Sainsbury's carrier bags, but I didn't think he'd come all the way out to the airport to pick up some groceries. He opened the boot, and in the glow of the courtesy light, I saw him lift the carpet and stow the carrier bags underneath. From the look of it, they were packed into the well where the spare wheel should be. Fitzgerald slammed the boot shut, then got into the Cosworth. He bounced the car round in a tight three-point turn, then he was off, leaving a cloud of dust hanging in the moonlight. I didn't even think about trying to follow him.

Instead, I waited to see who else was lurking inside the garage. I didn't think that anyone who owned a motor like that was likely to be spending the night there. Besides, with Richard behind bars, I had nothing better to do with my Sunday evening.

It was a long half-hour before there was any sign of life. With no warning, the door swung open. Before I had the chance to see who emerged, the inside light snapped off. A tall, burly man in an overcoat came out and turned his back to me as he fastened a couple of big padlocks that closed the heavy steel bars protecting the doors. Then, still with his back to me, he headed towards the Mercedes. I backed out of the hedge, coming out on the track out of his sight, and raced back towards the road as his engine started. I reckoned I had a couple of minutes while he turned the big car around. With a bit of luck, he'd be heading the way my car was facing and I might be able to pick him up. If I lost him, at least I had the car registration number to go at.

I dived behind the wheel of the Peugeot just as his headlights swept the hedge opposite the gap. The gods were smiling. He drove away from me, so I started the engine, left the lights off and followed. I was beginning to feel like I'd got the sucker role in a very bad road movie.

We were only a mile from the main road. I let him glide off before I switched my lights on and rejoined the respectable. I hoped this wasn't going to be a long chase, because my fuel gauge told me I'd soon be running on fumes. At least Mercedes

Man didn't drive like a speed freak. I suppose when you're driving round in that much money you don't need to prove anything to anybody.

We cruised through Wilmslow, the town where car dealers aren't allowed to sell anything that costs less than five figures. They're all here – Rolls Royce, Porsche, BMW, Mercedes, Jaguar, even Ferrari. Just before the town centre, the Merc turned right and, a couple of hundred yards down the road, he pulled on to the forecourt of a small car pitch. EMJ Car Sales. Even the second-hand motors were all less than three years old.

The driver got out of the car and let himself into the car showroom. A light came on inside. Now at least I knew where Terry Fitz had come by his trade plates. And why he seemed to go for seriously expensive motors. Five minutes later, the interior light snapped off and the driver got back into his Merc. I still hadn't had a good enough look at him to attempt identification. We drove back into the town centre. It was quiet; not even the designer clothes shops had attracted late-night browsers. We passed the station and headed out of town. By now, I had a shrewd suspicion where we might be headed.

Prestbury has more millionaires per head of population than any other village in England, according to the media-hype types. The only way you'd guess from hanging round in the main street is from the motors parked outside the deli and the *chocolatier*. They don't have sweetie shops run by Asians in places like Prestbury. They don't have anything that isn't one hundred per cent backed up by centuries of English Conservative tradition. But then, in Prestbury, you don't get the kind of *nouveau* millionaire celebs that give the paparazzi palpitations. We're talking captains of industry, backroom boys and girls, the high rollers whose names mean nothing to anyone outside a very select circle. You can tell it's posh, though. They haven't got pavements or streetlights. After all, who needs them when you go everywhere by car or horse?

About a mile from the centre of the village, the Merc signalled a left turn. I signalled right, then killed my lights and pulled on to the verge. Someone was going to have a major tantrum when they saw my tyre marks in the morning. I jumped out of the car and sprinted towards the gateway he'd entered. I crouched behind the gatepost. The deeply incised letters told me I was outside Hickory Dell, the land that taste forgot. The house was built on the side of a slope, a split-level monstrosity that could have housed half Manchester's homeless and still have had room for a wedding reception. A four-car garage bigger than any house on my estate stood off to one side. One garage door was open, the drive outside it spotlit with high-wattage security lights. I heard the soft slam of a car door, then the heavy-set man emerged. As he swung round to check the door was closing behind him, I got a good look at his face.

I'd seen him before, no question about it. The problem was, I didn't have a clue where or when.

17

I stopped running and took a couple of seconds to work out exactly where I was. I could feel the prickle of sweat under my helmet as I swivelled my head from side to side. I turned sharp right and started running again. As I rounded the next corner, my heart sank. I'd hesitated too long. The tank was heading straight for me, blocking the entire width of the street. Desperately, I turned back, in time to see the helicopter closing off my retreat by dropping a block of what looked remarkably like granite into the street.

Resigned to defeat, I pulled off my helmet and glove. In the next playing area, Davy was still inside his helmet, one hand on the joystick that controlled the tank, the other punching the air triumphantly. I hate kids. They're *always* better at the computer games where hand–eye co-ordination is vital.

I tapped the top of his helmet and undid the straps. Reluctantly, he let go the joystick and

climbed out of the seat. 'Time up, cybernaut,' I said.
I glanced at my watch. 'They'll be closing soon.'
The brand new VIRUS Centre (Virtual Reality
UniverSe, I kid you not) had proved to be the
best possible way of amusing Davy without doing
my head in. It had only opened a month before,
and secretly I'd been dying to try out the twenty
game scenarios promised in their lavish brochure.
I'd been wary about coming on a bank holiday
Monday, but it had been surprisingly quiet. I
blame the parents. Not that I'm complaining –
their absence gave me and Davy a lot more scope
for enjoying ourselves.

I suppose I should have felt guilty, indulging
myself with swords and sorcery while Richard
was still languishing, but he seemed to think that
his son's enjoyment was just as important as my
attempts to get him released. Besides, Alexis had
had to go into the office anyway to do some
last-minute work on the child porn exposé that
would launch the *Chronicle*'s latest campaign. At
least I'd pitched her into trying to find out who
lived at Hickory Dell.

We headed back to the car via the souvenir
shop. 'Enjoy yourself?' I asked. Pretty redundant
question, really.

'It was boss. Top wicked.' I took that to mean
approval. 'It was a lot better than Ice World,'
he said judiciously. "Skating gets boring after a
while. Your ankles get sore. And the other stuff
was pretty boring. You know, all that discovering

the South Pole stuff. The models are really naff, and they don't *do* anything. 'S not surprising there was hardly anybody there,' he added, dismissing Alexis's attempts to entertain him.

'Wasn't there?' I asked, more for something to say than out of interest.

'There was *no* queues,' he said indignantly. 'Anything worth doing always has queues.' He looked around the souvenir shop, where we were the only customers. 'Except this place,' he qualified.

How bizarre to be part of a generation where queues are a sign of approval. Me, I'd pay money to avoid standing in line. I'm the driver everyone hates, the one who jumps the queue of standing traffic on the motorway and sneaks in just as the three lanes narrow to two. I nearly said something, but Davy was already delving through a box of transfers.

I left him to his browsing and ambled over to the ego board by the door. It displayed five-inch by three-inch colour photographs of the creators and senior staff of the VIRUS Centre, captioned with their names and executive titles. They all looked interchangeable with the mugshots on the board down the local supermarket. I turned back to check on Davy, and suddenly my subconscious swung into action. No queues at Ice World, coupled with the ego board, had finally woken my memory. The answer had been there all the time, only I'd been too dozy to spot it.

*　　*　　*

When we got back, Alexis was sitting in my conservatory, trying to look like she was engrossed in the evening paper. I knew she was only pretending; Chris gave the game away. 'You were right,' she said to Alexis in a surprised voice. 'It *was* Kate's car. Hello, you two. Have a good day?'

That was all the encouragement Davy needed. He launched into a blow-by-blow account of the VIRUS Centre. Like an angel, Chris steered him off towards the kitchen, seducing him with promises of fish fingers and baked beans. I collapsed on the sofa and groaned. 'Thank God for contraception,' I muttered.

'I don't know what you're going on about,' Alexis said. 'He's good as gold. You want to spend a day looking after my nephew. He's hyperactive and his mother's the kind of divvy who fills him up with E numbers. Any more complaints from you and I won't tell you what I've found out today.'

I closed my eyes and leaned back. 'The occupant of Hickory Dell is Eliot James,' I intoned. 'Boss man at Tonik Leisure Services. Owners of, among other things, Ice World. Which, if what Davy says is right, must be struggling. If you're half-empty on a cold bank holiday Sunday morning, you're not going to weather the recession indefinitely.' I sneaked an eyelid half-open. Alexis's expression moved from fury to disappointment to amusement. Luckily for me, it stopped there.

'Nobody loves a smartass,' she growled. 'OK, clever clogs. So what else have you dug up about

196

Jammy James while you've supposedly been off entertaining me laddo? I mean, I don't know why I bother putting myself out when you just bugger off and do it yourself anyway!'

I sat up and tried to look apologetic. 'I haven't been doing any digging, I promise you. Like I said this morning, I knew I'd seen him before, I just couldn't get a handle on it. Then Davy told me Ice World was as lively as Antarctica on a Saturday night, which set me wondering how these theme parks cover their overheads when the punters haven't got enough money to take the family out on a bank holiday. We were in the souvenir shop, and they've got one of those boards with the flattering photos of the top brass that are meant to make you think this is a really user-friendly oper ation. I was staring at that, and then I remembered that I'd seen the guy I trailed on one of those ego boards. Add that to the personalized number plate on the car . . .'

'What personalized plate?' Alexis protested. 'You never said anything to me about a personalized plate!'

I gave a guilty smile. 'I . . . ah . . . I forgot to mention that. TON 1K. Sorry. I've got a lot on my mind.'

Alexis shook her head. 'I don't know. It's worse working for you than for my brain-dead newsdesk. So what else have you remembered?'

'That's it,' I promised. 'Have you got anything?'

Alexis pulled a face. 'Bits and pieces. Nothing

197

really. But I've arranged to meet one of my contacts in half an hour, and he's promised me the full SP on Jammy. Oh, and by the way – Ruth's coming round at nine o'clock for a powwow. And so's Della.'

'What?' I howled.

Alexis shrugged. 'Della rang up after Ruth had arranged to come round. I thought they might as well come together to save us having to go over everything twice.'

'Oh God,' I groaned. 'I don't suppose it occurred to you that I might not want them to know the same things?'

Alexis looked amused. 'Which one were you planning on lying to – the lawyer or the copper?'

I left Davy to Alexis and Chris, and headed for the office to develop the films I'd shot in Carlisle. In the cool silence of the darkroom, I concentrated on the job in hand, forcing myself to switch off from the ins and outs of the case. That way, I hoped, my subconscious would get on with processing the information in peace, and come up with some useful inspirations.

I shoved the finished prints into a folder, and headed downstairs to the Mexican restaurant to fortify myself for another soul-destroying visit to the cells. The place was empty, except for one guy sitting alone at a table towards the rear of the restaurant. He gave me a brief glance as I entered, then returned to the magazine he had propped up beside his bowl of chilli. With a jolt of surprise, I recognized the menacing bouncer from the Lousy Hand. If he was a regular here – and I couldn't see any other reason for frequenting the place on a bank holiday Monday, since the food isn't that great – it explained why he'd seemed familiar at the club. Relieved to have cleared that one up, I settled into a window table with my back to his cold eyes and ordered some guacamole and a plate of frijoles. As I ate, I thought about the evening ahead.

Now I'd calmed down, I was pleased Alexis had fixed up the brainstorming session, because I suspected that the dynamic between the four of us might just spark off some fresh ideas. I was desperate for any insight that might take us a step nearer getting Richard out of jail. The hardest thing about being grown up is realizing there are no magic formulas to release the ones we love from pain. Maybe that's why I enjoy computer games so much; you get to be God.

The girls were ready and waiting when I got back from the nick. Alexis had taken charge in my absence. I found it hard to recognize my living room. A flip chart on an easel had materialized from somewhere, and she'd arranged the chairs so we could all see it. She'd also found my cache of Australian Chardonnay and distributed glasses to the other two. I mumbled that I'd stick with the vodka and disappeared into the kitchen to fix myself a lemon Absolut with freshly squeezed pink grapefruit juice. By the time I got back, Alexis was copying some complicated tree structure from her notebook on to the flip chart. Ruth and Della looked as bemused as I felt.

'Alexis, I don't want to be difficult, but . . .'

'Chris is putting Davy to bed, so you don't have to worry about him butting in, if that's what's bugging you,' she said, not even pausing.

'It wasn't, actually. I just wondered what you were doing.'

'I need the diagram to explain about Jammy's empire,' Alexis said in the condescending tones I use to small children and she uses to news editors.

'Maybe Kate could bring us up to date,' Ruth said. 'Then perhaps we'd all have a clue what you're up to, Alexis.' Ever the diplomat.

It took a disturbingly short time to fill everyone in on my weekend activities. 'I waited till James went into the house, then I came home,' I finished up. 'Oh, and I've developed and printed up the films I shot in Carlisle.'

There was a slight pause. I could see Alexis gathering herself together to leap into the breach when Ruth said, 'I'm impressed, Kate. When you told me how little we had to go on, I thought we had as much chance of establishing the identity of the real criminals as I have of becoming Lord Chief Justice.'

'You're right, Kate's done an impressive job, but the Drugs Squad are going to have mixed feelings about it,' Della said ruefully. 'They've been chasing this crack epidemic for some time now, and while there are senior officers who are going to be bloody glad to get a solid handle on it, a lot of people are going to be very pissed off at being shown up by a private eye. And a woman private eye at that.'

'Tell me about it,' I sighed.

'And then there's the question of the accused,' Della went on. 'I've only been in Manchester a matter of months, but that's long enough to know that Eliot James is a name that means money, power and influence.'

Alexis finally managed to get a word in. She jumped to her feet. 'And that's where I come in,' she announced. 'I've been doing some digging into Mr Eliot James.' She picked up her marker pen and attacked the flip chart. For a full fifteen minutes she blinded us with science, taking us on a whirl-wind tour of Jammy James's leisure and property empire, his constant efforts to muscle in on the Olympic bid consortium, the parlous state of his marriage and the debts, loans and mortgages that, added together, put him in what building societies euphemistically call a negative equity situation.

'It's like Maxwell,' she concluded with a flourish. 'On the surface, it looks like everything's hunky-dory. But underneath, there's this huge iceberg of debt ready to smash into Jammy's hull and turn Tonik into the Titanic.'

'She's got a way with words, that girl,' I said. 'Ever thought of becoming a writer, Alexis?'

Della was shaking her head in amazement. 'I think I'll just go and shoot myself now,' she said. 'This has been a bad evening for the police. First, Kate does the Drugs Squad's job. And now you do my job. From what you've said, it looks very like our Mr James is trading while insolvent, so we're looking at one criminal offence at least. I think when the boys from the DS have finished with him, I'll be wanting a word.'

Ruth, who had been unusually quiet, said, 'It certainly explains why he needs the kind of cash injection that the drugs trade can bring. It does, however, give me a slight problem.'

'You're not his brief, are you?' I asked, the cold hand of panic squeezing my chest.

'Thankfully, no,' Ruth said. 'But he does play golf with Peter. My husband,' she added for Della's benefit. Peter hadn't been at Mortensen and Branningan's Christmas party, where the two women had first met. 'And he's supposed to be coming to dinner on Saturday.'

'Who with?' Alexis demanded cheekily. 'The wife or the mistress? Both, incidentally, called Sue. I suppose that way he doesn't run the risk of using the wrong name in bed.'

'Ignore her; it's gone to her head, getting something right for once,' I said.

'Yo, wait till I break this little gem in tomorrow's paper!' Alexis exclaimed.

'No way!' Ruth shouted.

'Don't you *dare*!' Della thundered in unison. 'We

want Jammy James nailed down watertight, not leaping up and down about trial by media.'

'Never mind that,' I butted in. 'Personally, I don't give a toss about nailing Jammy James. This is about getting Richard out of jail. And you printing daft stories in the *Chronicle* is not the way to do that, so forget it, Alexis, OK? What comes next, Ruth?'

Ruth spoke slowly, measuring what she said as she spoke. 'Kate's right, Alexis. I know this must be burning a hole in your notebook, but I think it would be disastrous for Richard if you wrote a story about this.'

Alexis pulled a face. 'All right,' she sighed. 'But when I *can* write about it, I want all of you to talk to me on the record.'

We all nodded wearily. 'Ruth?' I asked.

'Kate, you're going to have to talk to the police. You're also going to have to persuade them to move quickly; the sooner the better from Richard's point of view.'

Della interrupted. 'On that point, they'll already be anxious about how current your information is. These days, most drug dealers alter their distribution patterns every few weeks. Eliot James's team might not be doing that, but as far as the Drugs Squad is concerned, stress that this is up-to-the-minute info and the situation could change any day. There is one significant gap in your evidence, however, which might make them cautious.'

'What's that? Something I've got time to fix?' I

asked anxiously. I'd been right to decide I needed other people's eyes on this case.

Della pulled a face. 'It's not exactly a matter of time. It's a matter of legality. We don't know what's inside this shed out at the airport. If it's just an empty shell, it's not going to be easy to establish a direct connection between James and Fitzgerald. A good brief would argue that James had gone there for reasons entirely unconnected with the drug trade; he could even postulate a hypothetical third party that they were both there to meet.'

I nodded, grateful for the advice. 'Supposing I had that information, how quickly is quickly, in Drugs Squad terms?'

Della shrugged. 'I don't know this lot well, but given your info they should be able to plug straight into the surveillance. If this team is as busy as your material suggests, they could have the bare bones of their evidence within twenty-four to forty-eight hours.'

'Which means what, in terms of Richard's imprisonment?' I asked Ruth.

She bought time by lighting a cigarette. 'Best case, you talk to the Drugs Squad first thing and they stand up in court and support my bail application. Chances of that: almost nil. Worse case, they use your information, make a bundle of arrests and refuse to accept Richard was an innocent bystander. Chances of that: probably low. Most likely scenario, if you get to the Drugs Squad tomorrow, when I argue for bail on Wednesday, it will be refused but the magistrates will agree to a short remand, say till Thursday or Friday; to give the police the chance to evaluate the fresh evidence.'

My disappointment must have been obvious, for Alexis hugged me and Ruth shrugged apologetically. 'Well, we'd better get you fixed up with an appointment to see the Drugs Squad, hadn't we?' Della said briskly. 'Where's the phone?'

I pointed it out, and she wandered into the conservatory to make her call. I watched her through the patio doors. Her face was animated, her free hand expressive. Whatever she was saying, she wasn't pleading. As she ended the call, I remembered something else I wanted to talk to the Drugs Squad about. I turned to Alexis. 'Do you know if Cherie Roberts has been around today? Or if she's left me a note?'

Alexis shook her head. 'Not that I know of. Chris didn't say anything.'

Typical, I thought. Just as well I wasn't relying on Cherie to help get Richard out of jail.

18

It was midnight before I got the house to myself. Much as I enjoy their company, I couldn't wait for the three of them to go home. Ironically, they probably thought they were doing me a favour, keeping me from brooding over Richard's absence. And of course, I couldn't explain why I wanted rid of them, not with two of them being officers of the court. My impatience wasn't helped by the fact that I'd stopped drinking after my first vodka; if discovering what the shed contained was the key to releasing Richard, then I was going to have to get inside there. Preferably before my nine o'clock appointment with DCI Geoff Turnbull of the Drugs Squad.

I went through to my bedroom and changed into the black leggings and black sweat shirt I save for the sort of occasion when nobody I want to impress is likely to see me; illicit night forays, decorating, that sort of thing. I didn't have any black trainers, but I did have a pair of black canvas hockey boots which I'd bought in a moment of madness years before when they'd briefly looked set to be the next essential fashion item. I'd been a first-year student at the time, which is as good an excuse as any. I stuffed my hair inside a black ski cap, and I was all set. I know the Famous Five burned corks and rubbed their faces with the ash, but I couldn't bring myself to do anything that ridiculous. Besides, I had to drive right across town to get to the airport, and I didn't rate my chances of convincing any passing traffic cop that I was on my way to a Hallowe'en party.

On my way out the door, I stopped in my study and picked up one of those compartmentalized mini-aprons that tradesmen stuff with obscure tools. Mine contains a set of lock picks, a glass cutter, a kid's arrow with a sucker on the end, a couple of pairs of latex gloves, a Swiss Army knife, a small camera with a spare film, pliers, a high-powered pencil torch, a set of jeweller's screwdrivers, a couple of ordinary screwdrivers, a cold chisel, secateurs and a toffee hammer. Don't ask. Before I set off, I filled up a mini jug kettle that runs off the car cigarette lighter. Like I said, don't ask.

Less than half an hour later, I was cruising down the country lane I'd been in the night before. I pulled up in the same gateway and plugged in the kettle. As the water boiled, I lifted the lid and let the car fill up with steam. I got out and looked at the windows, satisfied. Anyone passing would be more likely to be jealous than suspicious.

I set off, hugging the infested hedgerows, just in case. I eased round the corner of the track, and saw with relief that there were no cars parked outside the shed. I crept slowly round the edge of the clearing till I was parallel to the big front doors. A quick look around, then I slipped across into the shadow of the shed. I took out my torch and shone it on the lower of the two padlocks. My heart sank. Some locks you can pick after ten minutes' training. Some locks give experts migraine. This wasn't one of the easy ones. I wished I'd brought Dennis with me. I gave it twenty minutes, by which time my hands were sweating so much inside the latex gloves that I couldn't manipulate the picks properly. In frustration, I kicked the door. It didn't swing open. I just got a very sore foot.

I shone the torch on the other padlock, but it was another of the same. The steel bars didn't look too promising either. Muttering the kind of words my mother warned me against, I skirted the corner of the shed and worked my way down the far side. Although it didn't look much, it was actually a deceptively solid building. I'd have expected to find the odd loose board, perhaps even a broken window. But this shed looked like it had been given a good going over by the local crime prevention officer. There was one window on the airport side, but it was barred, and behind it was opaque, wire-reinforced glass. I reached the far corner, but I couldn't get down the back of the shed at all because of the insidious creeping of the undergrowth. Frankly, I doubt if Mickey Mouse could have squeezed through that lot. With a sigh, I turned back. No chance. That was when the spotlight pinned me to the wall.

At least, that's what I thought at first. I froze like a dancer in a strobe, not even daring to blink. Then, as the light swept over me and my brain clocked on, I realized it was only the cyclops headlight of a tow truck from the cargo area. I threw myself to the ground and wriggled back to the front of the shed. Not a moment too soon. As I reached the doors, a battery of floodlights snapped on, bathing an area fifty yards away with harsh bleaching light. A truck was towing a train of boxes from one cargo holding area to another. This wasn't the time or place for burglary, I decided.

I inched backwards on my stomach towards the short drive leading to the road. And that's when I spotted the skylight. Gleaming in the blackness of the roof, it reflected the lights like a mirror. Even though it was a good twelve feet above the ground, the really exciting thing about it was the two-inch gap at the bottom. I gauged the distances involved, and saw there was a way inside the shed.

Getting out again was going to be the problem, I realized as I hung from the edge of the skylight, torch between my teeth. I tried to direct the beam downwards, to see what I was going to land on when I let go. I saw what looked like a chemistry lab constructed by a bag lady. If I dropped from here, I was going to end up either impaled on a bunsen burner or shredded by the shards of a thousand test tubes. That probably explained why the skylight on the blind side of the roof was open. Even with fume hoods, cooking up designer drugs is a disgustingly smelly occupation. The chemists doubtless decided the need for fresh air was greater than the security benefit of being hermetically sealed. At least having a factory out in the middle of nowhere meant there weren't any neighbours to complain about the pong.

With a groan, I flexed my complaining shoulder muscles and hauled myself back up and out again. I sat on the edge of the skylight and stared into the night. I'd only let myself over the edge in the first place because my torch hadn't been powerful enough to reveal the contents of the shed. And if the torch wasn't, the flash probably wouldn't be either. I had to come up with another idea, and quickly. I'd already had to wait an hour for the cargo area to go dark again, and I didn't know how long it would be before they took it into their heads to shuffle the packing crates again.

I could come up with only one possibility. Sighing, I eased myself off the skylight until my feet were in the guttering. Spread-eagled against the roof, I edged along until I came to the end of the roof. Slowly, cautiously, I slid down the corrugated asbestos until I was crouching, most of my weight on the guttering. I gripped the edge and half rolled off the roof, stretching my legs downwards as far as they would go. Then, thanking God for all the Thai boxing training I'd done, I gradually let myself down. I couldn't feel the roof of the Peugeot under my toes. I'd just have to pray I was in the right place. I released my handholds.

The drop was only a few inches, but it seemed to last minutes. Gasping for the breath I'd been holding, I slithered down the hatch back on to blessedly solid ground and opened the boot. I lifted the carpet, and there, tucked into the spare wheel, was the answer to my prayers. I grabbed the tow rope, coiled it round me like a mountaineer, gently closed the hatch and clambered back up the car and on to the roof.

I fixed the rope to a downpipe that was conveniently near the skylight and dropped it through the hole. I bit on the torch again and slowly started the precarious descent. Needless to say, the tow rope wasn't long enough to take me all the way to the floor, but it left an easy drop of a couple of feet, and I'd be able to reach it again if I moved a lab stool under it.

Getting in was the hard part. Doing the business with the camera was easy. I just started by the doors and worked my way through the shed, photographing the battered equipment, the jars of chemicals, the lists of instructions taped to the walls above the benches, and the plastic bags of white crystalline powder that made my gums numb. I don't know a lot about the drug world, but it looked to me as if there was much, much more than a bit of crack coming out of Jammy James's kitchen.

What there wasn't was paperwork. No filing cabinets, no safe, nothing. Wherever Jammy James kept his records, it wasn't here. I decided I paid enough in taxes. I'd done most of the work; it was time the Drugs Squad did their bit.

Wearily, I shifted a lab stool under the rope and climbed on top of it. My shoulder muscles were threatening to phone the cruelty man as I dragged myself up the rope and over the sill. I carefully lowered the skylight, restoring it to its previous position, give or take a millimetre or two. Then I untied the rope, did my crab imitation along the roof again. This time, the transfer of weight from feet to arms didn't go quite so smoothly; my shoulders were too tired for a gradual lowering, and my arms jerked uncomfortably in their sockets, making me let go sooner than I should have. I wondered how I was going to explain the depression in the roof to the car-leasing company.

My body wanted to get into bed as soon as possible, but my head was singing a different song. I had two films from the shed that needed developing. It would help my case if I could show the prints to Turnbull. The devil on my shoulder told me to go home and crash out for a few hours, then go into the office early to develop my films. But I knew myself well enough to know what my reaction would be when the alarm shattered my sleep at seven. And it wouldn't be to leap out of bed bright-eyed and bushy-tailed, ready to rush to the office and fill my lungs with the noxious fumes of photographic chemicals. With a groan, I shoved *The Best of Blondie* into the cassette player and opened the window all the way. If cold air and Debby Harry's frantic vocals couldn't keep me awake, nothing would.

I managed nearly four hours' sleep. Never mind what Richard owed me in fees; he owed me more sleep than I'd ever catch up on. For once, it wasn't Davy who woke me. It was Chris. She stuck her head round the bedroom door, followed by a hand waving a mug of coffee like a white flag. 'Come in,' I grumbled. 'Time is it?' I would have rolled over to look at the clock, but I couldn't find the energy.

'It's quarter past eight,' she said apologetically, sliding round the door and holding out the mug at arm's length. Alexis had obviously warned her I'm not at my sparkling best first thing.

'Shit!' I growled, as I leaped upright. Or rather, tried to. As soon as I moved, my shoulders went into spasm, and I let out a muffled screech of pain. I managed to shuffle up the bed enough to drink without a straw and seized the mug gratefully. 'Sorry I yelled. I'm in pain, and I've got to be at Bootle Street nick first thing with my brain firing on all four cylinders. So far, it's not looking good.'

Chris tried a smile that turned into a *Spitting Image* grimace. 'I just thought I'd better tell you that I'm off to work now,' she said. Belatedly, I noticed she was suited up, her hair dried and sprayed into the kind of neatly sculpted shape that Frank Lloyd Wright would have turned into an art gallery. 'Davy's had a shower and breakfast, and he's dressed and sitting in front of breakfast telly, which should keep him quiet for approximately twelve minutes, which is when the next news bulletin is due.'

'Has Alexis left?' Pointless question. Alexis is invariably at work by seven.

''Fraid so,' Chris apologized. 'She said she expected to be finished by three, and that you should ring her at the office if you wanted her to pick up Davy later. I'm really sorry we can't help out today.'

'Don't be,' I said. The power of speech seemed to have returned with the second mouthful of coffee. 'You two have done more than enough. Richard owes you.'

Chris smiled, a genuine one this time. 'I know you'll find it hard to believe, but we've enjoyed ourselves. I live with Alexis, don't forget, so I'm used to dealing with the demands of small children, and she loves having someone to play with.'

'You're not getting broody, are you?' I asked suspiciously. It's bad enough that all my straight friends seem to be hellbent on repopulating the world without the lesbians joining in.

'Building a house is more than enough to be going on with,' Chris replied as she headed out the door. In the hall she turned back and gave me a mischievous smile. 'Ask me again in a couple of years.'

If my neck hadn't seized up, I'd have turned my face to the wall. As it was, I gulped the rest of the brew and slowly, excruciatingly, dragged my body out of bed and into an upright position. I walked to the bathroom stiff as a guardsman. Unfortunately, I'd slept too late to have a bath so had to settle for a shower. I tried to relax as the hot water did the business, but I'd only been under for a couple of minutes when I heard Davy's voice outside the door.

'Kate?' he shouted. 'Can I play with your computer?'

'Not here, Davy. I've got to go to work in a minute, so I thought maybe you'd like to play on my machine in the office.' I spluttered.

Silence. That was more unnerving than anything he could have said. I switched off the shower, wrapped myself in a bath sheet and opened the door. He leaned against the wall, looking dejected. My breath stuck in my chest. The line of his body, the angle of his head, the slight frown was so like his father it hurt. He looked up through his long lashes at the sound of the door opening. 'When's my dad coming home?' he asked plaintively.

I managed to get my lungs working again. 'Not for a couple of days, I don't think. I spoke to him on the phone last night, after you'd gone to sleep. He said he misses you too and he'll get back as soon as he can get a plane. I'm sorry, I know I'm not a lot of fun.' I hugged him. Surprisingly, he didn't pull a face and draw away. He hugged back.

'It's not that,' he said. 'I'm having great fun. I just wish he was here too.'

You and me both, pal, I thought but didn't say.

I broke my personal land speed record getting out the door that morning. Dressed in under five minutes, second cup of coffee down the neck in less than a minute, breakfast one of the Pop Tarts I'd bought for Davy. It tasted like sugar-coated polystyrene, but at least it raised the blood sugar level. By the time I parked on the single yellow line round the corner from the office, I was almost functioning.

I hustled Davy up the stairs and into my office, checking the clock as I walked through the door. Seventeen minutes till deadline. Shelley was already at her desk, earphones in, fingers flying over the keyboard. I strode past her with a little wave, shooing Davy into my office. I switched on my PC, showed him the games directory and made him promise not to interfere with any of the other files on the machine. He dumped his backpack by the desk and was absorbed in Lemmings 2 before I'd had time to walk back out. I closed my office door behind me and perched on Shelley's desk, nailing what I hoped was a pathetic and appealing smile on my face.

'No, Kate.' She hadn't even looked up from her

screen. 'I am *not* a child-minder and this is an office, not a crèche.'

'I know it's not a crèche. A crèche is what happens when two BMWs collide in Sloane Street.'

'Not funny,' she retorted, not pausing long enough to let her sense of humour kick in.

'Please, Shelley. He'll be no trouble. Just for this morning. Just till I can get back from court. I promise I'll sort something else out for tomorrow.'

'There's no such thing as an eight-year-old boy who's no trouble. I'm a mother, don't forget. I've told the same lies you're telling now.'

'Shelley, please? I have a meeting with the Drugs Squad in ten minutes. Richard's freedom depends on it. I don't think they're going to be mega-impressed if I turn up with Davy in tow.' I was practically begging. I'd done so much of it lately it was beginning to become second nature. Another bad habit to lay at Richard's door. What's worse is that it doesn't work.

I got up from the desk and went into Bill's office, where I helped myself to his portable TV, a gift from a grateful client who had Mortensen and Brannigan to thank for the ending of his little software piracy problem. I marched through the outer office, wrestled with the door handle and staggered into my office, where I put it down on one of my cupboards. 'There's the TV, in case you get fed up with the computer,' I said to Davy. I can't swear to it, but I don't think he even looked up.

I stalked back into the office and gestured over

217

my shoulder with my thumb. 'Look at that. You're telling me that's more than you can cope with? God, Shelley, am I disappointed in you.'

When all else fails, go for the ego. The only trouble is, sometimes the ego bites back. Shelley smiled like Jaws and said sweetly, 'Just this once, Kate. And by the way, Andrew Broderick's been on again. He says if he doesn't get his car back soon he's going to have to come to some arrangement about reducing our fee.'

There's nothing like keeping the customer satisfied. I checked the fax machine on the way out, but nothing had arrived from Julia. I hoped that didn't mean it was going to be one of those days. Not when the next item on the agenda was a close encounter with the Drugs Squad.

19

Q: What's the difference between a schneid watch and a policeman? A: Schneid watches keep good time. By the time DCI Geoff Turnbull deigned to fit me into his busy schedule, I'd worn a furrow in the floor tiles of the front office. I was getting more wound up than an eight-day clock.

When he finally appeared, it took all my self-control not to bite his head off. Instead, I smiled sweetly and meekly followed him through the pass door into the real world of the city centre nick. We stopped outside a door that said DRUGS SQUAD – PRIVATE. I thought at first that was a joke, till I saw Turnbull pull out a key to unlock the door. He noticed me noticing and said, 'You can't be too careful, the stuff we have in here. These days, we've got more civilian support staff than we have coppers, and some of them have got more loyalty to their bank balances than they have to The Job.'.

How to win friends and influence people, I

thought as I smiled what I hoped would pass for agreement and approval. I followed him into an overcrowded office, crammed with desks, VDUs, bulging files, and not an officer in sight. The walls were lavishly adorned with colour photographs of villains. By the look of the pics, most of them were snatched, like mine. If anything, mine were sharper. Maybe Turnbull would be so impressed with my work that he'd offer me a job as a police photographer.

Turnbull's personal office was partitioned off in one corner. He'd managed to bag the only window, not much of a deal since it looked out on a brick wall all of five feet away. He squeezed his rugby player's frame behind the loaded desk and gave me the hard stare with small sharp blue eyes. He couldn't have looked less like my idea of a Drugs Squad officer. I'd expected an emaciated hippy lookalike with a distressed leather jacket and a pair of jeans. Either that or a flash bastard dripping with personal jewellery who could pass for a major dealer. But Turnbull looked like the only drug you'd suspect him of using was anabolic steroids. He lived up to his name: short curly hair with a forelock like a Charolais, the no-neck and shoulders to match, with the gut of a man whose stomach muscles have given up the unequal struggle with Boddingtons Bitter. I put him in his late thirties, well along the road to the coronary unit.

He rubbed a beefy hand over his jaw, massaging plump flesh. 'So, you're Miss Kate Brannigan,' he said consideringly. He managed to make the 'Miss' sound like an obscenity. 'Not much of you, is there?'

I shrugged. 'Enough to do the job. I don't get many complaints.'

He leered automatically. 'I bet you don't.'

I raised my eyebrows and gave him the bored look. 'DCI Prentice told me you were the person to talk to. I've got some information for you on one of your cases. Richard Barclay?'

'Oh aye,' he said, his Yorkshire accent deliberately exaggerated. 'The boyfriend.' He picked up his phone and dialled an internal number. 'Tommo? Any time you like.' He replaced the receiver and shook his head. 'I suppose you expect me to believe your fella's been fitted up? Well, you're in for a disappointment. It wasn't Drugs Squad officers that picked him up, it was Traffic, and even if they wanted to plant drugs on him, they wouldn't have access to anything like those amounts. So you're barking up the wrong tree there.'

'I don't think he's been fitted up,' I said patiently. 'But the drugs in the car were nothing to do with Richard, and the sooner you realize that, the lower the compo's going to be for the wrongful arrest.'

Turnbull guffawed. 'Was that a threat creeping out of the woodwork? By heck, Miss Brannigan, you like living dangerously.'

Before I could reply, a doorbell sounded. Turnbull leaned back and pressed a button on the wall behind him. I heard the door of the main room open behind me. I resisted the temptation to turn around and see who owned the heavy feet crossing the floor towards me.

Somehow, I wasn't too surprised when the custody sergeant from Longsight walked into Turnbull's office. 'That her?' Turnbull asked.

The sergeant nodded. 'No question about it, sir. That's the woman who purported to be Miss Hunter's assistant the other night. She claimed her name was Kate Robinson.'

'Thank you, Sergeant. I'll talk to you later.'

'Sir,' the sergeant said.

We both held our peace as the feet retreated back across the Drugs Squad office. Turnbull stared at me, a triumphant little smile on his cupid's-bow lips. I kept my eyes on his, determined not to show any weakness. As the door closed behind the custody sergeant, Turnbull said scathingly, 'It's not just you amateurs that can make deductions. I've been wanting to talk to you, Miss Brannigan. DCI Prentice's phone call just made it a bit easier for me to get you in here without a brief hanging on our every word. Especially since your brief's left herself wide open to charges of unprofessional conduct. I'm sure the Law Society would be fascinated to hear about her interpretation of professional ethics. And now we both know there's at least one offence I can hang on to you for, mebbe we can cut the crap and get down to the business.'

I said nothing. When his bluster ran out, he was

going to have to charge me or let me go. Either way he was going to have to listen to what I had to tell him. And I felt sure that his threats against Ruth were emptier than a dosser's bottle. The last thing coppers like him want to do is to antagonize the tightly knit club of criminal solicitors. Turnbull carried on staring at me and started drumming his fingers on the desk. Then he opened his desk drawer and took out a packet of cigars. When I rule the world, the European Court of Human Rights is going to outlaw the obtaining of confessions under cigar- and pipe-smoke torture.

He lit his panatella, the only slim thing about him, and said, 'Soon as I heard the story behind this car, soon as I heard that technically it was your responsibility, I wanted to talk to you. I mean, what better cover for a drug dealer's wheels than supposedly investigating some daft car-finance scam? Count yourself lucky you didn't spend the weekend in the CDC like your boyfriend.'

I shook my head. Clearly, I wasn't going to get anywhere being sweetness and light. Time for no more Ms Nice Guy. 'I don't believe I'm hearing this,' I snarled. 'I come along here with enough information to close down a major drug ring and hand you a bloody great score sheet of arrests, and you treat me like *I'm* the criminal? Jesus, it's no wonder you lot are always whingeing you don't get support from the public. If you threaten to arrest everybody that tries to give you a tip-off, it's a bloody miracle anybody tells you what day it is.'

He leaned forward and sneered. I bet he wouldn't have if he could have seen how badly his teeth needed a scale and polish. I was surprised his breath didn't strip them down to the bare enamel on a daily basis. 'You were supposed to be the bloody lawyer the other night. I shouldn't have to tell you that it's an offence to withhold information about a criminal offence. So cough, Miss Brannigan, or I'll have you banged up so fast your head'll spin.'

I stood up and leaned on Turnbull's desk. I was getting good and tired of being jerked around by the legal system. 'Listen, Turnbull,' I said coldly. 'You threaten me once more and I walk out that door and you don't get another word out of me till you've formally arrested me, cautioned me and allowed me to talk to my solicitor. I might not be a qualified lawyer, but I'd be willing to bet I'd score more points than you on a PACE quiz. Now, are we going to talk like grown-ups, or are we going to carry on playing silly boys' games?'

'Let's be clear about one thing,' he said, still not willing to let the macho bravado slip. 'I'm not doing any deals with you. None of this "I show you mine and you let my boyfriend go" routine. As far as I'm concerned, Mr Richard Barclay's in this up to his fancy tortoiseshell specs.'

I raised my eyes to the ceiling and sighed. 'I just love a man with an open mind. Mr Turnbull, by the time you've heard me out, you'll be dying to release Richard, because if you don't, you're going to look like dickhead of the year after the papers have finished with you. And that's *not* a threat, it's my considered opinion.'

'Sit down,' he growled. 'Let's hear what you've got to say.'

Ignoring his order, I leaned against the wall. I took my miniature tape recorder out of my bag and pressed the 'record' button. 'Since you don't seem inclined to tape our little chat, I'll do it for you,' I said. 'It'll save me having to come back later and make a statement. I know all your instincts tell you not to believe a word that anybody in custody says, but in this instance, you really should have listened. That's all I did. The only clue in Richard's story, as far as I could see, was the business with the trade plates. So I did what any good copper should do: I followed my instincts.' Turnbull looked like he wanted to throttle me, but the part of him that had taken him to the rank of DCI was obviously dying to know what I'd dug up, and right now his curiosity was stronger than his belligerence.

I took him through it from start to finish, omitting only the details of how I came by the photographs of the inside of Jammy James's kitchen. 'Careless of them, leaving the door unlocked, but then, you just can't get the help these days,' I finished up, taking the pics out of my bag and spreading them in a fan across Turnbull's desk.

He poked at the pics with the end of a Biro, as if they'd soil his fingers. Then he shook his head. 'You expect me to believe this taradiddle?' he asked scornfully. 'Eliot James? As in, Eliot James who plays golf with the Chief Constable? Eliot James who runs charity schemes for under-privileged kids at his leisure centres? *That* Eliot James?'

'The same,' I said. 'Having friends in high places doesn't stop you being a crook. Look at the Guinness trails. And if doing charity work was a guarantee of staying out of jail, the Krays would still be running London. Look, James is hanging on to his business empire by his fingernails. Check it out. Go down Ice World, The Dinosaur Adventure, Laser Land, or any of his leisure complexes. They're all empty. His cash flow doesn't. The only reason DCI Prentice isn't running a full-scale fraud inquiry into the sleazeball is that she thinks the drugs angle deserves the first bite of the cherry. But if you're not interested, I know she'll be after James like a greyhound out of a trap.'

Turnbull leaned back in his chair. The legs sounded like an avant-garde string quartet. 'It's funny, isn't it, how you've managed to find all this out so easily when we've been trying to get something on this mob for ages?' he speculated. 'If I was a suspicious man, I might think it was because you and your boyfriend were in it up to your eyeballs, and you decided to shop the rest of the team to try and get him off the hook. You wouldn't be the first private dick caught out by the recession who decided

226

to turn their limited knowledge of crime on its head.'

The only thing that stopped me being arrested for assaulting a police officer was the realization that I'd be as much use to Richard as a chocolate fireguard if I ended up behind bars too. So I smiled sweetly at the insult. 'If I was going to turn to crime, Mr Turnbull, I wouldn't have to leave the house. Computer crime. That's where the real, no-risk money is these days. And I've forgotten more about computers than you'll ever know. Look, I'm not asking you for a major favour. I haven't once said, I'll tell you what I know in return for you letting Richard walk away from all of this. I'm handing you all this on a plate, and all I'm asking is that you don't oppose Ruth Hunter's request for a short remand so you can start to test the value of what I've given you.'

'And that's all, is it?' he asked, utter disbelief riddling his voice like a virus in a computer.

'Pretty much, yeah. You see, Mr Turnbull, in spite of your performance this morning, I happen to think you're an honest copper. I don't think you want innocent men put away just to make your clean-up rate look better. And I know the strength of what I've given you. I think after forty-eight hours you'll have the same gut feeling I've got about Richard's innocence, and I don't think you'll be opposing bail then. But I'm not asking for any promises.'

'Just as bloody well,' he grumbled, 'for you'd not

227

be getting any.' He stared down at the photographs on his desk, slowly sifting through them, assessing what he was seeing with the eyes of an expert. Turnbull eventually looked up. 'So, what has Ruth Hunter told you to ask for?'

'I want you to call the Crown Prosecution solicitor and ask that they don't oppose Ruth's request for a short remand.'

'That it?'

'That's it. Now, are you going to give me something back, or am I going to develop profound amnesia about the events of the last three days?'

He grinned. 'You know, for a girl, you're not short on bottle. OK, I'll do it. I can't say fairer than that, now can I?'

'That's fine,' I said. 'You won't mind if I hang on while you make the call?'

This time he laughed delightedly, his hand making a half-hearted gesture that, if I'd been a bloke, would have turned into a clout on the back that would have brought my breakfast back. 'You're not a Yorkshire lass by any chance, are you? No? Pity.'

I waited while he did as I'd demanded. He was no more charming to the Crown Prosecution Service's solicitor than he'd been to me, but he seemed to achieve the right result. On my way out of the door, I said, 'By the way – Mr Broderick wants to know when you're going to release his very expensive motor from your compound.'

Turnbull snorted. I almost expected him to paw the ground. 'He's been on to you as well, has he? You tell your Mr Broderick that he can have his poncey set of wheels back when I'm good and satisfied that it's going to yield up no more clues to me. And that could be after your boyfriend's trial. Now, bugger off and let me get on. Oh, and leave me that tape, will you? Like you said, it'll save me having to keep you here all day making a statement.'

I handed the tape over with a grim little smile. 'One other thing,' I said. 'Nothing to do with Richard. You know those transfers that kids use – temporary tattoos, that sort of thing?'

Turnbull nodded. 'I've got a seven-year-old that gets in the bath looking like a merchant seaman. What about them?'

'Ever heard of them being impregnated with drugs and used to get kids high?'

Turnbull pulled a face. 'I've heard rumours, but I've never actually come across a case. It's one of them urban legends, isn't it? It always happens to a friend of a friend's cousin's dog. Crap, as far as I'm concerned. If I was wanting to get kids stoned, I'd just stick something in sweets or fizzy drinks. Helluva lot easier. Why d'you ask?'

'Like you said, urban legend. A friend of a friend's cousin's dog asked a doctor I know about it. She said the same as you.' I got to my feet. 'Sorry to have troubled you. Thanks. For phoning.' And

229

I was gone, quitting while I was still ahead. Let's face it. Telling Geoff Turnbull about Davy's brush with the hallucinogens wasn't the way to get his daddy out of jail.

20

I walked back through the office door on the
stroke of twelve. The door to my office was closed.
I raised my eyebrows in a question at Shelley. She
pursed her lips and said, 'I had to shut the door
in case any clients walked in.'

Curious, I opened my door a couple of feet and
stuck my head round. I saw instantly what she
meant. Davy was still intent on the computer,
but now Bill was sitting next to him, clutching
his own joystick. Neither of them looked up at the
sound of the door. I cleared my throat. Bill glanced
up. As soon as he realized it wasn't Shelley with
some troublesome business query, I could see his
attention leave the game and focus sharply on me.
He got up, saying, 'I've got to go and talk to Kate,
Davy. Thanks for the game.'

Davy didn't even look up as he said, 'But Bill,
you've got one more life!'

'Well, since you've still got four, I guess I'll
have to concede. You win,' Bill said, pretending

231

to be petulant about it.

In the glow of the screen, Davy grinned, his body shifting strangely in the chair as he controlled whatever it was that was currently conquering the universe. Bill steered me out of the room and through into his office. 'He's a nice kid,' Bill said. 'No bother.' I was beginning to wonder if there was something wrong with me. Was I the only person on the planet who liked to live in a child-free zone?

Bill sat down and stretched his long legs in front of him. 'So, how did it go?'

I filled him in on the weekend's events. Maybe I should just ring Richard Branson and ask him to release it on CD. It would save me a lot of time. Then I ran through my interview with Geoff Turnbull.

'You think he really will keep an open mind about Richard?' Bill asked.

'I doubt it. I think the only chance he's got is for Turnbull to make a lot of arrests. When he realizes none of them even know Richard's name, he's going to have to unclamp his jaws from off Barclay's leg.'

'But he did go along with the short remand request?'

'Sure, but that's no skin off his nose, is it?' My early jubilation at getting Turnbull to look properly at my evidence had evaporated. I wondered fleetingly how the families of the Guildford Four and the Birmingham Six had put up with this dislocating ordeal for the years it had taken them to have their loved ones released. I took a deep breath. 'And now,' I said, 'I want to ask you a favour.'

'Ask away,' he said. 'Hacking? Bugging? Your wish is my command.'

'None of the above. It's just that I've had enough aggro for one day. Will you phone Andrew Broderick and tell him what Turnbull said about the car? It's hard enough keeping my head together without having to deal with someone else's disappointments.'

Bill jumped up and engulfed me in a bear hug, his thick blond beard tickling my ear. 'Poor old Katy,' he said softly. 'It's not always easy, being as tough as old boots, is it?'

I let myself be held, wallowing in the illusion of security. There's something very solid about Bill. I felt like I was being given a tranquillity transfusion. After a few minutes, I drew back, standing on tiptoe to kiss his beard. 'Thanks,' I said. 'Now, I'm going to take Davy for a swim and a pizza, and then the pair of us are going to get a pile of videos and completely indulge ourselves.'

'You deserve it,' Bill said. 'You've done a helluva job, considering you started with virtually nothing to go at. Richard's a lucky guy.'

'What do you mean, lucky? When he sees our bill, he'll be wishing he was back inside,' I said. 'See you in the morning, Bill. Unless you want to come round and play computer games with Davy tonight?'

'I'll pass,' he said. 'I've got some rather different games in mind for tonight. Abstinence makes the heart grow fonder, you know.' Somehow, I found it hard to believe the heart was the organ in question. I wondered who the lucky woman was this week. One day, he's going to meet one with fancier footwork than him, and that'll be a battle worth seeing. Till then, he's working his way through the intelligent female population of the north of England. He once told me he's never been to bed with a woman yet who didn't teach him something. I don't *think* he was talking about sex.

There were only a couple of dozen people in the fun pool at Gorton, so Davy and I made the most of the slides and the waves, treating the place as our personal pleasure dome. Although my shoulders screamed in complaint at first, the water therapy seemed to help. Afterwards, both ravenous, we scoffed huge pizzas and enough salad to keep Watership Down's bunnies going for a week. Then we hit the video shop and chose more movies than we'd have time to watch. I didn't care. Part of me felt a holiday sense of release. I'd done everything I could to get Richard freed. Now all I could do was wait, and I owed it to Davy to do that as cheerfully as possible.

As we drove across Upper Brook Street and into

Brunswick Street, the traffic slowed to a crawl. I couldn't see what the problem was, only that there was no traffic heading past us in the opposite direction. Eventually, craning my neck, I could see that the road ahead was cordoned off, and that traffic was being diverted down Kincardine Road by a uniformed policeman. Curious, I swung the car out of the queue, and indicated to the policeman that I wanted to turn right, heading back home. He gave me the nod, and I pulled round the corner and parked. I couldn't help myself. There's no way I could ignore something looking that interesting on my own doorstep. At the very least, it looked like someone had raided the local post office. I sometimes wonder whether I chose the career or it chose me. I turned to Davy and said, 'Wait here a minute. I just want to see what's going on.' He flicked a glance heavenwards, sighed and pulled a comic out of his backpack.

I got out of the car and locked it up, then cut through the council estate so that I'd emerge at the mouth of a narrow alley off Brunswick Street, but further down than the road block. I was almost opposite the pelican crossing, and I could see that there was a second road block a little further down in the other direction. On the pedestrianized little shopping precinct on the other side of the street, two police cars and an ambulance were standing, doors open, just outside the post office. Around them milled a bewildered looking knot of people, police officers trying to keep them away from the

235

person the ambulance crew were crouched over. The wailing cries of a child rose and fell like a siren. While I watched, another pair of police cars arrived.

One of the ambulance crew stood up and shook his head while his colleague continued to crouch on the ground. There was a commotion at the heart of the crowd, then a stretcher was loaded into the ambulance. The spectators parted, and the ambulance reversed on to the road and sped off. The crowd stayed back long enough for me to see a policewoman ushering two young boys into the back of a police car, which shot off in the wake of the ambulance, blue light flashing. It was hard to be certain from that distance, but they looked disturbingly like Wayne and Daniel.

By this time, I was a question mark on legs. I'd also spotted a familiar mane of black hair bobbing around on the fringes of the crowd, tapping people on the shoulders and thrusting a tape recorder in their faces. I checked that none of the cops were looking my way, then I nonchalantly nipped out of the alley, crossed the street and headed for Alexis. If anyone had tried to stop me, I'd have insisted I was on my way to a dental appointment in the precinct. If the police were suspicious enough to check it out, Howard's receptionist knew me well enough to back me up.

As I drifted closer, I could see the police officers were working their way through the crowd, taking names and addresses rather than attempting statements. I could hear odd snatches of shocked conversation: 'all over in seconds . . .'; '. . . bala-clava over his head . . .'; 'thought it was a car backfiring . . .'; 'police should *do* something about them druggies . . .' Alexis was over on the far side, tape recorder shoved under the nose of a uniformed inspector. I took my notebook and tape recorder out of my handbag and rushed round the fringe of the crowd to Alexis's side. I arrived in time to hear him say in harassed tones, 'Look, I can't tell you any more now, you'll have to wait till we have a clearer idea ourselves.' Then, seeing me and falling for my instant disguise, he added, 'And I haven't got time to go through it all again. Get the details from her,' he said, gesturing towards Alexis with his thumb. She turned and clocked me. Her face, already paler than usual, seemed to go even whiter.

'For Chrissake, what are you doing here?' she hissed.

'I could say the same to you. What's happened? Somebody taken a pot at the post office? And where's the rest of the pack?'

'Still on their way, if they even know about it. I just happened to be driving back to your house when it all came on top. Kate, you've got to get out of here! Now! Move it!' Alexis started hustling me away, back towards the side street where I'd left my car.

'Why?' I protested. 'What's it got to do with me?'

237

'Where's Davy?' she demanded, still shooing me away from the crowd and back across the street.

'He's in the car.' We'd reached the opening of the alley and I stepped in, then stopped in my tracks. I wasn't going another pace further until she enlightened me. 'What is going on, Alexis? What happened back there?'

She ran a hand through her unruly hair and pulled a crushed packet of cigarettes out of her bag. She lit up and took a deep drag before she spoke. 'I'm sorry, but there is not a gentle way of saying this. Cherie Roberts just got killed,' she said.

I felt like I'd been punched in the chest. The air emptied out of me like a burst balloon. 'A robbery? She got in the way?' I asked.

My face must have betrayed my hope that this had been no more than a horrific accident, a tragic and malignant twist of fate, for Alexis turned her face away and shook her head, smoke streaming down her nostrils in twin plumes. 'No. It was a hit.'

I squeezed the bridge of my nose between my fingers. I didn't want to believe what Alexis was saying. 'That can't be right,' I said half-heartedly. 'For fuck's sake, she was no big deal. She was just another single mum, trying to get through the days and keep her kids out of trouble.'

'I've covered too many stories like this over the last couple of years in the Moss and Cheetham Hill,' Alexis said bleakly, referring to the violent drug wars that have practically doubled Manchester's homicide figures. 'According to the eyewitnesses, Cherie was coming out of the post office after cashing her child benefit. There was a car parked on the other side of the road. When she came out, the car revved up, shot across the road, mounted the pavement and drove towards her. When they were a few feet away from her, she got blasted from the rear window with both barrels of the shotgun. It was, variously, a metallic blue Sierra, a silver Toyota, a grey Cavalier, and nobody's admitting to getting the registration number.'

I closed my eyes and leaned against the wall. I could feel the brick rough against my fingertips. 'Dear God,' I breathed. I'd asked her to find out who had given her kids drug-laced transfers. And two days later, Cherie Roberts was on her way to the mortuary, stamped with the familiar hallmarks of a drug-related murder. Suddenly, my eyes snapped open. 'Davy!' I gasped. I turned on my heel and ran down the alley, panic pumping the blood till my ears pounded with the drum of my heartbeat.

I rounded the corner, imagination painting scenes of bloodshed and violence that even Sam Peckinpah would draw the line at, making all sorts of ridiculous bargains with a god I don't believe in. I skidded to a halt by the car, feeling deeply foolish as Davy waved at me and mouthed. 'Hi,' through the glass. Alexis rushed up behind me, slightly breathless. 'We need to talk,' she said. 'What did you ask Cherie on Sunday?'

'The wrong question, obviously,' I said bitterly. 'I asked her to ask the kids who they got the transfers from. That's all. She must have taken it further than that. Shit, Alexis, I need a drink. Are you finished here, or do you need to talk to some more people?'

'I'm too late for the final edition anyway. I've got the eyewitness stuff for tomorrow's paper. It'll be a while now before the police issue a full statement. Let's go back to your place, eh?' She squeezed my arm sympathetically. 'It's not your fault, KB. It wasn't you that pulled the trigger.'

So why did I feel so guilty?

It took less than a minute to drive round to my house. I parked in the bay outside Richard's house and walked towards mine. Davy hung behind, bouncing up and down at the end of the path, waiting for Alexis to get out of the car so he could show her the videos we'd chosen. You can't see my porch from the parking bays. There's a six foot, gold and green conifer in the way. I'd never thought much about it before. But that afternoon, I was more glad than I can say that the tree was there.

I passed the tree and glanced towards my house. What I saw made me stumble and nearly fall. I regained my balance and took a couple of steps closer to make sure my eyes weren't playing tricks on me. Then I felt sick. The white UPVC of the lower half of the door was pocked with hundreds of little black puncture holes. The glass in the upper half was crazed and starred, no match for the close-range blast it had sustained. Whoever had terminated Cherie Roberts had left me their calling card.

21

I wheeled round as fast as I could and nailed a smile on my face as I headed back towards Alexis and Davy, in a huddle looking at videos. 'We might as well go in through Richard's,' I said, trying to sound breezy. 'I've got some paperwork to do later, and that way you won't have to worry about disturbing me.'

It didn't entirely work. Alexis looked up sharply at the cracked note in my voice. 'All right,' she said casually. 'His video's just as good as yours, and we're nearer the ice-cream there.'

I steered them up the path, carefully using my body to shield Davy from the sight of my front door. I needn't have bothered; he was so engrossed in his chatter with Alexis that he didn't even glance in that direction. She did, though, and I could see from the momentary tightening of her lips that she'd spotted the damage. I unlocked the door and Davy ran into the house ahead of us. 'What the hell's going on, KB?' Alexis demanded.

'Your guess is as good as mine,' I hissed. 'You think this happens all the time?'

Alexis put her arm round my shoulders and squeezed. 'OK, sorry. But we need to get him out of here,' Alexis murmured. 'It's not safe.'

'You think I don't know that? What can we do? Where can we take him?' I asked.

'I'll pitch him into coming to the pictures, then I'll take him back to our house. Fill him up with burgers and popcorn and let him crash out with us while you get this sorted out,' she said softly.

'Gee thanks,' I said, my frustration bubbling up to the surface. 'And how exactly do you suggest I go about that?'

'Calm down, girl,' Alexis protested. 'I was talking about getting the door fixed, not solving the mysteries of the universe.'

I sighed. 'Sorry. I'm kind of edgy, you know?'

Alexis put the other arm round my shoulders and gave me a quick hug. 'I'll go and get Davy before he gets stuck into one of those videos.' She headed down the hall. I leaned against the wall and took some deep breaths, doing the mental relaxation exercises my Thai boxing coach taught me. I heard her say, 'Hey, soft lad, you can't watch a film without popcorn. Tell you what, why don't we go to the proper pictures? Then we can go to the McDonald's drive-in near my house and take the burgers back and watch your videos there.'

'What are we going to go and see?' Davy demanded.

'Hang on a minute,' Alexis said. She emerged from the living room and said, 'Did I see the local freesheet scrunched up in the porch? They've got the multi-screen listings in, haven't they?'

'I think so,' I said, exhaling the last of the twenty breaths.

Alexis moved past me and picked up the crumpled newspaper that had been stuffed gratuitously through Richard's letter box some time over the weekend. 'You know, I really object to trees being cut down so that rubbish can be dumped in my porch without my permission or invitation,' I grumbled.

'I hate freesheets too,' Alexis said, flicking through the pages. 'Because they get distributed to so many homes, advertising managers just lie about how many people read the bloody things, so local businesses spend their limited budgets advertising in wastepaper rather than taking an ad in the *Chronicle*. So the number of pages we print decreases, so we don't hire as many journalists. And the freesheets don't take up the slack on account of they're crap editorially,' she added for good measure.

'Not that you're biased or anything,' I muttered. 'Found the listing yet?' As I spoke, a rumpled sheet of blue writing paper slid out from between the newspaper's pages and fluttered to the floor.

'Mmm,' Alexis said, frowning in concentration as she moved back down the hall.

Absently, I bent down and picked up the paper.

It was a sheet from a writing pad, folded in half. On the outside, in unfamiliar writing, I read: 'Kate Brannigan'. Before I opened it, I knew what it was. I closed my eyes until the wave of nausea passed, then, slowly, apprehensively I unfolded it.

The hand was uncertain but perfectly legible. 'Kate – I came round Monday afternoon but there was nobody in. I asked the boys where they got the transfers from, and they told me who's handing them out. I spoke to the lad and found out where he's getting them from, and there's more to it than the drugs. You're right, it shouldn't be going on, and I'm going round tonight to tell him so. If you want to come with me, come to my flat about seven o'clock. Yours sincerely, Cherie.'

I slid down the wall till I was crouching in a tight bundle. I'd let Cherie down. I'd been so busy running around being a hero for Richard that I hadn't made the time to check back with her. And now she was dead, all because I hadn't managed to prevent her from sticking her head into a hornet's nest.

I'd probably have stayed like that forever if I hadn't heard wagons roll from the living room. Davy was shrieking with delight over some movie or other, Alexis's rumble of enthusiasm a lower counterpoint. 'Come on then, I'll race you to the car,' I heard her say. I forced myself into an upright position and I'd managed to find something approximating a smile by the time Davy was close enough to notice.

'See you later, super troopers,' I said as they passed at a run.

'We'll be at our house,' Alexis said. 'Phone Chris and tell her, would you? Only, don't tell her why, she'll only get fear of loss. I'll tell her when she gets home.'

I watched them drive off in the car. I don't think I've ever been so sorry to see Alexis leave. I pulled myself together with the assistance of a strong vodka and grapefruit juice and cut through the conservatory to my house. I didn't think I was up to approaching from the front. What amazed me was that the place wasn't crawling with police. But then, my bungalow's on the end of the row. No one overlooks the front of it, and even though it's got a postcode that whacks my insurance up into the stratosphere, it's still the kind of area where people assume a loud bang is a backfire from one of the MOT failures that sit on bricks all over the council estate, and not the shoot-out at the OK Corral.

From the inside, the front door looked just about as lethal. Time to call in a favour. I rang the office, and told Shelley I was on my way in. 'Oh, and Shelley? I'd like to make a contribution to your household budget.'

'You what?'

'I need a new front door. Pronto monto. I mean tonight. Can you get Ted to see to it?' Ted Barlow is the man Shelley strenuously insists she's not actually, technically, living with. They fell in love

246

when he turned up in our office looking forlorn, with the bank about to foreclose on his conservatory business. While I was busy sorting out the mess, the pair of them gazed into each other's eyes and whispered sweet nothings. Now Shelley's got a conservatory that takes up a good half of her back garden, and Ted tends to answer her phone first thing in the morning.

'What's happened? Have you had a burglary?'

'I wish,' I said with feeling. 'Unfortunately, it's a little bit more personal than that. I'll tell you all about it when I come in.'

'What about a key? Shall I get him to come by the office and pick one up?'

I pictured the door. 'I think a key's a bit academic,' I said. 'If I can get the key in, I'll leave the outside door unlocked, OK? So if it's still locked, he'll know just to kick it in.' I couldn't believe the words that were coming out of my mouth. I was instructing someone to kick my door in? Sooner or later, somebody was going to pay for all this. For scaring me, for killing Cherie, for giving drugs to little kids.

I felt safer in the office. Illogical, I know, but fear and logic are hardly ever on speaking terms, never mind pals. I perched on the edge of the leather sofa in Bill's office and told him all about the latest crisis. 'I'm sorry to lay it all on you,' I apologized, 'but I need to talk it through.'

His blue eyes smiled. 'We're partners, aren't we?

247

In my book, that makes this as much my business as yours.'

'I know, but, I feel like it's always me that's in the shit up to the neck. I seem to be accident-prone these days. I remember when this agency never did anything more dramatic than prowling through somebody else's database. Now I seem to spend half my life in a state of panic.'

Bill chewed his beard and shrugged. 'So walk away from it.' He saw my look of instant outrage and grinned. 'You see?' he teased. 'You like answers too much, Kate. But this time, I think we really should walk away from it. This is one for the cops.'

I shook my head vehemently, my nervous fingers plaiting the streamers from the waste basket of his shredder. 'No can do, Bill. Sorry.'

Bill prowled the room like a huge blond bear who's forgotten where he left the honey jar. 'It's too much of a risk,' he insisted. 'These people are serious, Kate. They've given you a warning. If they think you're ignoring that, then they won't hesitate to give you the same treatment they dished out to that poor woman. And frankly, I haven't got the time to find another partner right now.'

'I *can't* go to the police, Bill. I'm not just being bloody-minded!'

'It wouldn't be the first time,' he said, a wry smile counteracting the bitter edge to his voice.

I stood up, his restlessness infecting me. I walked across to his desk and perched on the edge of it and explained. 'Bill, the Drugs Squad are supposedly checking out the info I handed over to them, and if it stands up, Richard will be released on bail on Thursday morning. If I go to the bizzies now and say, "Excuse me, some drug dealer's hit man's just taken a shotgun to my front door, but it's got absolutely nothing to do with the fact that you've got my partner locked up on drugs charges," they're going to fall about. There's no way they're not going to connect it to what's happened to Richard, and that'll be the end of any chance he's got of being turned loose.'

Bill stopped pacing and threw himself down on the sofa. He breathed out deeply through his nose. 'Kate, I don't want you to take this the wrong way, but hadn't you considered the possibility that it just might be connected to Richard's case rather than Cherie's death?'

'It's hard for me to get my head round the idea that there were two lunatics with shotguns wandering round Ardwick at the same time. The only credible explanation is that when Cherie fronted up whoever is pushing these drugs to kids, she mentioned my name. She might even have used me as an insurance policy. You know – "if anything happens to me, Kate Brannigan knows where to come looking". If that's what happened, then hiring some psycho with a sawn-off to kill Cherie gets even more cost-effective. It not only gets rid of someone who knows more than the dealer wants her to, it also serves as a warning to me to keep my nose out and to stay away from the cops investigating the shooting. And it lets everybody else who's involved with the racket know just what's coming to them if they step out of line. A real bargain, when you think about it,' I added angrily.

Bill said, 'But I don't necessarily think that there *were* two psychos driving round Ardwick with a shooter. Manchester isn't LA. Having a gun in your glove box or under your car seat so the girls all know you're a big man and the yobs all know to give you a wide berth is a different kettle of fish from being a hired gun. It could be that while there was only one gunman, there were two paymasters. That would explain why Cherie was killed and you were only warned.'

Suddenly, I saw the flaw in Bill's theory. 'It was *my* front door,' I said.

'Yes?' Bill said.

'Not Richard's. It was *my* front door. Don't you see?' I was excited now, banging the desk with my fist. 'If they'd wanted to warn me off the case, they'd have blasted Richard's front door. *He's* the one that's vulnerable, *he's* the one that's banged up with a load of villains, *he's* the one with the eight-year-old pressure point. Besides, the only people who know there's any connection between me and Richard are the Drugs Squad.'

Bill slumped in his office chair and chewed a pencil. 'And we trust the Drugs Squad not to have a leak? We think they don't have any bent officers who might just be in Eliot James's golf club?'

I sighed. 'I don't exactly *trust* Geoff Turnbull. Not even on Della's say-so. But he's an ambitious man, and self-interest's one of the most powerful engines there is. I bet the thought of nailing a smooth operator like Eliot James is a bigger aphrodisiac than oysters to a man like Turnbull. And he'll want all the credit for himself; I doubt very much if he's told a living soul he got his information from a private eye.'

'I can't argue with that,' Bill said, resignation all over his face. 'So, what now?'

I told him. And since his only alternative was to betray me by going behind my back to the police, Bill reluctantly agreed to help where he could.

The main problem for me now was that I'd argued myself out of any chance of feeling secure. At least if I'd believed the shooting had anything to do with Jammy James and his merry men, I'd have known that the Drugs Squad were about to rob the gunman of any future playdays from that direction. Now, I had to live with the uncomfortable fact that some complete stranger out there wanted me to give up an inquiry so badly that they'd blown a hole in my front door. If I was going to stop them doing the same thing to me, I'd better find out who they were. And fast.

22

The rush-hour traffic had already started to build by the time I left the office. I sat smouldering in the jam at the top of Plymouth Grove, listening to GMR cheerily telling me where the traffic black spots were. I could have crossed town faster on foot than I was managing by car. I watched the seconds tick past on my watch, muttering darkly about what the transport policy would be when I ruled the world. It was twenty to five by the time I'd inched up Stockport Road and turned off into the car park behind the Longsight District Centre. I parked illegally as near as I could get to the Social Services office. I wanted to make sure I didn't miss my target.

Like the rest of the city's social workers, the family placement officer theoretically knocks off work at half past four. But like most of her colleagues, Frankie Summerbee knows that the only way to come close to dealing with her workload is to stay at the office long after the town hall bureaucrats have gone home. So, like most of her colleagues, Frankie's chronically over-tired, over-stressed and prone to making decisions that don't always look too wonderful in the cool light of day under cross-examination. That's what I was relying on this afternoon.

I've known Frankie almost as long as I've known Richard. Before he moved in next door to me, he lived in Chorlton-cum-Hardy, that Manchester suburb whose trendiness quotient rises and falls in tandem with the Green Party's electoral share. He lived in the downstairs flat of an Edwardian terraced cottage. Frankie had the flat upstairs. Luckily for her, that included the attic. I don't know if that had always been her bedroom, but after Richard moved in downstairs I suspect that sleeping at least two floors away from his stereo became an imperative.

Of course, as a trained social worker, she couldn't avoid helping him out; cooking the odd meal, picking up his washing from the launderette, grabbing a stack of pizzas every now and again as she whizzed past the chill cabinet in the supermarket on her weekly shop. I don't expect she got any thanks, but he did take her out to dinner a few times, and so she became another victim of the Cute Smile.

The bonking bit didn't last too long. I suspect they both realized after the first time that it was a big mistake, but they're both much too kind to have hurt the other's feelings by saying so. Luckily, Frankie also has the good social worker's ruthless streak, otherwise they'd probably both still be hanging on till the last minute every Saturday night because nice people come second. Under normal circumstances, I was glad she'd forced a return to uncomplicated friendship so he was unencumbered when he met me. After the events of the past few days, I wasn't so sure.

I could have short-circuited the waiting period by picking up my mobile phone and dialling Frankie's direct line, but I was glad of a breathing space to try to organize my thoughts into something approaching order. I didn't get one.

I'd been sitting there less than ten minutes when Frankie's spiky black hair appeared like a fright wig on top of a stack of files. The files teetered forward above a pair of black leggings and emerald green suede hi-tops. I jumped out of the car and rushed forwards to help her. 'Hi, Frankie,' I said, putting my arms out to steady the files as I stopped her in her tracks.

The hair tilted sideways and two interested brown eyes peered round the stack of files. Her granny glasses were slowly sliding down her nose, but not so far that she didn't recognize me. 'Hi, Brannigan,' she said. She didn't sound surprised, but then she's been a social worker for the best part of ten years. Nothing surprises Frankie any more.

'Let me help,' I said.

'The car's over there,' she said, sounding slightly baffled as I grabbed the top half of her pile. 'The red Astra.'

I carried the files over to the car and we did small talk while she fiddled with her keys and unlocked the hatchback. It wasn't easy, avoiding the subject of Richard's incarceration, but I managed it by dragging Davy's visit into the conversation two sentences in. We loaded the boot, and Frankie slammed it shut, then leaned against it, catching me eye to eye. Not many people manage that, but Frankie and I are so alike physically that if I ever get signed up to star in a movie with nude scenes I could get her to be my body double. 'This is not serendipity, is it?'

I shook my head sheepishly. 'Sorry.'

She sighed. 'You should know better.'

'It's not business, Frankie,' I said in mitigation. 'It's personal, and it's not for me.'

She raised her eyebrows and looked sceptical. I can't say I blamed her. 'I'm in a hurry,' she said. 'I've got a meeting this evening. I was on my way to grab a quick curry since I skipped lunch. If you think there's any point in telling me what you're after, follow me to the Tandoori Kitchen. You're buying. Deal?'

'Deal,' I said. I've always liked the Tandoori Kitchen. The food's consistently good, but the best thing of all is the chocolate-flavoured lollipops they give you when they bring you the bill. I wasn't particularly hungry, but I ordered some onion bhajis and pakora to keep me occupied while Frankie worked her way through the biggest mushroom biryani I've ever seen.

'So what's this favour you're after, Brannigan?'

'Who said anything about a favour?' I said innocently.

'A person doesn't need to have A Level Deduction to know you're after something more than a share in my poppadums when you turn up on the office doorstep. What are you after?' Frankie persisted.

So much for gently working round to it. I plunged in. 'You took a couple of kids into care this afternoon. Daniel and Wayne Roberts. Their mum was shot in Brunswick Street?'

Frankie nodded cautiously. 'Mmm?'

'I knew Cherie quite well, because Davy always plays with Daniel and Wayne when he's staying with Richard. Also, I helped her out when she was trying to get a divorce from Eddy, her ex.' I paused, but Frankie didn't lift her eyes from her curry.

Nothing for it but to soldier on. 'I was driving home with Davy this afternoon just after Cherie had been shot. The place was jumping with police and ambulance crews, and we saw the boys being taken away in a police car. Then when we got home, all the neighbours were talking about Cherie being shot. The bottom line is that Davy's in a hell of a state. He's terrified because Cherie's been shot, but he's even more frightened because Daniel and Wayne have been carted off in a police car.'

'Not particularly surprising,' Frankie said sympathetically. 'Poor Davy. So what do you want me to do?'

'I just wondered if there was any chance you could fix up for me to take Davy to see Daniel and Wayne this evening. I know it's bending the rules and all that, but I don't see how I'm going to get him to sleep otherwise. He's climbing the walls. He thinks Daniel and Wayne have gone to prison, you see.' I sighed and shrugged. 'I've tried to explain, but he won't believe me.'

'I wonder why not,' Frankie said drily. She gave me a shrewd look. 'Are you sure you're asking for Davy and not for yourself?'

'Give me a break, Frankie,' I complained. 'You know I don't do murders. Strictly white collar, that's Mortensen and Brannigan.'

She snorted, not a wise move when you're dealing with curry spices. After she'd finished spluttering and sneezing, she said, 'And Patrick Swayze's strictly ballroom. OK. I believe you. God knows why. But if I find out you've been lying to me, Brannigan, I'll be really disappointed in you.'

Just as well I'm not a Catholic or I'd never get out of bed in the morning with the weight of guilt on my shoulders. I smiled meekly and said, 'You won't regret this, Frankie.'

'Where is Davy now?' she asked. 'Is he with Richard?'

'My friend Alexis is looking after him. She was going to take him to the pictures to see if she could take his mind off what's happened.' I glanced at my watch. 'They should be back within the next half-hour or so.'

Frankie ran a hand through her spiky hair. 'I hope for your sake I don't live to regret this, Brannigan. I'll tell you what would make me feel happier, though.'

'What's that?' I asked, willing to go along with anything half-reasonable so long as I still had the chance to hit the boys with a few questions.

'I'd be a lot happier if Richard brought Davy along rather than you. Then I could be sure there wasn't a hidden agenda.' Frankie said calmly.

I hoped the dismay I felt didn't reach the surface. I pulled a face and said, 'You and me both. But the boy wonder is out of town tonight. He's gone to Birmingham to see some international superstar I've never heard of at the NEC. He went off this afternoon early. He doesn't even know about Cherie.'

Frankie sighed. 'I'll just have to live with it, then. OK. We've placed Wayne and Daniel with emergency foster parents in Levenshulme. Normally, it would take a few days to organize a visit while we checked out the credentials of the person claiming to be friends or family, but in this case, I don't see why we shouldn't speed the wheels of bureaucracy since I know both you and Davy. Besides, it might just help the boys to settle, feel less abandoned. After we've eaten, I'll find a phone box and call the foster parents, see what time will fit in with their arrangements.'

I put my mobile phone on the table. 'Have this one on me,' I said, nudging it towards her.

Frankie shook her head, smiling wryly. 'Since I've known you, I've come to realize what the essential quality of a private investigator is,' she said, reaching across and picking up the phone.

'What's that?'

'You simply don't recognize the point where the rest of the world backs off,' she said. 'Now, how do I work this thing?'

It was just after seven when Davy and I pulled up outside a trim between-the-wars semi off Slade Lane. The street was quiet; one of the few in the area that motorists driven demented by traffic don't think is a short cut to anywhere. I'd had a difficult half-hour with Davy, explaining what had happened to Cherie and the boys. I thought I should keep it low-key so I wouldn't frighten him, but I'd forgotten how small boys like things to be gory. He hadn't seen it happen right in front of his eyes, so it was no more real, no more frightening than a cartoon or a video. I was glad Frankie had gone off to her meeting; anything less like a terrified nervous wreck than Davy it would be hard to imagine.

You couldn't say the same for Daniel and Wayne. They sat huddled together on a settee in the front room. The television was on and their eyes were pointing at it, but they weren't watching. They didn't look up when the foster mother showed Davy and me into the room, but when she spoke, they both turned their heads towards us, a look of bafflement on their faces. They had the bewildered, desperate air we've all grown used to seeing in endlessly recurring TV film of refugees from disaster areas.

'Hi, lads,' I said. 'Davy and I were wondering if you fancied going to the ice-cream parlour.'

Wayne got to his feet and, after a moment, Daniel joined him. I felt like a monster, dragging these two shattered kids out of the nearest thing they were going to have to a home, just to satisfy my curiosity. Then I looked at Davy and remembered my front door. That reminded me there was a lot more at stake than my nosiness. 'Or we could go somewhere else, if you'd rather,' I said.

'It's good there,' Davy said anxiously, disturbed by his friends' silence.

'I want to go home,' Wayne said. 'That's where I want to go.'

. The foster mother, a bulky, comfortable-looking woman in her late thirties, stepped past me and gave Wayne a hug. 'You've got to stay with us for a while, Wayne,' she said in a soothing voice. 'I know it's not the same as home, but tomorrow we'll go back to your house and get your clothes and the rest of your stuff and you can be at home here, OK?'

'We'll go to the ice-cream place, then,' he said grudgingly to me. Wayne shrugged off the woman's arm and pushed past her into the hall, where he stood expectantly by the door. Daniel followed him, and, after a quick glance at me for permission, so did Davy.

'I'll have them back in an hour,' I promised.

'Don't worry about it,' she said. 'Quite honestly, love, the more worn out they are tonight the better.'

For the first twenty minutes, I said nothing about Cherie or the shooting. We pumped money into the Wurlitzer, we argued the relative merits of everything on the menu. Then I sat back and watched while the boys wolfed huge ice-cream sundaes, gradually returning to something approaching normal behaviour, even if it was tinged with a kind of hysteria. I even joined in some of their fun, dredging my memory for old and sick jokes. When I reached the point where the only one I could remember was the one about the Rottweiler and the social worker, I reckoned it was time to change tack.

'Davy got a lot of new transfers yesterday, didn't you?' I said brightly.

'Where did you go?' Daniel asked.

'VIRUS,' said Davy and proceeded to enthuse about the virtual reality centre.

'Maybe we could all go together the next time Davy's up,' I suggested. 'Show them your tattoos, Davy.'

He took off his New York blouson to reveal tattoos that spread up from his wrists and finally disappeared into the sleeves of his T-shirt. Wayne and

Daniel studied the intergalactic warriors and dino-saurs, desperately trying not to look impressed.

'Huh,' Wayne finally said. 'I've had ones just as good as that.'

'Where from?' Davy challenged.

'From Woody on the estate. You know, him that gave you a load last week.'

There is a god. 'I don't think I know Woody,' I said. 'Where does he live?'

'Up the top. Near the Apollo. Where the chip van parks,' Daniel said positively.

'Wasn't your mum going to go and see him last night?' I asked, feeling like I was walking on eggshells. It was the first time Cherie had been mentioned, and I didn't know how they would react.

Wayne stared into his sundae dish, scraping his spoon round the sides. But Daniel didn't seem bothered. 'Nah,' he said scornfully. 'It wasn't Woody she went to see. She'd already seen Woody and gave him a right gobful about giving things to us. And Woody said he was just doing what he was told to do, and she said he was a waste of space and who told him, and he said, the guy in the house on the corner. And that's where she went.'

'What guy is that, do you know?'

Daniel shook his head. 'Don't know his name. We don't go there.'

'What house is it?'

'You know I said where Woody lives? Well, if you was standing at the chip van and you looked across the street that way,' he said, gesturing with his right arm, 'it's the house on the corner. That's where my mum went last night,' he added.

I was impressed. 'Were you with your mum when she saw Woody?' I asked. Daniel's information seemed almost too good to be true.

''Course *we* weren't,' Wayne said contemptuously. 'She didn't even know we were out. We followed her. We always follow her. She says we're the men of the house and she needs us to take care of her, so we follow her, but she don't know. We watch and listen so we'll know if anyone did bad things to her and we could get them back later. She never saw us,' he added proudly.

'I wish I was that good at following people,' I said. 'It would come in really handy in my job. You'll have to give me lessons one of these days. Where did you learn your tricks? From the TV?'

Wayne shook his head, swinging it elaborately from side to side. 'Our dad showed us. He trained us to be silent and deadly, just like the Paras.'

I felt a chill in my heart. According to Cherie, Crazy Eddy hadn't been near the kids in years. 'When was this?' I asked casually.

'For ages. He just turns up at the common where we go with our bikes and takes us up Levenshulme and trains us. But he made us promise we wouldn't tell anybody because he didn't want Mum to know. But now Mum's not here, it doesn't matter about telling, does it?' Wayne's face crumpled and he rubbed his eyes savagely with his fists.

'No, it doesn't matter. Your dad must be really proud of you. When did you see him last?'

'We saw him yesterday,' Daniel said. 'But he's been around for ages. He came back at Easter.'

23

I knew that if I betrayed my surprise I wouldn't get another word out of Daniel or Wayne. Somehow, I had to keep superficially calm at the news that Crazy Eddy was back in town. I breathed softly and thought about something restful; a room freshly painted barley white, actually. 'I thought your dad worked away,' I said.

Daniel stuck his chest out like a sergeant major. 'He does. He's a warrior, my dad. He teaches whole armies how to fight like him. But when they've learned how to do it, he comes home and sees us.'

'Does he come home often?' I asked.

'Once or twice a year,' Wayne muttered. 'The first time was just after I was five. We were playing in the playground at school at break time and this soldier came up to us, and he crouched down beside us and said, "You know who I am, don't you?" And we did, because Mum had his picture on her dressing table.' At the mention of the photograph, something clicked inside my head. Wayne looked up and met my eyes. 'Do you think we can go and live with him now? Be soldiers with him?'

'You'll have to ask your foster mother about that,' I said, distracted by the piece of the jigsaw that had just fallen into place. 'Where does your dad stay when he's here?' I tried to sound casual.

'In the Moss. With a man that used to be one of his squaddies,' Daniel said. 'He's never taken us there. He's too busy training us.'

'Of course he is. It's a tough job, being a good soldier.' Out of the corner of my eye, I could see Davy getting restive. I pretended to be stern. 'And you soldiers are letting the side down now.' All three looked puzzled. 'Do you know what's wrong with this picture?' I asked, gesturing at the table. They all held their breath and shook their heads. 'Empty plates!' I mock-roared. 'Time for seconds! Who wants more?'

I didn't have to ask twice. After the waiter had brought the second round of ice-creams, I said, 'So what training were you doing with your dad yesterday?'

'Tracking and observation,' Daniel reported. 'We met Dad round the common, and then we went and hid across the main road, on the waste ground. We had binoculars, and we watched the outside of the flats and we waited for Mum to come out, then we trailed her and spied on her talking to Woody. Dad said she should keep her nose out of other people's business when we told him she was on about the transfers.'

'Did he know about the transfers, then?' I asked through a mouthful of chocolate hazelnut. I'd succumbed the second time around.

''Course he does,' Wayne said, scornful again. 'He told us to get the transfers off Woody and get the other kids to use them. He said they'd all want them and that way they'd do what we told them to. But we don't use the ones we take off Woody. Dad said that would be a sign of weakness, so we don't.'

Eddy wasn't wrong about the transfers being a sign of weakness. I couldn't help wondering just how much he knew about what was going on in the house on the corner. It was time I paid it a visit. But first, I had to keep my side of the bargain I'd made with myself. I'd had my needs met; now, Daniel and Wayne were entitled to the same thing. I dug my hand in my pocket and dumped a handful of change on the table. 'Who wants to play?' I demanded, gesturing with one thumb towards the array of video-game machines at the far end of the ice-cream parlour.

I kept half an eye on them as I struggled with the significance of what Wayne had told me without realizing. Now I knew why the big bouncer at the Lousy Hand seemed so familiar. It wasn't because he was a regular in the Mexican restaurant down-stairs from the office.

I'd once seen that photograph that Cherie kept

in her bedroom. She'd shown me it when she'd asked me to hunt her husband down. He'd been in uniform, the maroon beret of the Paras cocked jauntily on his head. He'd been nearly ten years younger too. But that scar clinched it. The man who was fingering cars for Terry Fitz was none other than Crazy Eddy Roberts. At the very least, it was a strange coincidence.

It takes more than bereavement to divert small boys from arcade games. By the time they'd fought in the streets, driven several grand prix, played a round or two of golf and done enough terminating to get us jobs with Rentokil, the effects of the afternoon's trauma had receded noticeably. When we all piled back into my car, the haunted look had left their eyes. I didn't doubt that it was only a temporary respite, but even that was enough to ease my guilt at having taken advantage.

I dropped them off, promising that we'd keep in touch, then I drove Davy back to Alexis's. Of course, he was fired with curiosity as to why they'd moved back to their house and why he was staying with them there instead of with me in Coverley Close. Luckily, he was tired enough to be fobbed off with the excuse that Alexis and Chris needed to be at home now they were back at work because all their clothes and stuff were there. Alexis greeted him like a long-lost friend and hustled him off to the spare room, where she'd moved the video and the portable TV from their bedroom. I made the coffee while she made sure he was sufficiently engrossed in *The Karate Kid* for the dozenth time.

'You all right, girl?' Alexis asked when she returned. 'You look about as lively as a slug in a salt cellar.'

'Gee thanks. Remind me to call you next time my self-confidence creeps above the parapet. I'm just tired, that's all. I've not had a decent night's kip since last Wednesday.'

'Why don't you crash out here now? You can have the sofa bed in the study.'

'Thanks, but no thanks. I've got to go and sit outside a house in the dark.'

'Hey, the sofa bed's not that bad,' Alexis protested, joking. 'I've slept there myself.'

'Sorry to hear that, Alexis,' I said, pretending deep concern. 'I hadn't realized your relationship was in such a bad way.'

'Hey, carry on getting it that wrong and you could get a job on the *Chronicle*'s diary column.'

'Tut-tut' I scolded. 'And you the one that's always telling me how unfairly you journos are maligned for your inaccuracies. Anyway, enough of this gay repartee. I've got work to do, and you've got a child to mind. I'll call you later.' I headed for the door. 'And Alexis? I know you probably think I'm over-reacting, but don't open the door to anyone unless you know them.' I was through the door before she could argue.

I got in the car, revved up noisily, and drove round the corner. I gave it a couple of minutes, then turned back on to Alexis's street, stopping as soon as I had a clear view of the path leading to the house. I picked up my mobile and dialled a familiar number. It rang out, then I heard, 'Hello?'

'Dennis? It's Kate. Are you busy tonight?'

'I don't have to be,' he said, his voice too crackly for me to hear whether he sounded pissed off or not.

'I need a major favour.'

'No problem. Whereabout?'

I gave him brief directions and settled back to wait. OK, so I was being paranoid. But like they say, that doesn't mean they're not out to get you. There was no way I was leaving this street until I was sure that Davy, not to mention Alexis and Chris, had someone to watch over them. And there was no minder I'd trust more than Dennis. He had an added advantage. Years of earning his living as a burglar had developed in him an astonishing ability to stay awake and alert long after the rest of us are crashed out snoring with our heads on the steering wheel. If he was sitting outside the house in his car, I'd feel a lot less worried about the possibility of Jammy James wanting to use me or Davy as a lever against Richard. Not that I believed for one minute that the demolition of my front door was a message from James. I just thought it was better to be safe than sorry. Or something.

While I was waiting, I wondered how Richard was coping. I felt bad about missing the evening's visit, but I figured he could live without seeing me for a day. Whereas, if I didn't do all I could to finger the people who were responsible for the holes in my door, he might have to get used to the idea of not seeing me again. Ever. It wasn't a comforting thought.

The house on the corner of Oliver Tambo Close wasn't the ideal place for a stake-out. The chip van's presence meant a constant flow of people up and down the street, as well as the gang of local yobs who hung round the van every evening just for the hell of it. Add to that the general miasma of poverty and seediness up this end of the estate, and I knew without pausing to think that the Peugeot would stick out like a sore thumb as soon as that evening's rock audience from the Apollo had gone home. I swung round by the office lock-up and helped myself to the Little Rascal van we've adapted for surveillance work.

I stopped behind the chip van, bought fish, chips and cholesterol and ostentatiously drove the Little Rascal back round the corner on to the street running at right angles to Oliver Tambo Close. From the tinted rear windows of the van, I had a perfect view of the house, front door and all. I pulled down one of the padded jump seats and opened my fragrant parcel. I felt like I'd done nothing but eat all day, yet as soon as I smelled the fish and chips, I was ravenous. I sometimes think we're imprinted with that particular aroma while we're still in the womb.

While I tucked in, I checked out the house. I'd once been inside one of the other houses on the estate demanding action against the toerag who'd been anti-social enough to smash my car window and walk off with my radio cassette. Sparky, who runs the car crime round here, wasn't too pleased about a bit of private enterprise on his patch, especially from someone who was too stupid to work out which cars belonged to locals and which were fair game. Incidentally, he's not called Sparky because he's bright; it's because he uses a spark plug whirling on the end of a piece of string to shatter car windows. Anyway, I thought it was fair to assume this house would have the same layout as Sparky's. It looked the same from the outside, and Manchester City Council's Housing Department has never been renowned for its imagination.

The door would open into a narrow hall, the kitchen off to the right and the living-room to the left. Behind the kitchen was the staircase, a storage cupboard underneath. I'd gone upstairs to use the bathroom and noted two other doors, presumably leading to bedrooms. That checked out with what I could see of the house on the corner. My job wasn't made any easier by the vandals who had busted the streetlamp in front of it. I could see heavy curtains were drawn at every window, even the kitchen. That was unusual in itself. If you've *got* curtains for all your windows in Oliver Tambo Close, the Social Security snoopers come round and ask where you're getting your extra income from.

I could see a crack of light from a couple of the windows, but apart from that there was no sign of life until nearly half past ten. The front door opened a couple of feet and spilled a long tongue of pale light on to the path. At first, there was no one to be seen in the doorway, then, sudden as sprites in an arcade game, two kids barrelled down the hall and out on to the path. They were both boys, both good-looking in the way that most lads have grown out of by adolescence. Unfortunately for the teenage girls. I'd have put them around nine or ten, but I'm not the best judge of children's ages. One had dark curls, the other had mousey brown hair cut in one of those trendy styles, all straight lines and heavy fringes that remind me of BBC TV versions of Dickens.

The two boys seemed in boisterous, cheerful moods, pushing each other, staggering about, giggling and generally horsing around. They stopped on the corner and pulled chocolate bars out of the pockets of their jeans. They stood there for a few minutes, munching chocolate, then they ran off down the street towards the blocks of flats where Cherie Roberts had tried to bring her kids up as straight as she knew how. A slow anger had started to burn inside me when those kids appeared on the path, all alone at a time of night that's a long way from safe in this part of town. Apart from anything else, it's an area that's always full of strangers in

273

the evening, since the city's major rock venue is just round the corner. If a child was lifted from these streets, the police would have more strange cars to check out than if they clocked every motor that cruises the red-light zone.

I bit down on my anger and carried on watching. About twenty minutes later, the door opened again, more widely this time, and a young man appeared. He couldn't have been more than five-six, slim build, blond, late twenties, cheekbones like chapel hat pegs. He had his jacket collar turned up and sleeves rolled up. Clearly no one had told him *Miami Vice* is yesterday's news. He walked with a swagger to a Toyota MR2 parked at the kerb. I toyed with the idea of following him, but rejected it. I didn't know that he was anything to do with the drugs being foisted on kids, and besides, chasing a sports car in a delivery van is about as much fun as that nightmare where you're sitting an exam and you don't understand any of the questions, and then you realize you're stark naked as well.

So I stayed put. The MR2 revved enough to attract the envy of the chip-van gang, then shot off leaving a couple of hundred miles' worth of rubber on the road. Ten minutes later, the door opened again. This time, the hall light snapped off. Two men emerged. In the dimness, it was hard to see much, except that they both looked paunchy and middle-aged. They walked towards my van, near enough for me to see that they both wore

Sellafield suits – those expensive Italian jobs that virtually glow in the dark. Surprisingly, they got into an elderly Ford Sierra that looked perfectly in keeping with the locale, and drove off.

I carried on with my vigil. There were no lights on that I could see, but I figured there might still be someone in the bathroom, or the bedroom at the rear of the house. The chip van packed up at midnight, and the gang wandered off to annoy someone else. By half past midnight, it had started to drizzle and the street was as quiet as it was ever going to get. There was still no sign of life at the house. I unlocked the strongbox in the floor of the van, and helped myself to some of the essential tools of the trade. Then I pulled on a pair of latex surgical gloves.

I got out of the van and walked towards the narrow alley that runs up the back of Oliver Tambo Close so the bin men have more scope to strew the neighbourhood with the contents of burst black rubbish sacks. As nonchalantly as possible, I made sure I wasn't being watched before I nipped smartly down the alley. The house on the corner had a solid fence about seven feet high, with a heavy gate about halfway along. Luckily, one of the neighbours was trusting. A couple of doors down was a dustbin. I retrieved the bin and climbed on top of it.

The rear of the house was in darkness, so I scrambled over the fence and dropped into a tangle of Russian vine. Come the holocaust, that's all there will be left. Cockroaches and Russian vine. I freed myself and stood on the edge of a patchy lawn staring up at the house. There was a burglar alarm bell box on the gable end of the house, but I suspected it was a dummy. Most of them round here are. Even if it was for real, I wasn't too worried. It would take five minutes before anyone called the cops, and by the time they got here, I'd be home, tucked up in bed.

The back door had two locks, a Yale and a mortise. The patio doors looked more promising. You can often remove a patio door from its runners in a matter of minutes. All it takes is a crowbar in the right place. Only problem was, I was fresh out of crowbars. With a sigh, I started in with the lock picks. The mortise took me nearly twenty minutes, but at least the rain meant nobody with any sense was out walking curious dogs with highly developed senses of smell and powerful vocal cords. When the lock clicked back, I stretched my arms and flexed my tired fingers. The Yale was a piece of cake, even though I couldn't slide it open with an old credit card and had to use a pick. Cautiously, I turned the handle and inched the door open.

Silence. Blackness. I slipped into the carpeted hall and left the door on the latch. Slowly, painstakingly, I inched forward down the hall, my right hand brushing the wall to warn me when I reached the living-room doorway. As my eyes grew accustomed to the dark, I made out a patch of lesser blackness on the left. The stairs. As I drew level,

I paused and held my breath. I couldn't hear a thing. Feeling slightly more relaxed, I carried on.

The living-room door was open. I moved through the doorway tentatively, scared of tripping over furniture, and closed the door softly behind me. I switched on the big rubber torch I'd taken from the van's glove box and slowly played it over the room.

It was like two separate rooms glued together in the middle. In the far end of the room, the walls were painted cream. There was a cream leather armchair, a pair of school desks with child-sized chairs, and a pair of bunk beds complete with satin sheets. Where there should have been a light fitting hanging from the ceiling there was a microphone. At the midpoint of the room, a camcorder was fixed on a tripod, flanked by a couple of photographer's floodlights.

The other half of the room, where I was standing, was like the distribution area of a video production company. There was one of those big video-copying machines that do a dozen copies at a time, a desk set up for home video editing, boxes of Jiffy bags and shelf upon shelf of videos, one title to a shelf. Titles like, *Detention!*, *Bedtime Stories* and *You Show Me Yours* . . . There were also sealed packets of photographs. Now I began to understand why kids were being handed free drugs that would smash their inhibitions to smithereens and make them see the funny side of being exploited to hell. I could only come up with one explanation of what was going on here, and the very thought of it was so sickening that part of me didn't want to hang around checking the evidence. The only thing that forced me to do it was the thought of some smartass from the Vice Squad doing the 'so if you didn't look at these videos, how do you know they weren't Bugs Bunny cartoons?' routine on me.

I picked a title at random and slotted it into the player on the editing desk. I turned on the TV monitor. While I waited for the credits to come up, I slit open a packet of photographs. Twelve colour five-by-sevens slid out into my hand. I nearly lost my fish and chips. I recognized the blond man who'd left earlier in the Toyota, but the children in the shots were, thank God, strangers. I'd have been fairly revolted to see adults in some of those poses, but with children, my reaction went beyond disgust. At once, I understood those parents who take the law into their own hands when the drunk drivers who killed their kids walk free from court.

If the photographs were bad, the video was indescribably worse, all the more so because of the relentlessly suburban locations where these appalling acts were taking place. I could barely take five minutes of it. My instincts were to empty a can of petrol on the carpet and raze the place to the ground. Then common sense prevailed and reminded me it would be infinitely preferable if those bastards ended up behind bars rather than me. I switched off the video and ejected the tape. I picked up the photographs and stuffed them inside my jacket. I grabbed another couple of videos off the shelf. The night relief at Longsight police station were in for an interesting shift.

I stood up. I heard a sickening crunch. My eyes filled with red, shot through with yellow meteors. A starburst of pain spread from the back of my head. And everything went black.

24

Mosquito. Unmistakable. High-pitched whine circling my head, in one ear and then in the other. Bluebottle. Low, stuttering buzz mixing in with the mozzy. You wouldn't think two little insects could make enough noise to give you a splitting headache, I thought vaguely as I surfaced.

Then the pain hit. You know when you catch your finger in a door? Imagine doing that to your head, and you'll start to get the picture. The sharp edge of the agony snapped my brain back into gear. In the tiny gaps between waves of pain and nausea, I started to remember where I'd been and what I was doing when something seriously brutal put my memory on pause.

As that memory returned, so my senses started to catch up. I still couldn't force my eyes open, but my hearing had recovered from its dislocation. I wasn't hearing a mozzy and a bluebottle. I was hearing a voice. The words drifted in and out, like listening to a pirate radio station on the edge of its transmission area. 'I don't fucking *know* how she got in,' I heard. 'I was fucking sleeping, wasn't I? Look, it's your job to sort out problems . . .' The voice tailed off. The silence was blissful.

Moments later, the voice started yapping again. This time, I registered that it was a man. 'I don't give a shit what you're doing. Look, you're paid to do this sort of thing. I'm just paid to copy videos and *be* here, not whack people over the head with tripods. You'd better get your arse over here now and deal with this cow.' Silence again. Then the voice, higher pitched, angry. 'You've already been paid once to warn her off, and it didn't work, did it? So you'd better come round here and finish the job or else I'll have to ring Colin and tell him you're not prepared to turn out, and he won't be pleased about that, not being disturbed this time of night.'

It finally dawned on me that this was me he was talking about. If I'd had the energy to be afraid, I'd have been gibbering. As it was, the immediate prospect of being executed helped focus my mind even more. My eyes still refused to open, but I became aware of a shooting pain in my shoulders and managed to work out my position. I was suspended by my wrists, which were manacled by something warm and solid that was biting into the flesh. My hands were jammed up against what felt like hot and cold water pipes. My body was dangling, my legs were crumpled under me, not actually taking any of my weight.

281

Before I could test whether it was possible to shift my weight to my feet without making a noise, the voice started yammering again. 'Look, it's your responsibility. She's got to be dealt with, and now. She's seen the videos, for God's sake. You might want to spend the next ten years being buggered by some Neanderthal in the nick, but I don't.' He paused. 'Fine. You better be here, that's all, or I'll be right on the phone to Colin. And if you want another wage packet like today's, you won't want me doing that.' I heard the sound of a phone being slammed down. The jangling crash cut through my head like a blunt axe, snapping my eyes open.

I closed them to a slit at once, eager to look like I was still out for the count. If I had any chance of getting clear of this place before the hit man arrived, it was by playing dead and hoping my captor would leave me alone. Through my lashes, I could see I was in the kitchen, the fluorescent light a stab behind the eyes. At the far end of the room, the man who'd been using the wall-mounted phone turned towards me. He was tall and slim, his gingerish hair tousled from sleep. He had a neat, full moustache that jutted out like a ledge above thin lips and a sharp chin. The bleary eyes he focused on me narrowed vindictively. 'Bitch,' he said, savagely tightening the belt of his towelling dressing gown.

I knew him. Not his name, or anything like that, but I knew him. I'd seen him around, in the local shops, and in Manto's café bar on one of the handful of occasions I'd been in there waiting for Richard. We were on nodding terms, talking about the weather in the corner-shop terms. It was hard to get my head round the idea of being trussed up by someone I knew. I've never had the slightest desire to explore S&M, and I sure as hell didn't want to start now.

He turned away from me and picked up the kettle. He filled it up and switched it on. While he was waiting for it to boil he came over to me. I let my eyelids sink shut and tried to ignore the cramps that were sending spasms of agony from my lower back muscles through my shoulders and down into my triceps. I let my body hang limp. I was just fine till he kicked me in the ribs.

I think I passed out again for a moment, for the next time I cracked my eyes open he was pouring boiling water into a teapot. I had a funny feeling that he wasn't going to offer me a cup. I took the opportunity of his back being turned to check out my position.

I was handcuffed to water pipes, each about an inch in diameter. What was holding me up was the brackets that were screwed into the wall to keep the pipes in place. What worried me most of all was that I wasn't wearing my jacket or my cotton sweater. I was stripped down to my sports bra, and the entire length of my arms was covered in temporary tattoos. No wonder I was feeling out of it. The gratuitous kick had given me a vague feeling that I ought to be really, really angry, but

I couldn't seem to get worked up. However, I was a long way from being totally stoned. Maybe the lack of circulation in my arms and hands had slowed down the process of absorption. Just how long had the tattoos been in place, and how long did I have before I became a silly giggling maniac?

While I worried about this, Moustache was brewing his tea. He poured himself a mug, gave me a last glance and walked out of the room. Judging by the shuffle of his slippers, he'd only gone as far as the living room.

I knew I didn't have a lot of time. The hit man was on his way, and I needed to be free and clear by then. Taking a deep breath, I shifted round so the soles of my feet were on the floor. Gradually, I allowed my legs to take the weight off my shoulders. For a moment, the pain in my shoulders vanished like magic. Then the pins and needles set in. From my hands to my shoulders, I twitched with a million stabs of irritation. I bit my lip to gag the whimpers that I couldn't stop escaping.

Slowly, inch by cautious inch, I straightened my legs, relieving all the strain on my arms and shoulders. It seemed to take forever, especially since I had to do it all in silence and the pounding in my head seemed to be growing rather than subsiding. When I was upright, I took stock again. The pipes looked pretty strong, but there were a couple of bends in them which might indicate weak points. The downside was that my arms were weak, my muscles twitching with pain. On the other hand, I had nothing to lose since the hit man was already on his way.

I took a deep breath and raised one leg, placing the sole of my foot against the wall, on a level with my hips. Then, gritting my teeth, I leaned back, taking my weight on my arms again, and swung my other leg up, bracing it against the wall on the other side of the pipe. With all my strength, I straightened my legs, pulling back against the handcuffs as hard as I could, my weight lending maximum force to my efforts.

At first, nothing happened. The cuffs dug into my hands, thankfully in a different place to the weals from my earlier suspension, but nothing moved. Then, suddenly, one of the brackets popped out of the walls like the pearl stud on a tight cowboy shirt. Another bracket followed it almost at once, and the pipe came away from the wall, bowing dramatically towards me. I bent my legs slightly, then prepared for a final, all-out effort. With a grunt that Monica Seles would have been proud of, I straightened my legs and hauled with everything I had. Just when I thought I would dislocate my shoulders, the pipe snapped about five feet from the ground and I crashed to the floor.

The roar of gushing water mingled with the roar of anger from behind me. I dragged myself upright and hauled my hands over the broken ends of the pipes, fast as I could. Even so, Moustache was on me as I swivelled round to face him. He'd grabbed the first thing to hand, which was the kettle, swinging it at my battered head. I did a staggering sidestep, as much to get away from the scalding blast of the hot pipe as to avoid the kettle. Moustache got the hot water straight in the face as the momentum of his running blow carried him past me and into the wall.

His scream would have been music to my ears if my head hadn't been splitting. Instead, all I wanted to do was shut him up. I aimed a Thai boxing kick at the crook of his knee. It was a pretty feeble kick, but he was off balance anyway. He dropped to his knees like a sack of spuds and I brought my clenched hands, complete with nasty sticking-out bits of handcuffs, down hard on the back of his neck. With a groan like an abandoned harmonium, he slumped against the wall and slithered down into the growing pool of water like something out of a Tom and Jerry cartoon.

I leaned against the sink, trying to catch my breath. I looked at the inert body crumpled at my feet and realized that all I had to do was walk away to get my own back for that gratuitous boot in the ribs. Given the rate the water was pouring into the kitchen, it wouldn't be long before Moustache said good night, Vienna.

Call me a wimp, but I couldn't do it. I crouched down, grabbed his hair and hauled his poleaxed head out of the water. I yanked him on to his back and propped him in a sitting position between the wall and the sink unit. I'm too nice for my own good.

Keeping one eye on him, I backed across the kitchen to the phone. Using both hands, I picked up the receiver and tucked it into my left shoulder. I punched in a familiar number and listened to it ring out. I was starting to panic when it reached the thirteenth ring: it's not easy being patient when you know someone's on their way to send you to the crematorium.

Just as I was about to abandon the phone and leg it, the ringing stopped and a blurred voice muttered, ''Lo?'

'Della? It's Kate. This is an emergency. Are you awake?'

There was a grunt, then Della said, 'Getting there. What is it?'

'Della, there's a guy on his way to kill me. It'll take too long to explain it all now, but he's the hit man who killed Cherie Roberts, the single mum who got blown away this afternoon? He's coming after me!' I could hear the hysteria rising in my voice, and I was overwhelmed by the urge to giggle.

'Kate? Are you pissed?' Della asked incredulously.

'No, but I think I've been drugged,' I said. 'I swear this isn't a wind-up, Della. I know it's not your beat, but you've got to get a posse out here right away, double urgent. This guy's a paid killer.

287

And he's after me!' Even to me, my voice sounded like Minnie Mouse.

'OK, calm down. Where exactly are you?'

'I'm in a house on the corner of Oliver Tambo Close, near the Apollo. The house is full of kiddy porn. They've been drugging the kids to get them to perform,' I gabbled.

'Later, Kate, later,' Della interrupted. 'I'm going to hang up now and get the local lads to send the area car round there pronto. And I'll be there myself as soon as I can. But I want you to get out of there right now. Don't hang about. Just get out. Go back to your house and I'll meet you there.'

I snorted with insane laughter. I was beginning to feel really silly. 'I can't go there,' I giggled. 'He knows where I live. He's already blown my door away.' Before she could make another suggestion, the line went dead. Not the way it goes when someone hangs up on you. This was dead, hollow, a void. Suddenly, I didn't feel like giggling any more. Somewhere outside the house was the man who had been sent to kill me. And his automatic first action was to cut the lines of communication.

I checked my pockets for the van keys, but they weren't there. Wildly, I looked around the kitchen. I spotted them on one of the worktops, along with my wallet. I paddled through the water and picked them up, stuffing my wallet in my trouser pocket. In the kitchen doorway, I hesitated, water flowing like a spring stream round my ankles, trying to decide whether the assassin would approach from the front or the rear.

I didn't wonder for long. With a crash that reverberated round my skull, the back door slammed against the wall. I didn't even wait to look. I whirled round to the front door. The gods were on my side, for the key was in the lock. I turned the key, pulled it out of the lock and yanked the door open. I was through it and had it closed in the time it took the hit man to travel the length of the hall. I shoved the key in the lock and turned it. Then I stumbled and weaved down the path, my breath coming in ragged sobs.

I'd reached the pavement when the night exploded in a pair of catastrophic bangs. I turned to look back at the house. The door was hanging drunkenly on one of its hinges, and the silhouette of a man was pushing it aside. In his right hand; he carried a sawn-off shotgun. I drew in my breath in a horrified moan and ran for my life.

Now I was swerving madly by design as I approached the van. I pressed the burglar alarm remote-control button, which unlocks the doors as well as deactivating the alarm. I was barely at the back of the van, and I could hear him gaining on me. Then, suddenly, the sound of his footsteps stopped. I knew he was taking aim. Desperately, I threw myself into a rolling somersault round the rear of the van to the passenger side, putting the van between him and me.

Weeping with fear, sweating in spite of the cold

night air on my freshly grazed skin, I scrambled to my feet and staggered along the side of the van to the passenger door. I grabbed the door handle like a lifeline and pulled myself into the cab. I had the presence of mind to lock the doors behind me. I fumbled the key into the ignition at the second attempt.

I was still cuffed, so driving wasn't going to be easy. I swivelled round to shift the gear stick into first, then released the handbrake. Movement at the edge of my peripheral vision made me swing round to look out of the driver's window. The shock of what I saw nearly had me stalling the engine. As it was, I let the clutch out way too fast and the van bucked forward in a series of jumps like a kangaroo on acid.

In my wing mirror, I saw him step back involuntarily to avoid having his feet run over by the van's rear wheels. Crazy Eddy Roberts, locked somewhere on the slopes of Mount Tumbledown, clutching his gun like mothers clutch frightened children. A man who'd lost touch with human feelings to the point where there was nothing difficult about taking a damn sight more than thirty pieces of silver to kill the mother of his children.

For a fraction of a second, our eyes locked. The engine was screaming a protest at still being in first, so I took my hands off the steering wheel to change up into second. When I looked in my mirror again, the twin barrels of the gun gleamed dully in the distant streetlights as Eddy swung it up towards me. I put my foot down and grabbed the steering wheel. I could feel the van fishtailing as I tried to wrench the wheel round to clear the oncoming corner.

I heard the boom of the gun as the window shattered. I'd lost control of the van almost simultaneously. I hit the kerb at speed and clipped a lamppost. As the van toppled over on its side, the last thing I saw was a pair of flashing blue lights.

25

I couldn't believe how blue the sea was. It glittered under Mediterranean sunlight like one of those crystal beds that New Age fanatics have lying around their living-rooms. I propped myself up on one elbow and watched the lumbering half-tracked harvesters further down the beach, gathering and refining the spice that had caused the planet wars that had ravaged Dune for a generation. Suddenly, the sand shifted, only feet away from my leg, and the head of a huge, carnivorous sandworm reared up. The ferocious jaws opened, to reveal Moustache's face.

I swam up the levels to consciousness, passing from dreaming to awareness via that state where you know that you've just been dreaming, but you're not quite awake. My head felt like an oversized block of stone, though there didn't seem to be as much pain as I remembered enduring before the accident. The accident!

My eyes snapped open. I was in a small room,

dimly illumined by lights glowing through frosted glass from the corridor outside. I tried to lift my head, but it was too much of an effort. Instead, I shifted my feet to check I was still functioning below the neck. You put your left leg in, you put your left leg out . . . Yeah, the lower limbs all did the hokey cokey. I breathed deeply. There was a bit of pain from my ribs and chest, but nothing felt broken, which was pretty miraculous given that I hadn't been wearing my seat belt when I crashed the van. I raised my right arm, which seemed fine, apart from the puffy bruises that ran round hand and wrist like designer bangles by the Marquis de Sade. My left arm had no watch on it, only grazes from shoulder to wrist, and a drip running into the back of my hand, which was more than a little disconcerting.

I moved my head to one side, trying to see if there was a clock anywhere. To my surprise, Della was fast asleep on a plastic bucket chair next to my bed. I felt mildly outraged. Someone had tried to kill me tonight, and she should have been down the police station, going through the hoops of the Police and Criminal Evidence Act to make sure Crazy Eddy spent the foreseeable future living at the taxpayers' expense in a room with a bucket to piss in and bars on the windows. Then a horrible thought struck me. What if Eddy Roberts had managed to give the plod a body swerve? What if Della was Greater Manchester Police's idea of a bodyguard? What if Crazy Eddy was still out there with his pump-action double-barrelled shotgun packed with cartridges with my name on?

I opened my mouth. My brain said, 'Della?' but my mouth was too dry to play along. All I managed was a sort of strangulated croak.

She must only have been catnapping, for her eyes opened at once. Momentarily, she had the startled look of someone who has lost track of where she is. Then her conscious mind checked in and she sat bolt upright, staring at me with undisguised relief. 'Kate?' she said softly. 'Can you hear me?'

I tried to nod, but it wasn't in my repertoire yet. I waved my arm in the direction of the locker, where there was a jug of water and a bottle of orange juice. 'Drink?' I mouthed.

Della jumped up and poured a glass of water. She leaned over me and tipped the glass to my lips. Most of the water went down my cheeks and on to the pillow, but I didn't care. All I was concerned about was getting some in my parched mouth. The water was warm and stale and blissful. I didn't want to swallow, just hold it there in my mouth. Della gave me a concerned, anxious look as I waved her away.

Finally, I let the water trickle down my throat. 'Thanks,' I said in something approaching my normal voice. 'What are you doing here? Shouldn't you be down the cells beating a confession out of that mad bastard with the shotgun?' She gave me an odd look. 'You did *catch* him, didn't you,'

I demanded, panic gripping my chest and turning my stomach over.

'We caught him,' Della said grimly. 'The officers from Longsight got slightly over-enthusiastic with their truncheons when they realized he had a gun. Your assailant has a broken collar bone and a shattered wrist, you'll be sorry to hear.'

'Is that why you're here and not down the nick taking a statement?' I asked.

Della looked awkward. 'Actually, no,' she said, shifting in her seat. 'Kate, this isn't the same day,' she said in a rush.

I frowned. 'Not the same day? What do you mean?'

'You called me in the early hours of Wednesday morning.' She glanced at her watch. 'It's now four forty-seven a.m. on Thursday. You've been out cold for over a day.'

'Over a day?' I echoed foolishly. I couldn't take it in. I had no sense of having lost a day of my life. I felt like I'd woken up from a strange dream after a brief spell of unconsciousness. Did people feel like this when they came out of comas that lasted weeks or years? No wonder they felt dislocated. I'd only lost a day and I felt like I'd stumbled into an episode of the *Twilight Zone*. I managed a twisted grin. 'You know it's a bad case when the only way you can catch up on your sleep is to get unconscious.'

'I'm glad you can joke about it. We were starting to get really worried. The doctors gave you a brain scan and said there seemed to be no damage, but they couldn't say how long you'd be out.'

'Does Richard know?' I asked.

'I discussed it with Bill and Ruth, and we decided not to tell him before this morning's hearing. It seemed the best solution.'

'Yeah,' I sighed. 'He couldn't have done anything, and they wouldn't have let him out unless I was really at death's door. It would only have had him climbing the walls. The last thing he needs right now is to be charged with assaulting a police officer.' The only good thing I could see about having lost an entire day was that I wouldn't have to wait so long to see Richard again. With luck, he'd be out on bail by lunch time.

'How are you feeling?' Della asked.

'Took your time asking, didn't you?' I teased.

Della looked hurt for a few seconds, before it sank in that I was at the wind-up. 'Listen, Brannigan,' she said, pretending to be stern, 'I don't have to be here. I'm not on duty. I'm here out of the goodness of my heart, you know.'

'Thanks,' I said, meaning it. 'I'm impressed. I've never known you go this long without a cigarette voluntarily. Actually, I don't feel too bad. A bit woozy, that's all. And my head's throbbing. And now I'm awake, they'll probably give me something for that. At least I know I'll be out of here in a few days. How's Crazy Eddy handling it, being locked up in a cell?'

Della stiffened to attention again. Her face shifted

from concerned friend to alert copper. 'You *know* who this guy is?'

'Why? Don't you?'

She looked faintly embarrassed. 'As it happens, we don't. He won't say a word. He had nothing on him that would identify him, and his prints don't seem to be on record. Who is he?'

'His name's Eddy Roberts. He's an ex-Para. He got invalided out a couple of years after the Falklands war because he was out to lunch and not coming back. He's supposedly been working all over the globe as a mercenary. He's been back in Manchester since Easter. Apparently working as a hired gun. Among other things.' I stopped, suddenly exhausted.

'Kate, I know you've been through it, and I'm sorry to have to keep on at you. This isn't the time to take a formal statement, but this is really important information. How do you know all this? Have you been chasing him?' She had the good grace to look ashamed of herself.

I gave one of those laughs that turns into a cough halfway through. 'No, Della. He was chasing me, remember. The reason I know so much about Crazy Eddy is because his wife and kids told me. Eddy Roberts used to be married to Cherie Roberts. The woman he blew away outside the post office on Tuesday.'

That was revelation enough to shatter Della's official cool. 'You mean, that wasn't a professional hit job? It was a domestic?'

'It was a hit job all right. Cherie had found out about the child porn racket. And I expect she threatened that she'd spill the beans to me. The fact that Eddy used to be married to her was, I suspect, totally irrelevant. If anything, it probably made it more exciting.'

'And that's how you got involved? Through Cherie?'

I was growing wearier by the second, but I forced a smile. 'I thought you weren't taking a statement?' Della started to apologize but I waved it aside. 'Only joking, honest. No, I got involved because Davy came home stoned out of his mind.' I gave Della the thirty-second version of events around Oliver Tambo Close. I'd just got to the bit about interviewing Wayne and Daniel when we were interrupted.

She was only in her mid-twenties, but the night sister was fierce. 'Is the patient awake?' she demanded. 'Chief Inspector, I gave you strict instructions to ring for a nurse if the patient showed signs of coming round. You've got no right to inter-rogate her on my ward without my permission.'

'It's my fault,' I butted in. 'I wanted to know what had happened.'

The sister busied herself with my pulse. 'You're in no fit state to discuss it,' she said firmly. 'Chief Inspector, I'm going to have to ask you to leave. You can come back after Mr Rocco has seen the patient and if he decides she's fit to be inter-viewed.'

Della got to her feet meekly and winked. 'See you soon, Kate,' she said.

'I hope so,' I sighed. 'Oh, Della – before you go . . . Sister, can I ask the officer one question?'

The sister smiled, unexpectedly. 'If you must. But keep it short,' she added, frowning pointedly at Della.

'The van. What sort of state is it in?'

'Amazingly enough, it's just superficial damage. You'll be relieved to hear it's not a write-off, according to Bill last night.' She edged towards the door. 'Thanks for your help, Kate.'

I watched her retreating back while the sister bustled about doing sisterly things to my reflexes. She asked me who the Prime Minister was, and I told her about the pain, so she gave me some pills once she'd finished her neurological observations. The last thing I remembered as I drifted into sleep was being grateful that I hadn't written off the Little Rascal. It was only seven months since another homicidal nutter had sent my last company car to the great scrap yard in the sky. Any more of that, and the insurance premiums were going to be higher than the price of a new set of wheels.

The next time my eyes flickered open, I thought I was hallucinating. There, sitting on the uncomfortable chair, brown hair flopping across his forehead, eyes intent behind his glasses, was Richard. Seeing me waken, a slow, joyful smile spread across his face. I'd never seen a more welcome sight. 'Hiya,

Brannigan,' he said. 'You're not fit to be let out on your own, are you?' He stretched out an arm and gripped my right hand tightly. The bruises sent out a protest bulletin on all frequencies, but I didn't care.

'You're a fine one to talk,' I said. 'This is all your fault anyway.'

'I had a funny feeling it was going to be,' he said, grinning. 'I see the blow to your head hasn't improved your grasp of logic. They tell me you've not got brain damage, but I told the consultant different. He said there was nothing they could do about the state you were in before the accident. So I'm just going to have to live with it.'

'Did you get bail, or was it Group 4 that escorted you to court this morning?'

'The police withdrew their objections to bail, and they let me go without conditions. Ruth says they'll drop charges once they've nailed the real guys in the black hats and cleared me. I came straight here, you know. I didn't even go home for fresh clothes and a joint. You did a great job, Brannigan.' He released my hand and dropped to his knees, hands clenched in supplication. 'How can I ever repay you?'

'I'll think of something,' I said. 'You can start by giving me a kiss.'

He jumped to his feet. 'I'll have to close my eyes,' he said, mock-seriously.

'I look that bad?' I demanded, suddenly discovering a new anxiety. I put my hand up to my head, discovering a thick turban of bandage that extended halfway down my forehead.

'Two lovely black eyes, two lovely black eyes,' he sang. 'And a whopping great bruise on your jaw. Linda Evangelista won't be worrying about you taking her place on the catwalk for a while.' Before I could say anything more, he stooped over me and kissed me gently on the lips.

'Call that a kiss?' I snarled.

It got better after that.

When he finally came up for air, he said softly, 'I love you, Brannigan.'

'Don't go getting soft on me,' I murmured. 'You're only saying that because I got you out of jail.'

'And you took care of my kid. I've heard all about what went on. Bill came to court this morning and told me how you'd ended up in here.'

'Speaking of which,' I interrupted before he got hopelessly sentimental in the way that only cynical journos can. 'Where is Davy?'

'Alexis took the day off to look after him. They've gone off to some fun palace this morning. She told Bill she'd meet me here ...' he glanced at his watch. 'In about ten minutes, actually.'

'God, you'd better not let him in here if I'm as much of a sight as you seem to think I am. He'll have nightmares for weeks.'

'Brannigan, you're talking about a kid who thought *Dracula* was a fun movie. I don't think a couple of bruises and a heavy-duty headscarf are going to freak him out. He knows you were in a car crash. The only thing I'm worried about is what he's going to tell his mother.'

Epilogue

On the first day of Davy's summer holidays, the three of us giggled our way along Blackpool prom on the open top deck of a tram. I was wearing a baseball cap that said 'Kiss me slow'. Tacky, I know, but it covered the uneven hair growth. At least it wasn't stubble any more. I'd been less than thrilled to discover I had a bald patch where they'd had to shave me when they stitched up the hole that Moustache's tripod had made in the back of my head. The hair seems to be coming back just fine over the scar, but it's knackered my attempts at growing my hair. I'm back to short and spiky. *Passé,* sure, but I hadn't had a lot of choice. And I didn't look too much like a punk now the deep bruising had finally faded.

Davy had insisted on coming back north for part of the summer because he'd had such a good time at half-term. I can only presume he gave his mother a highly edited version of events, since she made no objection. We'd spent most of the day at the Pleasure Beach, only giving up on the white-knuckle rides when Richard dumped his lunch down the drain after a spectacular trip round the Grand National.

Now we were heading for the tower. Richard had decided that physically being on top of the world was the best way to symbolize the fact that as of tomorrow he'd officially be a free man. 'I can't wait,' he said as we queued for the lift.

'I didn't think you were into views,' I said.

'No, for tomorrow, stupid. I can't wait to hear the prosecuting solicitor saying they're dropping all the charges against me.'

I squeezed his hand. 'Me too.' It had been an interesting few weeks. In spite of his misgivings about my information, Geoff Turnbull had put full surveillance on Terry Fitz, Jammy James and the chemical kitchen. They'd swooped in the early hours of Friday morning. They'd actually caught Terry Fitz red-handed in a stolen Mazda MX5 halfway down the M40 with trade plates and five kilos of crack in the boot. A dozen bodies had been remanded in custody at Saturday morning's Magistrates' Court. According to Ruth, nothing had come up in the interviews that even remotely implicated Richard or me. The police had even managed to establish that James and his team of dealers still had no idea who had driven off in a 'stolen' car with a boot full of crack. Best of all, the police seemed to think they wouldn't need me to testify in court, which I reckoned significantly increased my chances of celebrating my thirtieth birthday. After all, Crazy Eddy wasn't the only hit man in Greater Manchester.

Speaking of Crazy Eddy, he'd been charged with murdering Cherie and attempting to murder me. According to Della, it looked like he was also going to be charged with a couple of other street shootings in Moss Side just after Easter. He was still doing the Trappist monk routine with all of the coppers who'd done their brains in trying to interview him. He hadn't even asked for a solicitor. Interestingly, it turned out that Terry Fitz had been in the Paras with Crazy Eddy, which was how Eddy had got involved as spotter for the car stealing racket. The police also suspected that Jammy James's outfit was responsible for recommending him to the child-porn merchants as a hit man.

There was another connection between the two teams. It turned out that James's mob were supplying the designer drugs for the kids to the child-porn gang in exchange for videos they could sell on through their own network. Or, in the case of one of Terry Fitz's cronies, hang on to for their own sick purposes. Which explained the mysterious Polaroid that had slipped down the side of the seat in the Gemini coupé.

The house in Oliver Tambo Close had been a proper little gold mine for the Vice Squad. Not only had they put a stop to the racket, they'd found the porn makers' mailing list, investigation of which was currently causing marital difficulties from Land's End to John O'Groats; or rather, from an executive housing estate in Penzance to a croft on the Shetland Isles. Served them right too. The only bleak piece of news was that the two middle-aged bastards who'd made most of the profits from the sleazy trade had legged it at the first sign of trouble. The word is they're somewhere on the Algarve, playing golf.

And the police had finally released Andrew Broderick's Leo Gemini turbo super coupé. In his shoes, I'd have been less than thrilled at being deprived of one of my company's flagship motors for so long, but Andrew was a happy man. More than two months had passed since Richard and I had started doing the groundwork to expose the fiddle that the car dealerships were up to. And not a single one of the cars we'd purchased had been reported sold to his finance company. Which meant Andrew had been absolutely right about the scam, and with every day that passed without the cars being notified, he had more ammo to fight the war for his new distribution system.

Not only that, but the vague hunch I'd had had paid off in spades. With all the aggro there had been the day after the bank holiday, I'd completely forgotten Julia was supposed to be sending me a fax. When I finally got out of hospital, it was sitting in my in-tray, buried in a pile of correspondence that Shelley had been carefully nurturing for me.

What I'd asked Julia for was a company check

on both Richmond Credit Finance and the chain of car dealerships that had been the main target of our investigation. It wasn't difficult to come by the information. The only reason we don't have it on-line ourselves is that it's more cost-effective for us to get the info from Josh than to subscribe to the appropriate database. Anyway, when I'd been able to get my eyes to focus properly, I'd compared the two sets of directors. Surprise, surprise. The managing director and principal shareholder of Richmond Credit Finance was the wife of the managing director and principal shareholder of the garages, an interesting coincidence that is currently occupying some of the working hours of Detective Chief Inspector Della Prentice.

So, instead of trying to bully us into cutting our bill, Andrew was keen to make sure we felt Mortensen and Brannigan were properly rewarded for our efforts. I wasn't about to argue with him.

After the tower, there was nothing for it but fish and chips. I suggested beating the traffic by going back to Harry Ramsden's in Manchester, and the idea was supported by two votes to one. To take Davy's mind off his disappointment, we challenged him to a race back to the car. We let him win, of course. He looked much more appealing than the Rolls Royce silver lady sitting on the bonnet of my slightly shop soiled, midnight blue Leo Gemini turbo super coupé GLXi. Some days you eat the bear.